P9-DGO-186

DOC FORD IS USED TO DEALING WITH SECRETS. BUT NONE AS DEADLY AS THIS ONE.

"THE MASTER has knocked one out of the park."
—*FLORIDA TIMES-UNION*

"White shows a new side to his talent, combining familiar themes and much-loved characters with a real flair for MADCAP ADVENTURE."
—*BOOKLIST*

"White smoothly combines history, action, and colorful characters into a SAVORY CONCOCTION easily devoured in a single sitting."
—*PUBLISHERS WEEKLY*

"A trove of REVEALING PRIVATE DOCUMENTS, rumors concerning a political assassination, a trip to Cuba—it's either today's headlines or Dr. Marion Ford's twenty-second adventure. Cuba provides the perfect setting."

ALSO BY RANDY WAYNE WHITE

DOC FORD SERIES

Sanibel Flats

The Heat Islands

*The Man Who
Invented Florida*

Captiva

North of Havana

The Mangrove Coast

Ten Thousand Islands

Shark River

Twelve Mile Limit

Everglades

Tampa Burn

Dead of Night

Dark Light

Hunter's Moon

Black Widow

Dead Silence

Deep Shadow

Night Vision

Chasing Midnight

Night Moves

Bone Deep

HANNAH SMITH SERIES

Gone

Deceived

Haunted

NONFICTION

*Randy Wayne White's
Ultimate Tarpon Book*

*Batfishing in the
Rainforest*

*The Sharks of Lake
Nicaragua*

Last Flight Out

An American Traveler

*Gulf Coast Cookery
(and recollections of
Sanibel Island)*

*Tarpon Fishing in
Mexico and Florida
(An Introduction)*

Available exclusively as
an e-book:

*Doc Ford Country
(True Stories That
Inspired Doc and
Tomlinson)*

**FICTION AS
RANDY STRIKER**

Key West Connection

The Deep Six

Cuban Death-Lift

The Deadlier Sex

Assassin's Shadow

Grand Cayman Slam

Everglades Assault

CUBA STRAITS

Randy Wayne White

G. P. PUTNAM'S SONS
NEW YORK

PUTNAM

G. P. PUTNAM'S SONS
Publishers Since 1838
An imprint of Penguin Random House LLC
375 Hudson Street
New York, New York 10014

The Library of Congress has catalogued the G. P. Putnam's Sons hardcover edition as follows:

White, Randy Wayne.
Cuba straits / Randy Wayne White.
p.   cm.—(A Doc Ford novel : 19)
ISBN 978-0-399-15814-8 (hardcover)
1. Ford, Doc (Fictitious character)—Fiction.   2. Marine biologists—Florida—
Fiction.   3. Political kidnapping—Fiction.   4. Cuba—Fiction.   I. Title.
PS3573.H47473C83   2015   2015002557
813'.54—dc23

G. P. Putnam's Sons hardcover edition / March 2015
G. P. Putnam's Sons premium edition / February 2016
G. P. Putnam's Sons premium edition ISBN: 978-0-425-28009-6

Printed in the United States of America
1   3   5   7   9   10   8   6   4   2

Book design by Meighan Cavanaugh
Cover design by Nellys Liang

For Bill and Diana

Amor cuerdo, no es amor.
(Sane love, is not love.)

—José Martí

You should enter a ballpark the way you enter a church.

—Bill "Spaceman" Lee

Sanibel and Captiva Islands are real places, faithfully described, but used fictitiously in this novel. The same is true of certain businesses, marinas, bars, and other places frequented by Doc Ford, Tomlinson, and pals.

In all other respects, however, this novel is a work of fiction. Names (unless used by permission), characters, places, and incidents are either the product of the author's imagination or are used fictitiously. Any resemblance to actual persons, living or dead, or to actual events or locales is unintentional and coincidental.

Contact Mr. White at WWW.DOCFORD.COM.

AUTHOR'S NOTE

I do not pretend to be an expert on Cuba, but I have a patchwork knowledge—the equivalent of personal snapshots assembled from many trips over a period of thirty-eight years. My Spanish on a good day is poor, my understanding of lingual nuances is nonexistent. My admiration for Cubans and Cuban Americans, however, is limitless. I am devoted to my Cuban friends, and sensitive to their circumstances, which is why we never mention, let alone discuss, politics, the embargo, or Fidel and Raúl Castro. They are as patriotic and loyal to their country as I am to mine. It has never been an issue on an island where there are better things to talk about, such as baseball, fishing, literature, and the ingredients of a good mojito. All references to politics in this book reflect the opinions of two fictional characters who are always at opposition: Marion D. Ford and Sighurdhr

Tomlinson. Blame them or blame me. My friends were not consulted, and they played no role whatsoever in writing this book.

The reader doesn't need to know this to enjoy *Cuba Straits*, I hope, but I want these facts and a few others out there.

My first visit to Cuba was in 1977, when, after a stop in Havana, I flew to the Isle of Pines, where I was lucky enough (sort of) to visit the prison where the Castros were imprisoned from 1953 to '55. Letters written from that prison, as you will discover, are key to the plotline of this book. I then enjoyed scuba diving reefs and wrecks that, at the time, were unexplored. The only disappointment on the trip, as I recollect, was using Soviet tanks and regulators that were prone to malfunction at inopportune times—at a hundred-plus feet on one occasion, although I'm guessing. We hadn't been issued depth gauges, let alone pressure gauges, so I'm still not sure where or why I ran out of air.

Nineteen eighty was a formative year for me, and thousands of Cuban refugees. For complicated reasons, Fidel Castro told his people that if the "blood of the Revolution" wasn't in their hearts, all they had to do was sign a paper and they were free to leave the island. When word reached the U.S., hundreds of private vessels mustered in Key West for the 112-mile trip to Mariel Harbor. I was aboard one of them. I spent more than a week in Mariel, and returned on a 55-foot grouper boat overloaded with 147 people, who, when we raised Boca Chica, took up this chant: *Libertad . . . Libertad* (Liberty . . . Liberty).

Witness such purpose and bravery, your life changes.

As a columnist for *Outside* magazine, I returned to the island many times afterward. Nineteen ninety-one was the beginning of what Cubans called the Special Time. The Soviet Union's collapse, and the U.S. embargo, multiplied the island's already considerable economic woes, and I remember renting a car at José Martí International, then being told, "We don't provide fuel," after I'd run out of gas within a few hundred yards of the airport. Even now, car traffic outside Havana is sparse, but, in those years, roads were deserted but for a half a million Chinese bicycles the government had purchased to solve the island's transportation problems. On that trip, I first saw children playing baseball with bats they'd carved by hand, and balls made of asphalt and wrapped with twine.

The pure joy with which they played—wow.

The memory stuck with me. In high school, I was a mediocre catcher (as my venerated coach, Bill Freese, will confirm), but I loved the game. My pal Gene Lamont (American League Manager of the Year, White Sox; now a Detroit icon) managed Kansas City's single A team at the time, and Geno came through in a big way. On my next visit, I brought along a hundred balls, my catcher's gear, and bags of bats and gloves, mostly major league quality. I returned to Florida with an empty backpack and bigger plans for the future. Enter William Francis Lee III—the "Spaceman" of Red Sox and Expos fame. I met Bill in 1989 when I was a bull pen catcher for a team in the short-lived Senior Professional League. I remember him walking onto the field in Winter Haven, spikes over his shoulder, wearing a Chairman Mao T-shirt, and me thinking, *Who is this left-wing loony?* but saying, at some later date, "Comrade, you'd fit right in playing ball in Cuba."

"Just got back" was his reply.

Bill is a genuinely brilliant man, and as generous as he is eclectic. Thanks to his contacts in Cuba, and those of Luis Tiant, we began taking our own team to the island along with busloads of baseball gear to give away to kids. We even made a documentary, *Gift of the Game*, that premiered at Fenway Park, and was issued by WGBH, Boston. It is a sweet, honest film that I recommend. Bill and Jon Warden (pitched for Detroit) are hilarious; Cuba's children, unforgettable.

Baseball, as you might guess, plays a role in this novel. My love of Cuba and Cubans, same thing.

I learned long ago, whether writing fiction or nonfiction, an author loses credibility if he's caught in a factual error. I take research seriously, and am lucky to benefit from the kindness of experts in varied fields. Before recognizing those who provided assistance, though, I would like to remind the reader that all errors, exagger-

AUTHOR'S NOTE

ations, and/or misinterpretations of fact, if any, are entirely the fault of the author.

My attorney friend Temis Giraudy López, of DeLand, Florida, and my nephew Justin White, Ph.D., were helpful in many ways, including offering their insights into Cuba and nuances of speech when translating Spanish to English. Much thanks goes to friends and advisers Bill Hauff, Ismael Sene, Capt. Tony Johnson, Dr. Brian Hummel, Dr. Dan White, Stu Johnson, Victor Candalaria, Dr. Marybeth B. Saunders, Dr. Peggy C. Kalkounos, Ron Iossi, Jerry Rehfuss, and Dr. Quirkous Miller. Sports psychologist Don Carman, once again, contributed unerring insights into human behavior, aberrant and otherwise, and his advice regarding Marion Ford's fitness routine is much appreciated.

Bill Lee, and his orbiting star, Diana, as always, have guided the author—safely, for the most part—into the strange but fun and enlightened world of our mutual friend, the Rev. Sighurdhr M. Tomlinson. Equal thanks go to Gary and Donna Terwilliger; Wendy Webb, my wife and trusted friend; Stephen Grendon, my devoted SOB; the angelic Mrs. Iris Tanner; and my partners and pals, Mark Marinello and Marty and Brenda Harrity.

Much of this novel was written at corner tables before and after hours at Doc Ford's Rum Bar and Grille on Sanibel Island and San Carlos Island, where staff were tolerant beyond the call of duty. Thanks go to Liz Harris Barker, Bryce Randall, Madonna Donna Butz, Capt.

AUTHOR'S NOTE

Jeffery Kelley, Chef Rene Ramirez, Amanda Rodriguez, Kim McGonnell, Superstar Ashley Rodeheffer, Christine Keller, Amazing Cindy Porter, Desiree Olson, Gabby Moschitta, Sam Ismatullaev, Mary McBeath, Michelle Gallagher, Mitch Larson, Twin Cities Rachael Okerstrom, Detroit Rachel Songalewski, Becca Harris, Sarah Carnithian, Cool Tyler Wussler, Yakh'yo Yakubov, Darlene Mazzulo, Jamie Kennedy, Tall Sean, Tall Shane, Boston Brian Cunningham, Becca Conroy, Lisa Kendrick, and Maria Jimenez.

At Doc Ford's on Fort Myers Beach: Lovely Kandice Salvador, Charity Owen, John Goetz, Deon Schoeman, Heriberto Ramos, Efrain Gonzalez, Jamie Allen, Capt. Corey Allen, Dear Nora Billheimer, Kassee Buonano, Angi Chapman, Astrid Cobble, Allison Dell, Mike Dewitt, Jessica Foster, Stephen Hansman, Jenna Hocking, Anthony Howes, Janell Jambon, Chris James, Kelsey King, Netta Kramb, Chad Mason, Bobby Matthews, Meredith Mullins, Katy Forret, Christiana McCrimmon, Kylie Pyrll, Reyes Ramos, Natalie Ramos, Dustin Rickards, Timothy Riggs, Sandy Rodriquez, Kim Ruth, Thomas Skehan, Heidi Stacy, Daniel Troxell, David Werner, Meliss Alleva, Eric Hines, Erin Montgomery, Ali Pereira, Brett Vermeul, Molly Brewer, Katie Kovacs, Erinn Fagan, Taylor Recny, Matthew Deverteuil, Nick Howes, Andres Ramos, Brandon Patton, Justin Voskulh, Ethan Janey, and Adrian Medina.

At Doc Ford's on Captiva Island: Lovely Julie

AUTHOR'S NOTE

Grzeszak, Hi Shawn Scott, Mario Zanolli, Alexis Marcinkowski, Adam Traum, Chris Orr, Erica Debacker, Heather Walk, Holly Emmons, Josie Lombardo, Joy Schawalder, Kelcie Fulkerson, Lenar Gabdrakhmanov, Spiking Nick Miller, Patti McGowan, Patti Tesche, Paul Orr, Ryan Body, Ryan Cook, Scott Hamilton, Shelbi Muske, Sonya Bizuka, Brilliant Ashley Foster, Cheryl Erickson, Mojito Greg Barker, Capt. Stephen Day, Yamily Fernandez, Hope McNulty, and Chelsea Bennett.

Finally, I would like to thank my sons, Rogan and Lee White, for helping me finish *Cuba Straits*, which is among my all-time favorite Doc Ford novels.

—*Randy Wayne White*
Telegraph Creek Gun Club
Babcock Ranch
Central Florida

25 Mayo, 1954

(From Raúl Castro
Prisión Federal
Isle de Pinos, Cuba)

My Querida Elma

... the censor's stamp must approve every letter that leaves here so I feel comfortable reaching out to you about a mutual friend. You will recognize the signature of the person I refer to. Over the years you and I have exchanged many letters including frivolous discussions of sports and baseball yet, at this time in history, nothing is frivolous. I am sure you understand why our previous correspondence in this matter must be kept in your secret heart, a place reserved only for me. My dear girl, yesterday we played the prison guards in the game all Cubans love, and it did not go well for my competitive brother, Fidelito ...

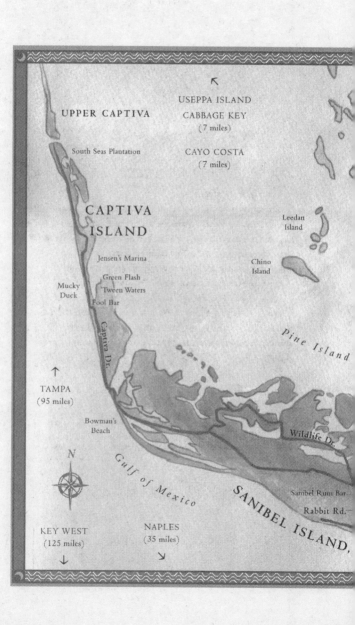

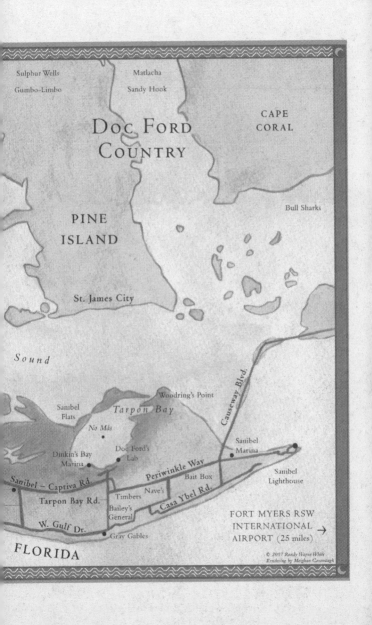

Sulphur Wells

Gumbo-Limbo

Matlacha

Sandy Hook

CAPE
CORAL

DOC FORD
COUNTRY

PINE
ISLAND

Bull Sharks

St. James City

Sound

Woodring's Point

Sanibel
Flats

Tarpon Bay

No Más

Causeway Blvd.

Dinkin's Bay
Marina

Doc Ford's
Lab

Sanibel
Marina

Periwinkle Way

Sanibel – Captiva Rd.

Bait Box

Sanibel
Lighthouse

Tarpon Bay Rd.

Timbers

Nave's

Casa Ybel Rd.

Bailey's
General

W. Gulf Dr.

Gray Gables

FORT MYERS RSW
INTERNATIONAL →
AIRPORT (25 miles)

FLORIDA

© 2007 Randy Wayne White
Rendering by Meighan Cavanaugh

At sunrise in November, Marion D. Ford, wearing shorts and jungle boots, jogged the tide line where Sanibel Island crescents north, and finally said, *"Screw it,"* tired of wind and pelting sand. To his right were colorful cottages—red, yellow, green—The Castaways, a popular resort during season, but this was Tuesday and a slow time of year. He went to the outdoor shower, thinking he'd hide his boots and swim through the breakers. He was ten pounds overweight and sick of his own excuses.

A porch door opened: a woman backlit by clouds of cinnamon, the sun up but not hot enough to burn through. "Want some coffee?" She cupped her hands to be heard. "Your dog's welcome, if he's sociable."

No idea who the woman was. Wearing a sweatshirt, with an articulate, strong voice that suggested Midwestern genetics: a descendant of dairymaids good at sports and baking pies. Late thirties, a rental compact in the drive, only one pair of sandals outside the door: a woman on a budget vacationing alone.

Ford said, "Can't. I'm punishing myself."

The woman replied, "You, too?" and walked toward him, started to speak but stopped, got up on her toes, focusing on something out there in the waves. "What in the world . . . Is that someone drowning?"

Beyond the sandbar, Ford saw what might have been a barrel but one thrashing appendage told him was not. He removed his glasses. "A loggerhead, I think. This isn't mating season, so it must be hurt."

"Logger-what?"

"A sea turtle." Ford handed her his glasses, jogged to the breakers, and duck-dived, still wearing his damn boots. The dog, which was a retriever but not a Lab or golden, swam after him. That was a mistake, too.

The turtle, barnacles on its back, was tangled in fishing line, and, yes, drowning. Ford had to alternately battle his dog, then the turtle, which hissed and struck like a snake while he maneuvered the thing through waves into the shallows. The woman was impressed. "You seem to know what you're doing."

"On rare occasions. Do you have a knife?"

"You're not going to . . . ?"

"Of course not."

The woman galloped to the cottage, her sweatshirt bouncing in counter-synch, legs not long but solid. *Nice.* She watched Ford cut the turtle free, inspect it for cuts, then nurse the animal back through the surf, where he side-stroked alongside for a while.

The woman was waiting with a towel, coffee in a mug, and water for the dog.

"Why not come inside and dry off? Or a hot shower, if you like, but you'll have to forgive the mess." The look the woman gave him was unmistakable—not that Ford often got that look from women he didn't know. "Three mornings straight I've watched you run past here"—an awkward smile—"so I finally worked up the nerve. Is it always this windy in November?"

Ford cleaned his glasses with the towel. "Nerve?"

"Old-fashioned, I guess. You know, speaking to strange men and all that." Another look, eyes aware, before she added, "I'm here all alone."

Ford tested several excuses before he followed the woman inside. He was thinking, *Why do the lonely ones choose islands?*

THAT NIGHT IN FORT MYERS, off Daniels Parkway, he was at Hammond Stadium, where the Minnesota Twins train, one of the practice fields, listening to his friend Tomlinson ramble on about something, but not really listening.

"Which is why," his friend concluded, "I won't even watch a game on TV without wearing the ol' codpiece."

Mentioning fish got Ford's attention. "You caught a cod? They don't migrate this far south."

"No, man—*my cup*. Until a woman finds an expiration date on my dick, I simply will not risk the Hat Trick Twins." Tomlinson rapped three bell tones from between his legs to illustrate, which proved nothing, because they were sitting in a dugout, under lights, wearing baseball uniforms, not in a bar watching TV. On the field was a Senior League team from Orlando, a left-hander warming up while the umpires kibitzed, game time stalled for no apparent reason.

Tomlinson muttered, "Geezus, what's the holdup?" He grabbed the fence, yelled, "Hey, blue—while we're still young, okay?" before returning to Ford. "You seem distracted, ol' buddy. Romantic problems or is it something unusual?"

Ford replied, "This morning I found a turtle tangled in fishing line—one of those crimped-wire leaders tourists buy at Walgreens. I assumed it was a loggerhead because they're so common. Now I don't think so."

"Was it dead? Goddamn pharmaceutical companies. They'd sell Pop-Tarts to diabetics if it bumped their numbers."

"The turtle was only about fifty pounds but already

had barnacles growing. See what I'm getting at? Even a young loggerhead or hawksbill would be closer to a hundred. Or maybe I'm wrong about that, too. I had him in my hands but didn't bother to notice details. Embarrassing, how little I know about sea turtles. Wouldn't you expect a biologist to notice what the hell species it was?"

Tomlinson knew the pitcher from Orlando or would not have yelled, "Joe . . . Hey, Joey—put some color in that rainbow. Slow-pitch is for commies, dude." This ultra-left-wing Zen Buddhist priest (he'd been ordained in Japan) and dope-smoking boat bum was a different person when he exited reality and entered a baseball field.

Joey flipped Tomlinson the bird.

Ford mused, "Now I'm thinking it might have been a Kemp's Ridley turtle, or even a Pacific Ridley. Two of the rarest in the world—the thing snapped at me like a dog, which is typical according to the literature. And its shell was too round. Had it right there in my hands; swam with it and still didn't dawn on me. If that's not a metaphor for something, I don't know what the hell is."

Ford hunched forward and retied his spikes, Tomlinson saying, "I should've never gotten rid of my old Kangaroos. These new Mizunos pinch my toe rings. I hate that." Then hollered through the screen, "Oh great, now I've got to piss *again*. Guys . . . I have a Masonic meeting tomorrow. Any chance we'll be done?"

Ford sat up. "Know what's odd? Two days ago, I was reading about sightings of Pacific Ridleys in the Cuba Straits. I just remembered. Olive Ridleys, actually, but they're the same thing. A few nests documented along this coast, too. Even north of Sarasota."

Tomlinson reverted to his role as Zen master. "Nothing accidental about coincidence, Doc. Hey—just listen, for once. You're being nudged toward something. Or away. Or into a new avenue of study. Karma seldom grabs a rational man by the balls."

"I didn't say it was a coincidence."

"Oh?"

"Not the Cuba part." Ford checked the bleachers—only a couple of wives in attendance—then found the main field, where stadium lights created a silver dome. Minnesota's minor league team, the Miracle, was playing St. Pete, a few hundred fans in attendance. He said, "You'll see when he gets here."

"Who?"

"*If* he shows up," Ford said, "you'll understand. A friend from Central America. He was drunk when he called, which might explain why he's late. Or might not."

That made perfect sense to Tomlinson. He nodded, fingering a scar on his temple hidden by scraggly hair—a figure eight that he insisted was an infinity symbol.

"Saving that Ridley is the coincidence. If it was a Ridley. The data goes back to 1953—one was caught in nets off Pinar del Río on Cuba's western coast. A few years back, a Ridley was photographed laying eggs near Sarasota. They're not supposed to be in the Gulf or Caribbean, but sea turtles are like underwater birds. They travel anywhere they want; flawless navigation systems, which suggests a magnetic sensitivity that's still not understood. It crossed my mind I've never actually seen a Ridley. Not confirmed anyway, which is why I'm pissed at myself about this morning."

Tomlinson's attention focused. "*Really?* You sure that's the only reason?" He said it as if envisioning a woman who was lonely and alone in her vacation cottage. Then added, "I hope you're not thinking about going back to Cuba. That's risking jail, man; a firing squad, from what I remember. Or has something changed?"

Ford shrugged, adjusted his protective gear, and buckled his pants. "I'll ask Victor to catch the first few innings. He might have gone to the wrong field."

"Vic? No . . . he went to his car to get eye black. What about Cuba? You know I'm right."

"Not him. The guy I was talking about."

Tomlinson said to Ford, whose spikes clicked as he walked away, "Not if I'm called in to pitch, you're not leaving. Hey . . . *Whoa!* Do you have a death wish or get dumped again? Dude . . . I can talk you through this."

THERE IS A FINE LINE between getting dumped and a relationship ended by the unanimous vote of one.

Ford thought about that as he walked past the spring training clubhouse, across the parking lot to the stadium, into a tunnel of noise and odors: popcorn, beer, and grilled brats. Cuba was also on his mind. What Tomlinson said would've been true a few years ago but might be okay now with the right cover story—or a companion with the right political ties.

The man he was searching for had those ties.

Ford spotted him in the outfield cheap seats, alone above the bull pen. The nearest cluster of fans was three sections closer to third base. The man had been watching relief pitchers warm up, not the game, but was now arguing with two security cops.

No doubt who it was, even from a distance. The man's size and his choice of seats would have been enough.

Baseball spikes are tricky on aluminum. It took Ford a while to get to left field and intervene on behalf of the man who was an old enemy and sometimes a friend—General Juan Simón Rivera, recently arrived from Central America via Havana.

"Tell them," Rivera said in English when he spotted Ford. "Tell them who I am. Perhaps they will understand that diplomatic immunity includes baseball and cigars."

He'd been smoking a Cohiba, that was the problem.

Ford replied in Spanish. "You want me to blow your cover, General?" This was safe to ask in front of two Anglo sheriff's deputies who resembled farmhands.

Rivera, the former dictator of Masagua, a tiny country that exported bananas and revolution, got control of himself. Decided, "Hmm. A man of my intellect is seldom a donkey's ass, but good point. Yes . . . better to indulge these fascists—for now." Spoke loudly in slang Spanish, then waited with regal impatience while Ford pacified the cops.

When they were gone, Ford endured a bear hug; they exchanged pleasantries—who was married, how many wives, how many kids. Rivera, finally getting to it, said, "I'm surprised you recognized me. I've come incognito for a reason."

Instead of signature khakis and boots, he wore a yellow Hawaiian shirt, a Disney visor, and flip-flops. Not enough to disguise a husky Latino with a gray-splotched beard and wild Russian hair, but Ford played along.

"A European tourist, General, that's what I thought at first. Very clever."

"Yes, I know."

"Oh, it took me a while."

Rivera expected that. It was a game they played, informal formality, but each man knew the truth about the other. He said, "Sometimes a wolf must blend with the sheep. Yet, not clever enough to fool you, my old catcher friend." He noticed Ford's uniform. "Why are you not on the field? I might even agree to pitch a few innings . . . *if* you have a large uniform. It doesn't have to be clean, but it cannot be an even number. I'm partial to the numbers three, nine, and thirty-seven." With his hands, he gestured *I think you understand*.

Santería, a mix of Catholicism and voodoo, was big on numerology, especially when it came to baseball. Rivera was devoted to the game. In Central America, he had built his own field in the rainforest and drafted soldiers based on their batting averages. He fancied himself a great pitcher whose politics had ruined his shot at the major leagues.

Ford replied, "General, my teammates would be honored. But, first . . . why are you here?"

"Always the same with you, Marion. Rush, rush, rush. Only bachelorhood has spared you ulcers, I think." Rivera nodded to the bull pen, where a pitcher who looked sixteen but was almost seven feet tall, sat with his hat askew. "That is Ruben. He's one of my protégés. The Twins have offered him a tryout, but a mere formality. Ruben's fastball rivals my own, yet he is a southpaw, as you can tell from his sombrero."

A joke. *Gorro* was Spanish for "cap." The general was in a pawky mood.

"He can't be from Masagua. I never saw anyone from Masagua much over six feet—except for you. Are you his agent?"

Rivera touched an index finger to his lips. "Unfortunately, the situation requires that Ruben pretends he doesn't know me. I can't explain right now."

Ford could guess where this was going but waited.

"I have an interesting proposition, Marion."

Ford said, "In Cuba."

"I told you as much on the phone. A nice chunk of silver in U.S. dollars if you agree."

Ford sensed trouble but also escape: turtles, isolated beaches, a land without cell phones—if he wasn't arrested. "I'll listen, but I don't do that sort of work anymore. Not if it's dangerous. Or political work—count me out if politics are involved." He hadn't ruled out human trafficking in deference to his own curiosity.

"Politics?" Rivera said. "I spit on the word. I piss on their speeches. To hell with their silly games. I am a freedom fighter—always—but have learned there are benefits to this free enterprise system of yours. A man is allowed to change, isn't he?"

"Only the small-minded hate change, General."

In clumsy English, Rivera replied, "You can say that twice. We will feast ourselves several days in Cuba. A week at most, every expense paid. But, first"—he hesitated while shifting to Spanish—"I have a little problem here that must be dealt with."

"In Florida?"

"Let us hope so." Rivera leaned closer to speak over the noise of the PA system. "I have lost a baseball player. Temporarily, I'm sure, but it would be unwise to contact your police."

"How long has he been missing?"

"Not 'missing'; 'wandered off.' Since this morning,

when I visited his motel—a place not far from here, with a large red sign. Without shoes or money, the lunatic could not have gone far."

"He's crazy?"

"Well . . . no more than most, but he's not as smart as normal men. And honest, very honest, which makes him unpredictable."

Ford had spent much of his life on the water and in baseball dugouts, which is why he asked, "Were his glove and bat missing? He could have worn spikes instead of shoes."

"I didn't think to check. I was too angry because a briefcase I entrusted to him was also gone. Nothing of value—some letters, a few photos. What I think is, the crazy fool took my orders to protect the case too seriously and carried it with him when he wandered off." Rivera demonstrated the size of the case by holding his hands apart. "An old leather briefcase. Not big, but well sewn."

Ford wondered about that, looking down into the bull pen, where the seven-foot-tall pitching prospect, sitting alone, was scrutinizing a Gatorade label. "Well . . . if the kid looks anything like Ruben, he shouldn't be too hard to find."

"No, he is a shortstop, and not so young. There is no birth certificate to prove his age, but his brain has not matured. Figueroa Casanova is the name he uses—but we are wasting time. Tomorrow, we will find Figuerito. Tonight, we must discuss this trip I've proposed."

Ford's mind returned to Cuba. The government there respected Juan Rivera; with Rivera, he'd probably be safe. But there were other concerns. "Would we be traveling . . . together?"

Rivera misread Ford's wariness and was insulted. "In my country, *generalissimos* do not travel like Yankee flamenco dancers or *maricóns*. Separately, of course, so bring a woman—two or three—all you want. I will provide you with a rental car and gas. Details can wait, but on a certain day we will rendezvous in the west of Cuba. A day or two there, shake a few hands, then back to Havana. Have you traveled the Pinar del Río region?"

Ford knew what "shaking hands" meant but pictured dirt roads and rainforest when he replied, "I'd have to think back."

"Magnificent countryside, and vegetables from the garden. There, every village has its own baseball *campo*, so you will have many opportunities to swing the bat." Rivera removed a cigar from his shirt, bit the tip off, chewed and swallowed. "Inferior pitching, of course, but on an island ruled by Fidel for fifty years, what do you expect?"

That was an odd thing for Rivera to say, and it would have been heresy in Cuba, but Ford was warming to the idea. He'd felt restless for weeks, but still had to say, "This can't be legal."

No, it wasn't. He could tell by Rivera's attempt to skirt the subject, which is when Ford decided, "Tell me anyway."

2

In his lab, Ford dropped three brine shrimp pellets into an aquarium while speaking to Tomlinson, who had an ice pack bag on his knee and a pitcher of beer on his lap. There had been a collision at home plate, but just bruises.

Ford said, "Rivera is smuggling Cuban baseball players into the U.S. He didn't admit it, of course. He came up with another story—a bizarre one you'll like—but I'm sure that's what he's doing. Now the heat's on in Cuba and Rivera wants me to go along, probably as a beard. Or who knows, with him."

"How bizarre?"

"The cover story? Just so-so, by your standards. He says in the late fifties, three American ballplayers buried their motorcycles and some guns the day Fidel Castro came to power. You know, rather than have their valuables confiscated. Thompson submachines, presentation-grade. But let's stick with the smuggling thread and I'll fill you in later."

Tomlinson moved the ice pack, fidgeting. "Were the bikes Harleys? If they were Harleys, the story is bullshit. No ballplayer would bury his Harley."

Ford took a patient breath. "Anyway . . . the U.S. has loosened sanctions, but Cuban players still need legal asylum from a third country before Major League Baseball will sign a contract. Most escape through Mexico. The drug cartels handle everything—boats, papers, even sports agents. But now Rivera has set up his own cut-rate version through contacts in Masagua. Or could be Nicaragua. Pretty much the same political players both countries. Oh—get this—for start-up money, he's been smuggling Cuban hard goods: cigars, paintings, historical items. Anything he can sell on the Internet while the Castro regime collapses."

Wind slapped waves against the pilings, sifting odors of saltwater and iodine through the floor. Tomlinson was still wearing baseball pants but had traded his spikes for Birkenstocks. He adjusted the ice pack and wiggled his toes as if they were cold. "For a while," he said, "I thought you were talking about the Juan Rivera I know—big guy from Masagua, a pitcher with a decent slider? The famous general. It's such a common name."

"That's him. You were pissed because he wouldn't give you a uniform when we were down there, then almost hit one out. That was more than, what, ten years ago? Now Rivera's caught in a squeeze between the Cuban government for stealing players and the Mexican cartels for horning in on their business. That's why he wants help, I think."

Tomlinson smiled, gave a sideways look. "Naw, you're messing with my head."

"Ask him tomorrow when he shows up. If he shows. We're supposed to help him find a shortstop who wandered off this morning."

"You're serious."

"After all your cracks about my lack of imagination, what do you think?"

That clinched it. Tomlinson placed the beer pitcher on the floor—a man trying to control his temper. "You're telling me that Juan Simón Rivera, the Maximum Leader of the Masaguan Revolution . . . the *generalissimo* of the goddamn People's Army . . . is smuggling ballplayers and selling shit on eBay—"

"On the Internet . . . Yeah, he admitted that much—"

"And profiting from the flesh trade? Gad, that's freakin' human trafficking, man."

"Well, depends on the ballplayer, I suppose." Ford thought that might get a smile. It didn't. "I could be wrong. Like I said, he gave me that story about motorcycles and machine guns. I can tell you the rest now or wait until we drive in to look for his missing shortstop."

Tomlinson didn't hear the last part. He got to his feet, chewed at a string of hair while he paced, limping a little. "That *bastard*. Is there not a shred of Euro socialist integrity left in our leaders? A feeding frenzy of mobster behavior—that's what's happening. Even to advance Utopian goals, it is totally bogus." He cringed and sighed. "Thank god Fidel and François Mitterrand aren't alive to see this day."

Ford, attempting subtlety, replied, "A lot of people would agree." He flicked on the aquarium's lights and noted movement among clusters of oysters at the bottom of the tank that had appeared lifeless but were now coming alive. "Watch this. It took only two days to condition the stone crabs—see that big female creeping out? Lights mean it's feeding time. At five days, even the barnacles started to respond."

Among the oysters, a mini-forest of lace blooms were sprouting, robotic fans that sifted amid a sudden flurry of crabs—dozens of crabs—most of them tiny.

Tomlinson said, "There you go—a feeding frenzy. I rest my case. Living entities perverted by the system to hide from the light—at least until some poor, innocent shortstop walks into the money trap. Now I understand why Rivera didn't have the balls to look me in the face tonight and say hello. Which is why I assumed it was a different guy."

Instead of pitching for Ford's team, the *generalissimo* had remained in the main stadium but was gone by the end of the game—a game they might have won if, in the ninth inning, down by two runs, Tomlinson hadn't tried to steal home. By all standards, a truly boneheaded play.

Ford asked, "Are you mad at the general or still mad at yourself?"

"Sure, rub it in. I didn't buy a plane ticket to fly back here and lose. Be aggressive—that's just smart baseball."

In October, Tomlinson had sailed his boat, *No Más*, to Key West for the Halloween freak show known as Fantasy Fest. That was three weeks ago, but he couldn't resist returning for a tournament that attracted teams from around the country, games played day and night at the best fields in South Florida.

"Stealing home with two outs? Down two runs?" Ford tried to sound neutral.

"Surprised everyone but the damn umpires, didn't I? Dude, spontaneity, that's just who I am." Tomlinson looked into the empty pitcher. "You're out of beer, Doc. Hate to say it, but I warned you this morning. Me sleeping outside in a hammock takes at least a six-pack—and that's before I knew we'd be searching for some poor dugout refugee from the slave trade. What's the shortstop's name? Just from how the name flows, I can tell you if he's any good."

Ford, walking toward the door, replied, "The 7-Eleven's still open, if you're desperate. I've got to find my dog."

FORD'S LAB was an old house on pilings in the shallows of Dinkin's Bay, just down from the marina, where, on this Tuesday night, people who lived on boats were buttoned in tight but still awake, watching monitors that brightened the cabins along A dock.

The dog was there, curled up next to the bait tank, probably tired from swimming all day. A picnic table allowed a view of the bay. Ford sat, opened his laptop while explaining to the dog, "I didn't renew my Internet service because it's so damn intrusive. And I don't want to be there when Tomlinson sneaks a joint. Or comes back with more beer."

The dog's eyes sagged open. His tail thumped once. He went back to sleep.

"People say you need Internet for research? What the hell's wrong with going to the library? I like libraries—or used to." Ford, using two fingers, banged at the keys. "Next time—I mean this, by god—Tomlinson is getting a hotel room and he can either ride his bike or call a cab. What kind of grown man asks to do a sleepover? His exact word: *sleepover*. Then bitches at me about not buying enough beer."

More hammering on the keys before he scanned the boats, some held together by epoxy and tape, others expensive yachts. "Crappy reception out here. You'd think one of these people could afford a decent router.

Hey"—he was speaking to the dog—"*Hey*, if I've got to sleep in the same house with him, you do, too. Your too-tired-to-walk crap isn't going to fool me twice. The way he snores, I get it, but I'm the one who needs sleep."

Ford zipped the laptop into its case, loaded the dog into his truck, and drove to Blind Pass, telling himself he would cast for snook along the beach on the good outgoing tide despite a waxing moon.

From the parking lot of Santiva General Store he could look across the road to the beach and colorful cottages of The Castaways, red, green, and yellow, although they appeared gray at eleven p.m. on this breezy night.

From the back of the truck, Ford selected a spinning rod—an intentional deception. All the cottages were dark but for one where a woman, opening the screen door, said, "I was hoping you'd stop by."

SHE HAD YET to request or offer an exchange of last names, or personal histories, which created a vacuum of protocol that, to Ford, felt like freedom.

He asked, "Need any help?" No lights on, the woman was in the bathroom, searching for something—a towel, it turned out.

"Not with you around. Wasn't it obvious? That was a new one for me."

"It seemed natural, just sort of happened."

The woman, voice husky, said, "I wouldn't mind if it happened again," and came back into bed.

Maggie, that was her first name. Whether it was her real name or short for "Margret" or "Marjorie," he hadn't risked inquiring. Intimacy with a stranger was a cozy tunnel untethered to the past, open at both ends. Secrets, if shared, would necessarily vanish at first light.

Seldom had Ford felt so relaxed.

Later, they talked some more. Him saying, "I know the Cuba idea sounds far-fetched, but it's an actual business proposition. Usually, I'd put it down on paper, a list of pros and cons, instead of bouncing it off you. You mind?"

Without using names, he had condensed Rivera's unusual cover story.

Maggie started to ask "What kind of business are you . . ." but caught herself and opted for a safer option. "Machine guns and motorcycles, huh? I guess we're all Huck Finn at heart. I've always wanted to go to Cuba—not that I'm fishing for an invite. I've got this place booked through Sunday." She tested the silence for awkwardness, then added, "Havana is beautiful, from the pictures. Have you been?"

He dodged that. "There are direct flights from Tampa now. That would make it easier."

"But is it legal? And, once you get there, is it safe? I read an article about an antiques dealer—he's from Miami, I think—that he's in jail, accused of stealing documents from the Castro estate. Paintings and stuff, too. And this other man who tried to smuggle in electronic equipment. Almost four years he's been in prison."

Ford's attention vectored. "Which Castro?"

"Well . . . I'm not sure, but they've both been sentenced to death by firing squad. Not the Castros, the men I'm telling you about. Or sentenced to life. Some terrible punishment. I'd have to find the article."

Ford settled back. "It wouldn't have made the news if it was true."

"You mean it *would* have made the news."

Too late to correct his slip. "Could be. You hear all kinds of rumors about that place."

"What I'm saying is, you need to confirm with your friend that what you're doing is legal. If he is a friend . . . or *she* is a friend. Either way." Her hand found Ford's thigh. "Sorry, none of my business. Tell me the rest."

He did, paraphrased a summary he'd written on a legal pad earlier in the lab:

On December 31, 1958, three American pitchers playing for the Havana Sugar Kings were delayed by extra innings and accidentally trapped when Castro's army came to power. The players—two from the Midwest, one from the Bronx—weren't politically savvy but knew it was dangerous to return to Havana until things cooled down.

They were cautious for good reason: Cuba's recent

dictator, flaunting Caribbean League rules, had personally signed their contracts after bribing them with cash and presents. Bribes included new Harley-Davidson motorcycles and three gold-plated Thompson submachine guns, each personalized and engraved LOYAL BEYOND DEATH—FULGENCIO BATISTA.

At the end of seventeen innings, when news about the coup circulated into their dugout, that inscription took on a darker meaning. Fulgencio Batista was the recently deposed dictator.

Everyone in Havana had seen their hot rod Harleys and gaudy rifle scabbards. No denying that. So the three Americans waved good-bye to the team bus, mounted their bikes, and lay low in western Cuba for a week. Ultimately, they swore a blood oath and either hid or buried their valuables before returning to the United States. Because of the embargo, they never went back.

Ford ended the story, adding, "My friend has a contact who claims to know where the stuff is. It would be fun, I think. Not for the money—if we recover anything, it should go to the players' families. That part we haven't discussed. Problem is, my friend might have invented the whole business just to lure me down there so I can help with something else."

Maggie, rather than ask the obvious, decided to have fun with it. "They buried their motorcycles . . . my god. That sounds unlikely. Probably hid them, don't you think? Even if they didn't, you should go. Adventure for its own sake. We get trapped in ruts, doing what's expected instead of what we really want." She squeezed his hand. "I don't mean to sound maudlin, but I've wasted too many years afraid to step off the high board."

Ford, loosening up, said, "Might be fun. There's a species of turtle down there I've never seen. Occasionally found in Cuba anyway. A Pacific Ridley. Not that I'm an expert—you were wrong this morning. So yeah, why not? As long as I don't have to spend too much time with this guy. He can be a lot of work."

"Then your friend is a man."

"Times two. I thought I made that clear."

Maggie—if that was her name—lifted the covers and sprawled atop him, her breath warm. "Good. I don't care what happens tomorrow, but tonight—I'll admit it—I'm glad you're not going with some ballsy woman."

"Jealous?"

"Envious," Maggie replied, "of any woman with that much nerve. This is my first vacation without training wheels"—she was repositioning her hands—"and, so far, I like the taste of freedom."

I n the morning, the retriever followed Ford past the marina office, where Mack, behind the counter, read the sports section as fishing guides fueled and iced their boats. No rush. Fog had displaced the wind with a stillness that dripped from the trees. Poor visibility required a late start.

Mack called out the window, "Were you there when police showed up at the stadium?"

Ford was on his way to the beach. "What do you mean?"

"That Senior League tournament. You had a game last night, didn't you?"

"Yeah . . . ?"

"Says here there were gunshots, but it could have

been a car backfiring. That a locker room was robbed and a couple of cars. Must have been quite a game."

"You're kidding. Cars were stolen or just broken into?"

"During a brawl," Mack replied, and resumed reading until Ford was inside. "Says here it started because a batsman scored four home runs in two games, which somehow caused a fight." He peered up through his bifocals. "Is a four-over considered a century? Or is it called a round-tripper?"

Twenty years since Mack had immigrated from New Zealand, but he still confused baseball with cricket. Ford approached the counter. "Mind if I see that?"

There were two stories about a game and resulting incident at an old Grapefruit League complex, Terry Park in east Fort Myers, miles from the Twins stadium, which Ford explained.

Mack, although disappointed, looked on the bright side. "I suppose there are enough ugly rumors about this marina, so I'm glad you weren't involved. Particularly"—he motioned in the direction of Tomlinson's mooring buoy—"you-know-who."

Ford scanned the newspaper for familiar names and zeroed in on yesterday's box scores. In the afternoon, a shortstop named F. Casanova had hit three home runs playing for the Dallas BMW Bandits. Last night, pinch hitter F. Casanova, playing for the Tallahassee Orthopedics, had *beaten* the Dallas team with a solo shot in extra innings.

Thus the brawl.

Was F. Casanova "Figueroa," the general's missing shortstop? More likely it was "Frank" or "Felipe," some baseball stud who sold his services to the highest bidder. It happened. Interesting, though, because the locker room and two vehicles had been damaged by forcible entry during the game. It brought to mind Rivera's missing briefcase.

There was something else: F. Casanova had vanished by the time police and the news reporter arrived.

Ford, after asking Mack's permission, tore out the page. "Tomlinson will want to see this. Is he around?"

"I sure as hell heard him when I got up to check for water in the rentals. Snoring. Before sunrise, even with this fog, I knew it was him from a hundred yards away. If sleep apnea didn't kill His Holy Weirdness, I suppose he went to breakfast. Did you check the rack for his bike?"

Ford went out the door, the dog at heel but jittery when a gaggle of pelicans parted to clear a path.

TOMLINSON'S BEACH CRUISER, with fat tires, AC/DC stickers, and a basket stolen from Fausto's in Key West, was outside Bailey's General Store, intersection of

Periwinkle and Tarpon Bay, a quarter mile from the marina. Only a few vans and lawn service trucks in the lot. Ford sat on a bench near a bulletin board, watching men exit with coffee and breakfast in Styrofoam containers.

Not Tomlinson. Two bananas, a bag of scones, and a six-pack of Corona for him.

"Damn it," he said, "forgot the limes." Then looked up from the bag in his hand. "What happened to you last night? I got up to piss around four, you weren't back. But I smelled coffee before sunrise."

Ford replied, "I actually got some sleep," and handed him the newspaper. "Keep an eye on the dog while you read. I'll grab limes while I get breakfast."

"You're welcome to a mango scone."

"Bottom of the page about a brawl," Ford said, "the teams from Dallas and Tallahassee. Oh"—he waited until Tomlinson had found the article—"the name of Rivera's missing shortstop is Figueroa Casanova. Take a look at the box scores."

"Is it 'Figueroa' or 'Figgy'? That makes a difference." Tomlinson stroked his beard while he read. "Geezus, the dude hit four dingers?"

"Could be a different Casanova."

"Not if his name's 'Figgy,' it couldn't. That's what I meant, just by the rhythm. A 'Fran' or 'Floyd' or 'Federico' couldn't hit his weight, not playing shortstop. And sure as hell wouldn't be my choice to pinch-hit with the game on the line. Yeah, gotta be 'Figgy' . . . 'Figgy Casanova.' What do you want to bet?"

Ford had refused a scone but decided to try one. "What I'm curious about is, the locker room was broken into. Did you get to that part?"

"Don't pressure me, Doc. It's too early for speed-reading. Besides, not all illegal immigrant shortstops are thieves. That is semi-racist."

"Spare me your guilt-ridden lectures," Ford replied, then explained about the missing briefcase. "Rivera said Casanova isn't smart, but he's loyal. When he wandered off, he left his street shoes and other stuff but took Rivera's briefcase. I'm projecting, probably no connection whatsoever, but see what I mean? Because that's what he'd been told to do: watch the thing."

Tomlinson liked that. "A position player you can trust, plus he hits for power. What do you think he'd charge to play for us?"

Ford, walking toward the electronic doors, didn't remind him their team had been eliminated after a misguided attempt to steal home. When he returned with a salt bagel and coffee, Tomlinson was still reading, but less enamored with the missing shortstop. "The dude went and double-crossed Dallas. He's nuts. You don't screw a team from a state that fries killers before the judge's truck is out of the parking lot. Why would the *generalissimo* trust Casanova with anything valuable?"

"Rivera said the briefcase contains some letters, personal stuff, nothing worth much. But it wouldn't be the first time he's lied to me. The man's tricky. He's got a very nasty edge—don't let the charm fool you." No reason to add that, during Masagua's first revolution, Rivera had put a bounty on Ford's head—ten thousand córdobas, dead or alive. But then, a few years later, at a baseball tournament in Cartagena, he had greeted him like a long-lost friend.

The *generalissimo*'s team needed a bull pen catcher, turned out.

"He claims he doesn't have a cell phone and wouldn't say where he's staying. So we'll have to wait until this afternoon—if he shows. I've got work to do in the lab anyway."

Something else Ford intended to do was check for articles about items stolen from the Castro estate.

Tomlinson had folded the page to "Senior League Tournament," "Today's Games." "Dallas is playing the Long Island Starbucks at ten a.m., Terry Park. A clash of cultures, man, in the loser's bracket. You know how grueling that shit is. Two or three games in one day and both teams desperate for players who can still walk. I think we've got a shot at starting."

Ford, fussing with the dog's collar, shook his head.

"Your call, man. You going for a run?"

"To the Island Inn and back, hopefully eight-minute

miles or better. Then pull-ups. I need to start pushing myself."

"Sure. Pain is a lot more fun than baseball," Tomlinson replied. "If I can get my van started, I'll let you know how things shake out."

IN 1921, a baseball-loving farmer donated cattle pasture east of Fort Myers in the hope of attracting a major league team to spring training. Connie Mack's Philadelphia Athletics obliged. Although teams changed through the decades—Pittsburgh, then the K.C. Royals—the baselines of the main diamond had not moved an inch since 1925.

Tomlinson loved that about Terry Park. He sat in his van, windows open, soaking up history while the morning sun baked the fog away. Senior League games didn't attract fans, so players' cars were clustered behind the stadium but not on the grass near the gate. That's why Tomlinson had chosen this spot, out here in the Bermuda flats, close to the old clubhouse, but not because the locker room had been robbed. He was a man who valued solitude for practical reasons—such as lighting a joint after amping up Springsteen's "Glory Days" until the bass vibrated in his heart. Then held his breath so long he had to relight the joint, which was okay, because he also valued ceremony.

Next up, Tomlinson decided, he'd play Warren Zevon, with the Stones on deck and Jimi Hendrix in the hole. No . . . Buffett was a better choice to hit cleanup. Captain Jimmy prolonged the amperage of a buzz; he sort of took the tiller until mist cleared unto another fine day.

This was a bold move that required a lineup change. Which is why Tomlinson was pawing through a box of CDs when a man, his face obscured by a towel, appeared in the van's mirrors. The man was barefoot and shirtless, all skin and muscle, built low to the ground, maybe five-five on a tall day, with baseball spikes slung over his shoulder and wearing a towel like a hoodie.

Tomlinson sat up straight, cupped the joint, and let his paranormal powers assist his eyes.

Hmm . . . were those Santería beads hanging from the guy's equipment bag? Yep. Beads of red and black. They hinted at the man's identity despite the towel over his head. If true, this was one ballsy finesse, attempting to sneak onto the field this morning after causing so much trouble last night.

Tomlinson made a clucking sound of approval and used a boney hand to motion the stranger closer. *"Aquí, amigo,"* he called. "Over here."

The little man tilted his head to sniff the air, sniffed again and appeared interested. Then started toward the van—which is when two sheriff's deputies exited the locker room and scanned the parking lot. An instant later, an equipment bag banged through the van's window. The little man followed, small and agile enough to land curled up on the floor like a cat. With his hands, he urged *Get moving*.

Tomlinson smiled down from the steering wheel. "Dude . . . I love your act already."

"My brother," the man replied, "that *pitillo*, it smells fine, but not so fine in jail, huh? Let me hold that thing while you drive."

"You're from Cuba, aren't you? A shortstop, I'd wager."

Figueroa Casanova formed a V with his fingers and accepted the joint with a smile.

WHAT FIGUEROA couldn't understand is why, after only five days in America, so many angry men had chased him, some with bats, but one with a *pistola*, and now police were after him, too.

"I come here, all I want to do is play baseball. In Cuba, we play all day, all night if there's no cane to cut or I'm not in jail. Why is such a simple matter so crazy? Amigo, my ears hurt, those men yell at me so loud."

Tomlinson pulled into the old armory, no cars around, just seagulls sunning themselves and shitting on haggard Humvees beyond the wire. The symbolism won him over, so he put the van in park. "Wait until your first iPhone, pal. Hell, or even a laptop if your ears are ringing now. The social media thing, Twitter and Facebook, they jackhammer into your skull. They'll infest your privates and suck your soul dry. In terms of decibels? S and M—social media, I'm saying—the shit's a relentless banshee scream that no silver bullet can silence."

Casanova had no idea what Tomlinson was talking about, so continued with his story. "General Rivera, he says to me, 'Figuerito, I promise all the baseball you want,' but then leaves me—although in a fine hotel, it is true. Two days, do I play baseball? Three days, same shit. I bounce the ball in the parking lot. I sit on my ass in that room with cold air. Then *bang-bang-bang* at the door—it's a *bandito* with this thing over his head—like a sweater with eyes, you know? A damn pistol pointed, so I grabbed my shit and ran. Brother, I have been running ever since. Well"—Figueroa paused to accept a freshly rolled joint—"not yesterday, when I hit three home runs. I trotted the bases out of, you know, respect for the pitcher. But those big gringos last night, when I hit a fourth, they chased me anyway." He reached for the lighter. "What's the name of that town where their team lives?"

Tomlinson was opening his cell. "Dallas, Texas," he replied, then left another message on the phone in Ford's lab. For half an hour and one fat joint they'd been talking, just driving and taking it slow to see what they had in common. There was Juan Rivera and baseball, now they were getting down to the nitty-gritty. This was the first Tomlinson had heard of an armed man breaking into Casanova's motel. It sobered him. "Any idea who it was? From his voice, or maybe you saw his car."

The shortstop was admiring the van's spaciousness. He shook his head. "A man sticks a *pistola* in my face, all I think about is, run. He wanted something, kept yelling at me, but how the hell do I know?" His eyes did another scan. "This thing's roomy, man. Last night, I slept on a bench outside 'cause of what happened. A golf course, I think. It was a field with flags."

"What do you think the guy wanted?"

"The *bandito*? Whatever he could get. That's why I left my money and shoes in the room. Nice shoes, and almost twenty dollars American. But guess what? Didn't matter. That man chased me, too." He went into detail, saying he didn't know where Rivera was staying, and that he was afraid to return to his fine hotel, the Motel 6 on Cleveland Avenue, so he had nowhere to stay. Then, peering through the windshield, asked, "Which way is Texas?"

Tomlinson pointed west.

"Let's don't take that road," Figueroa said, frowning.

"No way in hell, so don't worry. But help me make sense of what's going on here. The friend I told you about, Doc—his name's really Marion Ford—he knows

Rivera a lot better than me. He thinks Rivera's tricky. And, from personal experience, I know he's dangerous."

"Who?"

"The general."

"No, the other one. His name is Doc?"

"Marion Ford, he's my neighbor on Sanibel."

"Oh. Of course. All generals are dangerous. Why you think I ride a boat to Florida from Cuba?" Figueroa let that sink in for a moment. "Yes . . . what you say is interesting. The general has a bad temper, this is true. And always on the phone whispering. Secretive, you know? I think he is running from something, or afraid."

"Rivera gave you a briefcase to hang on to, according to Doc. Is that true?"

The shortstop patted the equipment bag at his feet, an oversized model carried by catchers, to indicate the briefcase was inside. "The general, he trusts me."

"Maybe that's what the robber was after."

"The case? Could be, yeah. I don't know 'cause I couldn't understand what he was saying."

"That's the confusing part. Your English is excellent— thank god or we'd need sign language. Or was it because you were so scared?"

Figueroa gave him an odd look. "Man, I don't speak English. What makes you say this crazy thing?"

Tomlinson tugged at a strand of hair and reconsidered the joint he had rolled. "You're shittin' me."

"Just Spanish. What you think we've been talking this whole time?"

"I'll be damned. You actually understand me?"

"Except for all the crazy shit you say. Smoke some nice *pitillo* before a game, yeah, I need it to slow me down. But too much"—he shrugged—"guess we all different. You a pitcher, huh? Left-handed, I bet." Talking, he reached, unzipped the equipment bag, and removed a briefcase.

"This is so freaking cool," Tomlinson murmured. He located his own eyes in the mirror, decided there were untapped worlds behind those two blue orbs. Among them, a cogent intelligence that might decipher why his new best amigo had been assaulted by a bandit.

The briefcase drew his attention. It rested in Casanova's lap: antique brass buckles, and leather of waxen brown, all handsomely sewn. "Hey . . . *that's* what that bastard *bandito* was after. What Rivera told my friend was a bald-faced lie, I think."

"Yeah?"

"Rivera claimed there's nothing valuable in there, but my cognitive senses reply, 'Bullshit.' Yes, a lie . . . a blanket deception designed to cover his ass—and all the more plausible because Rivera gave the briefcase to you. Why didn't the general hide the thing in his own room? *That's* the question. Dude . . . I can only think of one reason."

"'Cause the general knows I'm honest."

"That, too—or because *it's dangerous*." Tomlinson looked from Figueroa to briefcase.

The shortstop didn't want to believe him. "This?"

"Damn right, Figgy. Dangerous, sure, to have in your possession." Tomlinson bent to see a logo branded into the leather flap . . . no, three letters, one bigger than the others, but all too small to read until his nose had damn-near skewered the brass lock.

Figueroa was getting nervous. "I didn't ask what's inside. The general tells me to watch something, I watch it. He tells me not to look inside a briefcase, I don't look inside. As a child, I made a vow to a certain deity that I will not lie unless—"

Tomlinson, after inspecting the flap, sat up fast, saying, "Son of a bitch—I was right," but gathered himself when he saw the shortstop's face. The poor guy was ready to run barefoot through the streets again. So he took a breath—like, *No big deal*—and added, "On the other hand, Figgy, I'm seriously blazed. For instance, I didn't realize I spoke fluent Spanish until now."

This was true, although the initials on the briefcase suggested it was a big deal.

"God damn, brother, you scared me, actin' like you found something bad."

"Dude, look for yourself. We've got ourselves a situation here. Do the initials *F.A.C.* mean anything to you?"

"Nope. You want to open this case, you welcome, but it's up to you." The shortstop pushed the thing toward him and reached for the lighter. "All I promised to do is watch."

F.A.C. Tomlinson, after reconfirming those initials, decided, *It's got to be his.* Damn few people, even Cubans, knew that Fidel Castro's middle name was Alejandro. But that wasn't proof enough. He fiddled with the lock, part of him hoping it wouldn't open.

Cripes. Like magic, the flap peeled back to reveal what was inside. There were well-sewn pockets. They holstered reading glasses with wire cables and several antique pens. At the bottom was a stationery box adorned with a ribbon in the shape of a heart. The box smelled of lavender perfume, and had some weight when he placed it on his lap. This offered hope. A man, especially the leader of a revolution, wouldn't keep something so blatantly feminine in his briefcase.

Figgy, gazing out the passenger window, said, "Hurry up. I'm tired of pretending not to see."

Inside the box were letters. Several dozen . . . no, at least a hundred, written on paper that ranged from fine onionskin to postcards to cheap legal-sized. Even a couple of telegrams, all in Spanish.

Tomlinson said, "Dude, I'm going to need some help here."

The shortstop refused to turn his head. "If you can

speak it, you can read it. But, brother, don't read out loud 'cause I don't want to hear this bad thing you're doing."

Tomlinson let his mind go loose and picked out a letter at random. It had been typed; others were in cursive ink, written with a flourish that suggested a Jesuit education:

17 March '53

My Adored Gaitica . . . I saw Mirta yesterday, she said that she had spoken with Mongo by phone. I haven't been to the University since the softball game three days ago . . .

"Softball," the English spelling.

"Figgy, how do you say 'softball' in Spanish?"

"'Pig shit,'" he responded but didn't turn.

"Float on, *hermano*," Tomlinson replied, and skipped over several lines to:

There has been no blood shed until now. Havana is still in a sleepy state and nobody speaks on the buses. Last night they detained Dr. Agramonte and other Party leaders again. Fidel and I remain in hiding, although discreetly moving around a lot . . .

Huh?

He flipped the page over.

My regards to all and to you all the affection of your unforgettable love.

It was signed "Raúl."

What the hell was a letter written by Raúl Castro doing in a briefcase with his older brother's initials?

Tomlinson plucked out another letter, this one handwritten, three pages, dated April 1954 . . . and, my god, it was postmarked from prison on Cuba's Isle of Pines. There was a censor's stamp and red initials.

My Dear Little Doll . . . In the night I imagined you taking a bath in the washbasin and you were telling me in the mirror that you are too young to be so daring . . . I lay in bed rather absentmindedly and was soon in a state of ecstasy with thoughts of my sweet little girl . . .

Tomlinson spoke to Figueroa. "This one's hot. I think the guy's whacking off, which I don't blame him because he's in the slammer. You know? Locked up. But wait, let's see how it's signed . . ."

The shortstop covered his ears.

At the bottom of the third page:

You are always in my thoughts. Fidelito

Whoa! Jackpot.

Check the mirrors, lock the doors, check mirrors again. Tomlinson started the van.

They were on I-75, south of the Twins stadium, before he finally said to Figgy, who was calmer, "I'll tell you a great place to play baseball—you ever been to Key West?"

F ord was in his truck, crossing the bridge to the mainland, when Tomlinson phoned from a dugout where the Key West Fighting Conchs played, saying, "It's top of the seventh, our lives are in danger, and so is yours. Oh . . . and guess who's playing short-stop?"

It was late afternoon. The Gulf of Mexico, to Ford's right, was a horizon of cloudy jade; not much traffic this close to sunset.

"You're on the Keys? I don't understand a damn thing you're saying."

"Figgy Casanova," Tomlinson replied, then muffled the phone to watch Figgy dive to his right, deep in the hole, but come up dealing and throw a runner out at home. "Poetry, man. He's got a gun. Did you know his grandfather danced for the Moscow Ballet?" A pause, bleacher noise and whistling, before he added, "Seriously, Doc. Rivera's a traitor. The shit he's into could get us all killed. Plus, it's just morally wrong, you know? My conscience won't let me stand back and do nothing."

Marion Ford, who had survived jungles and violence, was a stickler for small concessions to safety. Among them, talking while driving. Past the toll station, where gravel and mangroves edged the bay, he pulled close to the water and parked. "Okay . . . go over that one more time. What's this about a gun?"

"I found Figuerito. He's with me. Dude's got a freakish arm; a true magician. And has this child-like quality. *Plus*, he's a full-on stoner—but, with him, it's more of a metabolism thing. Anyway, I had to get him out of Dodge, so I did, which gave me time to think. Thing is, Doc, if you're already committed to the *generalissimo*'s deal, I can't tell you much more. This wasn't an easy decision, *hermano*. Just keep in mind, Rivera's the problem. Not you. Oh, by the way—how'd your run go this morning?"

Assembling order from a scattergun conversation with Tomlinson required patience. "You're at a baseball game. I can hear that much. But are you really—"

"Yeah, Key West. Seven hours on the road, and we saw some Roy Hobbs players at the Arby's on Cudjoe Key. There's a wood bat tournament; the finals are today, so why not? Their team hasn't talked money yet, but it won't be a problem the way my man Figgy is picking it clean. The manager, this team from Indiana, he wants to adopt him—or give him a job at his Cadillac dealership."

Ford knew Tomlinson's sailboat was in Key West—an obvious link—but played it loose, saying, "And it'll be seven hours back. You *are* coming back?"

"Not through Hialeah. A black SUV tailed us clear to Homestead, so I took the back way to Key Largo and lost them in a convoy of bikers. That's why I turned my phone off—there's no running from a GPS, man. Didn't even stop at Alabama Jack's because—"

"Hold on. Why would anyone follow you? If you're worried it was Rivera, it wasn't. I'm on my way to meet him now. If this is paranoia, fine, but try to avoid the fantasy riffs. You're confusing me."

Ford heard the ting of an aluminum bat and more whistling. Had to wait awhile before Tomlinson replied, "Meeting the *generalissimo*, huh?" He sounded wary.

"You knew that. He's in a rental cottage near the Sky Bridge to Fort Myers Beach. He called about an hour ago."

More silence. "Doc, we've been friends a long time, and I want you to promise me something. Promise you won't tell that traitor fascist where we are."

"Okay. What *should* I tell him?"

"Nada, man. Rivera has played Figgy like a rube.

First of all, the little guy's age, he's closer to forty than thirty, so no major league team's going to sign him—especially without a birth certificate. Did you know that? No passport either."

"How does that prove the general's a traitor?"

"He's an asshole, too. In Figgy's mind, no birth certificate means he's ageless, but why get the guy's hopes up? Mostly, I'm pissed because of the briefcase. Rivera stuck him with it for a reason, almost got the dude killed. He'll get me killed, too, if he knows where we are."

What's in the briefcase? Ford wanted to ask, but held off. Through the mangroves, he watched fishermen wade the sandbar and a lone woman paddleboarding. Tomlinson had his quirks but also a gift for reading people accurately. Stoned or straight, his IQ was off the charts. If this wasn't paranoia, it was serious.

He waited for background noise to quiet. "I warned you about Rivera, remember? So whatever you say, sure. If you want, I'll help you pull some kind of switch, or just play dumb. Tell me what to do, I'll do it."

Tomlinson, reading Ford's mind, said, "After I tell you what's in the briefcase, you mean?"

WATCHING THE WOMAN PADDLEBOARDER, he left a message for a friend who owned Tampa–Havana air charters, then left another for his seaplane pilot pal,

Dan Futch. If Tomlinson panicked and turned his phone off, no contact, so Ford might need to fly out tonight, Thursday at the latest. A narrow window. Even in a clunky old Morgan sailboat, Key West to Cuba was only a full day's sail, two if the wind was wrong.

It all depended on Tomlinson . . . and if Juan Rivera would talk.

At McGregor Boulevard, he turned right toward Fort Myers Beach, still unsure if his pal was in danger or just reacting to THC and systemic guilt. The contents of the briefcase, albeit valuable, weren't as dangerous as he'd feared. It contained love letters to a young girl, nearly a hundred, written between 1953 and 1963 by two men who even then were the equivalent of Cuban rock stars.

Fidel Castro and his younger brother, Raúl.

Hearing those names, Ford had muttered, "Bastards," which Tomlinson assumed referred to Gen. Rivera.

Stand back, though, view the big picture: Having the briefcase wasn't that bad. They were personal letters, not political documents, according to Tomlinson. Never mind the brothers were writing to the same girl. Their mistress had saved them, plus snippets of poetry and a lock of Castro's hair, in a binder decorated with hearts and dried wildflowers. It was a totem of adolescence, Tomlinson had reasoned, from a girl besotted by two older, famous men.

The letters would bring cash from collectors, no

doubt, but weren't worth killing for, although Tomlinson disagreed—not that a man who didn't speak Spanish could be relied upon to judge. He'd only had time to leaf through the folder, fearing his van was being followed.

Figueroa Casanova was no help. He'd refused to participate due to a moral conflict, some childhood vow to never lie.

No matter. One thing Ford had learned after years of dealing with international intrigue types, power players such as Gen. Juan Simón Rivera: *everything* was potentially dangerous, *nothing* was what it appeared to be.

For Ford, it felt like arriving home without leaving Sanibel.

The *generalissimo* had called around five from a blocked number. He'd sounded subdued; didn't mention the missing shortstop, but did say, "Make sure you're not followed." That meshed with Tomlinson's claims. So at the Sky Bridge, Ford checked mirrors before turning left onto Main Street, which wasn't much of a street, just a long asphalt lane. For a mile, it separated the shrimp docks from a geometry of mobile homes fenced and spaced in rows, in contrast to weeds and Elvis-era rentals on the other side.

Rivera was, indeed, traveling incognito. Perhaps that's why he had provided directions, not an address.

Ford slowed, looking for a dirt road, and noticed a black Suburban behind him. He waved the vehicle around, used a pencil to jot the license number, and watched the SUV drive several blocks, then turn. Rivera's cottage was bayside, fifty meters past a house with dogs chained in back, and the first drive after a sign that read *Weekly Rates*. As described, a white Mustang from Hertz was in the drive.

Ford didn't pull in. Using his phone, he photographed the house, then drove to the end of the street before looping back and parking under a banyan tree. More photos. He scanned for neighbors and surveillance cameras. Cigar smoke and loud salsa music suggested Rivera was inside. In the back of the Mustang, an empty rum bottle warned the general had been drinking.

A training exercise, that's what this felt like. One of those hide-and-seek games at Langley or at the Blackwater facility across the Virginia line in Moyock, North Carolina. Evolutions, they were called, a new game for every day of the week. As demanding as the courses were, key elements couldn't be simulated, such as fear of the crosshairs, or an adrenaline spike that, in the real world, caused some men to vomit, others to freeze.

The cottage was faded wood on pilings. Ford was still in practice mode when he approached the front steps—then everything changed. The side door to the garage was open, but the main doors were closed. A small detail that seemed all wrong in this neighborhood.

He veered to get a different angle. Beyond a tangle of hibiscus, a black SUV had nosed into a lot where boats were racked, most covered by tarps. A man wearing coveralls and a tool belt was standing there. He pretended to inspect a boat but was actually eyeing Rivera's cottage—the cottage on stilts above the floodplain, so Ford was able to slip underneath the cottage into the garage unseen.

The same Suburban? He wasn't sure, couldn't see the license. Above him, through the floor, came music and a muffled bearish voice: the general talking, but a one-sided conversation . . . a phone call.

Talking to whom?

Ford moved to the window. The man in coveralls, no phone in hand, was crossing backyards toward the cottage. He was dressed like a cable installer, but cable guys drove vans, not black Suburbans.

FBI? An undercover detective, possibly.

When Cable Guy was closer, Ford decided, *No*. Feds and local pros don't mount sound suppressors on their weapons. This man had. From his coveralls, he'd produced a pistol with a lethal-looking tube on the barrel, now close enough to thump his shoulder against the garage while he paused and took stock.

Ford, on the other side of the wall, felt that thump, separated by half-inch particleboard, and knew this wasn't a stakeout. Cable Guy was a killer. At the very least, he was prepared to kill as quietly as ballistics allowed.

A pro—or too many movies.

It was the way Ford's mind worked.

Overhead, Rivera, still on the phone, turned the music louder, which proved the conversation was important, and began to pace. His weight sprinkled dust onto a floor that was packed shell, not cement, junk piled everywhere. The particleboard was slick like moldy bread. Spongy enough to put a fist through. But then what?

Ford's brain shifted from spy games to protocol.

There were two options: remove the asset (Rivera) from harm's way or neutralize the threat. Training didn't allow a third, which was to run like hell, although he was tempted. This was Rivera's problem, damn it. On the other hand, they shared a history, and "neutralize" didn't necessarily mean "kill."

In every garage are weapons: clubs and cutting edges and fire accelerants. He chose something milder, a can of Raid Wasp & Hornet Killer, and put an eye to the window. Cable Guy had rounded the corner and was opening a utility box. Part of his act or he was actually doing something, no way to confirm. Ford, an analytical man, went to the door, dropped to a knee, and waited. A lot could be learned from how a gunman entered a room.

Cable Guy was pretty good. Came through textbook-fashion: empty hand up as a shield, the pistol at high ready while his eyes scanned what is called the fatal funnel. Then stepped through to confront the room's unseen wedge, his shooting arm not fully extended, but enough. Also, he pivoted too slowly.

Ford, from his knee, grabbed the pistol, clamping hard enough to freeze the slide, and used the wasp spray while forcing the barrel down and away. Jetted the man's eyes and mouth as they wrestled for control, Ford thinking, *Pull the trigger, damn you.* That's what he wanted: freeze the slide until one muted shot emptied the chamber without cycling another round. With both hands free and the weapon disabled: end of story.

Instead, the pistol tumbled free. Cable Guy, rather than diving for it, charged blindly. Ford sprawled, spun behind, and used the wasp spray again, but sparingly: one blast in the mouth to silence the man, that's all. Gagging, the man crawled a few yards and pawed at his eyes.

Ford empathized. Spray had slipped under his glasses, and his left eye was tearing. The damn stuff was oily; it burned. He retrieved the pistol, and used a rag that wasn't too grimy. The pistol was a .22 Beretta with a mag full of subsonic hollow-points—a favorite of the Mossad and assassin pretenders.

Above them, Rivera was still yakking, oblivious. Outside, no sign of movement within the Suburban. Ford dropped the rag near Cable Guy's hand, saying, "Use this and keep your voice down. So far, this is just between us. Who sent you?"

The reply was emphatic but garbled, while Cable Guy scrubbed at his eyes.

"Any other weapons?"

A shake of the head.

Ford would have checked anyway. No billfold, no cell phone, but a mini Sig Sauer in an ankle holster, which he pocketed after clearing the chamber. The tool belt had a pocket—two tiny gel transmitters with alligator clips. In the breast pocket of the coveralls, a batch of freshly minted business cards: *Ace Cable & Utility / Largo, Florida.* No logo, but an 800 number. At the bottom: *Hector Spalding / Your Installation Specialist.*

Ford almost smiled. A fake name on a cheap card, yet it meant something to him. Since the 1930s, when the U.S. Marines introduced baseball to Nicaragua and Masagua—Cuba much earlier—spies, spooks, and hit men from Latin countries often deferred to their baseball gloves when choosing an American pseudonym. Wilson or Rawlings was a common fake name; Spalding, MacGregor, and Louisville considered more creative. In esoteric circles—the fifth-floor embassy types—"José Wilson" had become a euphemism for "Latino spy," an inside joke.

Ford, voice low, said, "This is a piss-poor cover story. Come to do a hit while the sun's still up, people around? That's stupid. Or whoever sent you is stupid. Do yourself a favor and talk."

Cable Guy, inhaling fumes, croaked, "Shit . . . how can I? This rag, man, it just makes it worse," yet continued to rub his eyes while toxic oil constricted his throat. The accent was Spanish—Cuban, possibly—but faint. A man who'd spent most of his twenty-some years in the States.

Ford said, "Don't do anything stupid," and went out the door. He returned with a hose, kinked, dripping water. He flushed his own eyes, then told the man, "Sit up—sit on your hands—and cross your legs. Now tilt your head back. No, damn it, keep your eyes open."

That didn't work very well, so he held the Beretta and watched Cable Guy wash his face, gargle and spit, repeating the process several times, before Ford kinked the hose again and jammed it under the door. "What's your name?"

"It's right there, man. You can't read?"

"Your real name."

"*Hector.* I need more of that hose, then maybe my throat'll work better."

"I'm not going to play question-answer."

"You got a problem, call the cops. You ain't no cop, and this shit in my eyes ain't mace, so we both go to jail. What you think about that?"

Ford said, "Not so loud," and picked up the wasp spray, which scared Hector more than the gun. After two false starts, Ford looked at his watch to show impatience. Didn't say a word—silence, the ultimate threat—even when Rivera turned the salsa music louder and clomped toward what might have been the bathroom.

Hector, listening, decided to strike up a conversation with his raspy voice. "You're wrong, what you said. I ain't stupid. A customer wants his ESPN working when he gets home. Nothing stupid about a repairman walking through yards, going into a house, while it's still light."

Ford waited.

"Assaulted me, doing my job."

He listened to more of this before pointing upstairs. "The guy you came to kill? If he finds out, he'll glue your eyes shut and cut off an ear. You still don't talk, he'll make you eat it. Your own ear. Super Glue or sometimes tape, that varies, but not cutting off an ear. It's what *he does*."

Hector sat at attention. "You actually seen him do that? I heard something similar, man, but figured it was bullshit."

"It's not."

"You were actually *there*?"

"I walked away. Why would I stick around? But I heard it happen at least twice."

"Guys screaming, you mean, then he makes them swallow, huh? Shit . . . they'd have to do some chewing first."

"I suppose so."

"Jesus Holy Mary. After that, he tells the prisoner—*interreges* is the right word—he says to them, 'Listen to what your gut tells you. I'll wait.' Or your 'inside voice'—something similar—is what I was told. Sounded like bullshit to me. Is it true?"

Rivera did everything with a flair, it was possible. Ford nodded.

"*No shit?* Why you think I came armed?"

Ford replied, "That's fairly obvious."

"No . . . not to kill the man, but as a precaution for my own personal defense. In the security business, that's what we're taught. Something else I was told"—Hector, becoming cautious, looked up—"well, that Rivera . . . *General* Rivera . . . was traveling with a . . . not a bodyguard, exactly, but some serious badass. You know, as in approach with extreme caution. Safety first, man. I'm not some crack addict. We have what's called a procedural checklist. That don't mean I came to kill anyone."

No need for more wasp spray. Ford, placing it on the ground, added flattery. "From the way you came through the door, I knew you'd had some training. Keep talking, maybe we can work this out."

"From how I handled myself, you mean? Same with you, when you grabbed my weapon—but I expected this psycho *Cubano*, not a gringo-looking dude. Not that I'm making excuses."

"Oh?"

Hector, speaking as one pro to another, said, "Tell me something. If I'd pulled the trigger, would it have blown up? I've heard different things about freezing the slide. Not from anyone with the balls to actually, you know, experiment, so I'm interested."

The temptation was to point the Beretta and demonstrate, but better to keep things moving. "Who told you I was Cuban?"

Hector, sitting on his butt in dirt, replied, "I'll talk, but I want my weapons back. That one there"—a nod at the Beretta—"don't belong to me. I'll lose my job, man, if I can't account for that suppressor. Don't screw with the ATF, right? And you've got to promise not to tell the general until I'm gone. Hey—is he really a general?"

After a long, uneasy silence while Ford stared, the man added, "I ain't saying *you're* crazy. This Cuban dude, I mean. More of a murderer than a pro."

Another chilly silence. "Man . . . by 'gringo,' I didn't mean no racial slur. That's what I was told: a *Cubano* who escaped and hooked up with Rivera. The big concrete jail in Havana—a prison asylum, I'm talking about, the one by the baseball field on your way to José Martí. You never been to Cuba?"

Ford thought, *Uh-oh.* "What's the guy's name?"

"The psycho Cuban?"

"Of course."

Hector sensed an opening. "Do I get my guns back?"

Ford picked up the wasp spray.

5

As applause died down, Figueroa Casanova, enjoying his first ride on a sailboat, waved both hands at the crowd on Mallory Square and asked Tomlinson, "Brother, how'd you get so famous in Key West? Must be a hundred women, but the men, even that juggler, they're clapping, too."

Tomlinson, at the wheel, was kicked back, steering with his feet. "Naw, man, they do this every sunset. Hey . . . mind digging out another beer?" He pointed, wearing frayed shorts and a T-shirt that read BUM FARTO, CALL HOME.

Figgy had puzzled over the strange American words, but his interest had moved on. "They clapping just because the sun goes down?"

"Like a tradition, yeah."

"Brother, you're too modest. Every day since I was born, the sun comes up, it goes down, except in prison—no windows in my cell, you know?—but I'm pretty sure it happened anyway. Why they so happy about night coming?"

Tomlinson cocked his head. "You did time? Why'd the pigs lock you up?" Which, even to him, didn't sound right in Spanish, so he translated, "Cops, I mean. Not 'time' as in clock time."

Figgy replied, "I don't need a clock to know night from day when I see it." He couldn't take his eyes off so much activity, flaming torches, cats jumping through hoops, and too many gringas with nice *chichis* to count. "No, this afternoon I'd of noticed any pretty fans from the dugout. Those women, they looking at you, brother." He opened the Igloo, grabbed two beers fast so as not to miss anything.

Tomlinson considered what he'd just heard while his eyes lived in the moment: tourists and locals packed along the seawall, tangerine clouds over the Tortugas, the air sweet with coconut oil, Gulf Stream jasmine, and some professional-grade weed that only a true pirate town could handle with dignity. A slow turn of the head and there was Key West Bight, the Turtle Kraal docks busy where he often tied his dinghy, although the sandy spot at the end of Simonton was better for swimming naked.

Whoops . . . His head jolted and pivoted the other way.

Christmas Island astern, a colony of sailboats floating where, three weeks ago, he'd moored *No Más* before taking a taxi boat, the *Magic Penny*, ashore. Then late this afternoon, after the ball game, the same in reverse but with a stop at Fausto's Food Palace to buy provisions, then another stop at Marine Hardware on Caroline. No charts of Cuba available, but hemp for a boom vang and extra shackles might come in handy, as would oil for the dinghy's little Yamaha outboard, boat and motor both secured forward atop *No Más*'s cabin.

The baseball team from Indiana had slipped a hundred bucks to Figgy, who'd picked the field clean and gone four for five with two RBIs. Only a Coors Light to the scraggly-haired pitcher who'd closed the game—no runs, but three duck-fart bloopers beyond the range of Indianola Cadillac's limping, over-the-hill fielders. Tomlinson was still peeved about that. But he had gotten the save and paid for provisions anyway.

No problem. He'd inherited a family fortune, but that wasn't the reason. The last thing he'd expected was the little shortstop to ask to accompany him to Cuba, and the chaos he'd recently escaped, all because of a promise he'd made to watch the briefcase.

The deal was done when Figgy finally perused the letters and saw what they contained.

Comrade, Tomlinson thought, *I am proud to have you aboard.*

Honor . . . conviction . . . loyalty—the little dude personified everything good about the Revolution, which, of late, had been made a mockery by snot-nosed dilettantes and political traitors. This sad truth had brought Tomlinson near tears more than once. He accepted the beer, sopping ice chips with his shirt, and toasted his new shipmate. "Solidarity, man."

Figgy was wary of political slogans. He demurred by asking what BUM FARTO, CALL HOME meant.

"That's what everyone called the guy. Bum. He was the fire chief in Key West years ago. One night, he got in his car and was never seen again. Farto, his real name. Seriously. Which reminds me . . ." Tomlinson checked his phone, seeing his last text to Ford, which read *Sailing south on a righteous mission. Stop your damn worrying.* He switched it off and added, "You can't be too careful down here on the Keys."

Figgy had refocused on a group of gringas, five or six with their *chichis* bouncing while they yelled something across the water. "Those women love you, brother. Modesty, yeah, that's sometimes good, but it won't get you no papaya. Maybe they'd enjoy a boat ride—make some hot oil with us. You think?"

Tomlinson smiled at the Cuban slang and checked Mallory Square. Yes . . . a redhead and a blonde he recognized—possibly several familiar faces jumbled back there in memory. Over the years, he'd dropped anchor in bedrooms from Duval to Cudjoe Key, but women always looked so different wearing clothes instead of body paint. He replied, "Those whom Key West does not kill, it enlightens. *That's* why we're not turning back."

It was more strange talk from this odd pitcher who didn't throw hard enough to break glass but had a pretty good curve. Figueroa liked him anyway, trusted the man's kindness and sophisticated manner. Felt comfortable enough to speak up when he didn't understand. "You mean 'kill' as in *putas* who rob? Or these island women, they exhaust a man's *pinga*?"

"Count on it," Tomlinson replied. "It's happened to better sailors than us. That's why I know when to pull anchor and haul ass to saner harbors." He stood to ready the mainsail. The shipping channel, busy with traffic and sunset pirate vessels, required an engine. Once clear of Kingfish Shoals, however, they would be free if there was wind . . . But, damn it, there was no wind. The low-pressure system had left a vacuum of calm that would make them a puppet of the Gulf Stream . . . until morning at least, according to the VHF under the helm, which he knelt to turn louder.

"But they're callin' your name, brother."

"Yeah? Think back to your Greek tragedies—'Beware the Sirens on the rocks' and all that. Odysseus dropped anchor and Circe, plus some other witch goddesses, drugged him, screwed the man blind, and kept him and his shipmates captives for a year."

Figueroa's eyes were fixed on Mallory Square. "They're witches?"

"Circe? Hell, yeah. Spellbinders, they all are."

"If Circe's the one I'm looking at, sometimes a year don't seem so long."

Tomlinson replied, "Hush a minute," and listened to NOAA weather's monotone: seas outside the reef three feet or less until morning, when a high-pressure band increases wind slightly to . . .

Figgy didn't attempt to translate those foreign words. Still waving at the eager gringas, he endured a sense of loss unknown since his first month in Havana's prison psychiatric ward. "Brother, isn't there some way?"

Tomlinson muttered, "Damn. Apparently not," and switched off the VHF.

Figgy suggested, "How about I swim to shore? Allow me, oh . . . just two hours. Shine a light and I will swim back. I don't doubt what you say about those witches, but I have never experienced this tragedy you fear."

Tomlinson slouched behind the wheel. "The weather gods usually ignore NOAA's doom-and-gloom bullshit when *No Más* goes to sea. Apparently, my vibe's out of kilter." He looked at the horizon, a turquoise glaze to Cuba, then at his new shipmate. "Mind rolling a skinny—my Spanish seems to be fading." Then: "What was that last thing you said?"

OVER MARGARITAS at Louie's Backyard, Tomlinson had to lie. "*Cerci* in Cuban means 'a beautiful, sensual woman.' *Women*, in your case. See? It's not that my amigo can't remember names." Explained this to three German nurses who had intercepted them after *No Más* was illegally anchored off Dog Beach, where their dinghy was tied—an Avon inflatable that had rocketed them to shore and was visible from their table near the tiki bar.

Next, a question about the shortstop's shoes. "Baseball spikes, we call them," Tomlinson explained. He signaled the bartender, indicated their empty pitcher, and called, "I think we're prepared to sail again."

Figgy disappeared after that with one of the Cercis who was infatuated with the rhythm of his name: *Figueroa Casanova*. Kept repeating it like lyrics to a song, which was okay. It warmed the long silences at a table where only Tomlinson spoke English.

Twenty minutes later, Figgy and Cerci reappeared from somewhere beneath the deck, both a little woozy.

"Mission accomplished," Tomlinson whispered. "Now, let's hit the dinghy and get under way."

Figueroa tapped his wrist as if he owned a watch. "You promised two hours. It is hardly dark yet. Oh"—he stole a look under the table—"thanks, my brother. Next time, I carry that with me."

The briefcase, he meant. He'd insisted they bring the thing, a last-minute fire drill that had tumbled Tomlinson into the water, but this was not the first time he'd used soggy bills to buy drinks.

On Thomas Street, they popped into Blue Heaven, the outdoor seating fragrant with frangipani and scrawny, scratching chickens. In response to the hungry look Figgy awarded the fattest hen, their server warned, "Don't you dare—they're protected." That hastened them on to Margaritaville and another frosty pitcher in tribute to a generous man. By then, a fourth Cerci had hinted she was seducible—this one from the Wolverine State, a stunning Ph.D. candidate who played rugby and had the scars to prove it. "I've got a room at the La Concha," she said into Tomlinson's ear. "Just me. Bring the Krauts, if you want, but no more than two, and no less than three."

Talk about cryptic. On a napkin was her room number, and an addendum: "Love the name Cerci. Much cooler than the name I've been using."

Hmm. Tomlinson was aware that women journeyed to Key West eager to try what was unthinkable back home, yet he fretted for the coed's innocence, and all the innocents who had run amok on the rocks of Bone Key. What to do?

He thought back. Long ago, he had earned his doctorate with a dissertation that became an international best seller: *One Fathom Above Sea Level*. A "fathom" being six feet—the distance between earth and one man's eyes. A line he'd written offered guidance: *When torn between doing what is morally right or the chance for a few hours of fun, never decide until morning.*

After that, the streets of Key West assumed their normal spatial focus, which is to say fuzzy . . . not unlike embedding marbles in one's eye sockets and watching the babysitter swim naked at nap time.

Cerci, the one from Berlin, had listened patiently to this tale of boyhood emergence, but Cerci, the Wolverine Ph.D., had bigger adventures in mind. "Eat this," she said.

Tomlinson considered the pill she squeezed into his palm. "Mescaline?"

"Think of it as a time capsule." A sharp, perceptive smile while she continued: "I *knew* it was you. I've read your book at least ten times, and the last chapter still makes me cry." A slight sniffle, then a brighter smile. "Mind if I snap a selfie to send a few friends?"

Her phone was on the nightstand, two topless fräuleins away.

Flash . . . Flash . . . Flash-Flash. Blinding, but the strobe helped the mescaline unfurl gently throughout Tomlinson's brain. Time to show some real American know-how and put his back into the task at hand.

He did.

Yes . . . this corn-fed Cerci was the real McCoy, a true spellbinder. Yet, some passage of time later, on Duval Street, Tomlinson experienced a disturbing moment of clarity when a bear-sized man shouldered him off the sidewalk and muttered what sounded like a threat in Russian. Then again, at the corner of Southard and

Margaret, when Figgy, standing shirtless, briefcase in hand, froze as he stared into the darkness of trees, where there were tiny columned mansions and row after row of stones.

"What's wrong?"

"Brother, we being followed. You see him?"

Tomlinson mustered his motor control and did a slow turn. "Hey . . . where'd our Cercis go? I've become very fond of that spunky little Wolverine."

"It because of him, brother. The witches, they all ran."

"What? That damn trollop . . . she used me like a hood ornament. *Shit* . . ." He searched his pockets, shorts still wet for some reason—oh yeah, they'd crashed Pier House Beach for a swim, but his dripping billfold had survived. His iPhone present, too, but iffy. "Well, she's no thief. I'll give her that much."

"Shhhh!" The Cuban clutched his Santería beads and stood motionless like a dog flagging a snake. Then gestured with his chin. "Outside the wall by the tree. See? I hope it's not him."

"Him *who*?"

"A *Santero* from my village, but an asshole. 'Cause of him, I got sent to the crazy prison for murder."

"Gad, Figgy. You killed someone?"

"Or could be that Russian who called you a pussy."

Sobering, to hear such words. "That's even more upsetting. No one's supposed to know I'm here."

"Santería, my brother." Figgy whispered the words as if they explained everything.

To Tomlinson, they did. Santería, voodoo, were mystic religions, and even a *Santero*, which was a novice priest, would have powers far beyond the norm. A Russian, not so much, but formidable—the guy had resembled the fruit of a Cossack screwing a grizzly. Tomlinson took stock. He squinted again, seeing rows of stones and flags and miniature stone mansions that were . . . mausoleums?

A *cemetery* . . . Christ, how had they stumbled this far off course?

Figgy nudged him. "No . . . he's behind us."

A turn of the tiller. Streetlights on Southard spilled pools of yellow onto asphalt, each pool smaller, block after block. Banyan trees shadowed sidewalks and the occasional utility gizmo, such as a fire hydrant or a post office drop box. After many seconds, Tomlinson relaxed and pointed. "Is that what scared you? It's just a mailbox, for christ's sake. How tall is this guy?"

"Even bigger than me, but that's not him. He must'a moved, the son of a dog." Figgy shuffled closer to the drop box, shoes clicking like a shod horse.

"Tell me something. Did Cerci give you a pill to eat?"

"Maybe. And some dollar bills that got the wrong pictures on them."

Deutschmarks, Tomlinson translated. "Not the German. I'm talking about the Cerci with small *chichis*. Or she could have roofied your beer. Frankly, I don't think that my little Wolverine is the squared-away feminist she pretends to be."

Figgy did it again: froze. His head swiveled shoreward to an antebellum house dark beneath trees, a few stars, but no moon showing. *"Madre de Dios,"* he murmured.

"Now what?"

"He's coming, brother—*run*."

The Cuban's spikes sparked toward the cemetery, briefcase swinging, while Tomlinson hollered, "Dude . . . you can't outrun mescaline."

Too late. Unless . . . unless the little shortstop's fears were reality-based. If so, darker forces might be at work here.

Beelzebub—still on my trail, huh? Good! Tomlinson, a pacifist by choice but a spiritual warrior by nature, had been anticipating such a visit. He hollered toward the shadows, "Pleased to meet you—now kiss my ass."

A fence of wrought iron separated the house from the street, metal cool to the touch. The gate wasn't locked when he tried it. Beside the porch, bushes parted with the tinkling of wind chimes. Two creatures appeared in the form of human shapes, one bear-sized, the other smaller. Teeth flashed a Rottweiler grin, followed by a cough of Russian.

Tomlinson stood his ground. Waited, expecting the worst, but the specters retreated. Soon vanished, as if circling behind the house.

More wind chimes on this dense, still night.

Tomlinson yelled after them, "Now who's the pussy?"

6

Upstairs in the rental cottage, Gen. Rivera said to Ford, "He came to assassinate me with a Beretta? I, too, like Berettas. At least that shows some respect."

Ford put the gelatin listening devices in the freezer and closed the door. "You need to pack up and get out of here, that's what it shows. Where's your suitcase?"

"You don't understand. I was on the phone with . . . well, a person I trust. He warned me about something they might try to do to me. Radiation poisoning—a horrible thing. Your hair falls out, and you shit yourself to death." At the window, Rivera opened the blinds to see where the Suburban had been parked. "You should have brought that *puta* to me. I know ways to make men talk."

Hector had talked, but Ford hadn't volunteered all that he'd learned. "Poison? Why?"

A shrug. "A microscopic grain of something, an isotope—already the name is gone. They jab you with a needle or slip it into food. From their rocket program. It's the way that . . . the way they do things now."

Jesus Christ. Rocket program—it had to be the Chinese or the Russians. No, it was the Russians. The over-complicated, Cold War style left little doubt. Ford asked, "Are you sure?"

"Two of my contacts in Cuba are dead. I just found out. Another is in intensive care. A woman . . . quite beautiful"—Rivera sounded sad and a little wistful—"who has, over the period of a week, lost her beautiful hair. A bullet—I'd much prefer a soldier's death. Shitting is no way for a man to die."

An hour after sunset, they dropped the Mustang at Hertz. On the way to the airport, Ford turned the radio off and said, "General, I need to know what's going on."

The former dictator replied, "I can't fly out until I've found Figuerito. How many times must I say this? That stadium sign we passed, why not stop and have a look?" They had already passed the Twins stadium, but the Red Sox complex was ahead, the lights of the practice fields aglow.

Ford seldom lost his temper but came close. "Goddamn it, Juan, I just saved your life. Enough with the bullshit. Why are they after you?"

Rivera stiffened but let it go. "The world has turned savage, old friend. I knew I was being followed, but I thought it was because of my new sports agency business."

"Smuggling baseball players, you mean."

"Phrase it how you like. What I'm telling you is, now I'm not so sure. I was cultivating a variety of businesses in Havana. At first, I thought the Mexican cartels, or the Cubans. That I might have stepped on the wrong toes. This American dream of yours can bite a man in the ass, which your propaganda fails to—"

Ford interrupted, "It has nothing to do with baseball. Russians don't give a damn about Cuban ballplayers." He had yet to allude to the contents of the briefcase but did now. "For the last decade, outsiders have been stealing collectibles from Cuba. Paintings, historic items. Suddenly, Russia and Cuba are allies again. You know what I'm asking you—the stuff you've been selling on the Internet."

Rivera rode in silence until he realized the turn to Southwest Regional was before the Red Sox complex. He slapped the dash. "I have to find Figuerito! Must I write my orders on paper?"

"I didn't enlist in your army, Juan. Tell me why the goddamn Russians are involved."

"I didn't say they were."

Stubborn bastard. Ford drove and used the silence to put together a workable premise. Letters written by Fidel Castro between 1953 and 1963—a tumultuous period. Batista ousted, 1959. The botched Bay of Pigs invasion, 1961. Next came the Cuban Missile Crisis; the Berlin Wall was erected. The CIA attempted to foil the execution of three hundred anti-Castro operatives, and they had botched the first of several attempts to take out Fidel. Then 1963: JFK assassinated, November 22nd. Oswald killed; Jack Ruby dies. The whole time, a lot of backdoor nastiness between clandestine agencies worldwide. Riots and protests fired by the accelerant of KGB money. East Berlin, Saigon, Nicaragua, El Salvador—same thing but financed by American dollars.

The biggie, of course, was JFK. Conspiracy theories about Ruby, the Mafia, and Fidel's orders to "Kill Kennedy" were still believed today.

But it was bullshit. Decades later, for professional reasons, Ford had studied details of the event. He had filled a folder with notes from investigations by the Warren Commission, the House Select Committee, and had even played a much later role in debunking Congress's antiquated confidence in so-called sonic experts. They had insisted that a lone gunman could not have fired three rounds—or was it four?—from a bolt-action rifle in less than six seconds.

Once again, bullshit. Yet, every twenty years or so,

some esoteric government agency ordered that it be proven. Ford was not a gifted marksman, let alone a Marine Sharpshooter, but even he could put three rounds into a moving target from only fifty-nine yards away— and in less than six seconds. An FBI shooter, using a clone of Oswald's rifle, had done it in only *four*.

But there was still one sensitive unknown out there. It had been overlooked even by fringe feeders like movie hack Oliver Stone and other conspiracy profiteers. The Castros didn't kill JFK, nor did the CIA, the Soviets, or the Mafia. The only valid question was: Did Fidel and the Soviets know, six weeks before the assassination, that Lee Harvey Oswald had visited the Cuban embassy and vowed to do exactly what he did?

Love letters. Ford tried to imagine why the Castros would reveal sensitive information to a mistress. It seemed unlikely . . . So why, fifty years later, did the Russians care?

"Damn it, Juan. Uranium poisoning? I'm not stupid. Talk to me."

Rivera set his jaw and glowered. That did it. Ford pulled off the road, his truck's headlights showing weeds and a yellow sign that read *Panther Crossing* while traffic sped past. "Okay, I'll try another approach. What's so important about that shortstop? He's too old to sign with a major league team—don't lie to me. Why did you bring him to the States?"

"*Lie* to you?" Rivera's temper bordered on the berserk. He was famous for it. He shifted his weight in the seat and glared. "You are calling me a liar?"

A stare-down, but it was the general who blinked when he realized what he'd just heard. "Wait . . . How do you know Figuerito's age? All I said was that he has no birth certificate."

"Tell me why it's worth risking your life to find him. Then I'll explain."

A light came on in the general's head. "By god . . . you know where he is."

Ford nodded, listened to a series of threats, before he repeated, "Tell me the truth."

It wasn't a long story, but he parked again—this time, in the airport's cell phone lot—to listen to Rivera conclude, "That's why I trusted Figuerito to keep the briefcase, even though I could find no electronic device inside."

"You still haven't said what's in there."

Rivera used his hands to say *I'm not done*. "The point is, I was still being followed. Now I'm worried they are following Figuerito, too. That they'll stick him with a needle, like my beautiful friend who has lost her hair. That's why I must find him, then return immediately to Cuba."

"I'll be damned. You actually care about the guy." Ford didn't pose this as a question.

"He is a simpleton, that shortstop, but very honest—

also crazy, from what I've been told. Perhaps these Russians will be the lucky ones if I find him first."

"You mean he's dangerous?"

Rivera replied, "I think not, but who can say what is in a man's head? My friend on the phone continues to warn me that Figuerito is a violent psychopath. Even the warden I bribed described him as a serial killer without conscience, so . . ." The former dictator lowered the window to watch a plane land, his mind slipping back in memory. A bemused smile formed. "Of course, as you know, there are people who say the same about me."

A LITTLE BEFORE TEN, Ford got an NA beer and sat at the computer in his lab. Across the room, the dog opened one yellow eye to watch, seeing Ford's familiar size, lighted water boxes and odors behind him, then heard the man's familiar voice.

"That damn Tomlinson, not a word since his stupid text. So maybe there's an email . . . if he wasn't too blitzed to find an Internet café."

Sailing south on a righteous mission . . . don't worry the text had read.

Ford used two fingers to rap at the keyboard, his wire glasses silver beneath a gooseneck lamp, while he spoke to the retriever: "If there's nothing to worry about, why the hell doesn't he call? At least have the courtesy to give me an update. Oh . . . I bet I know—a waterproof phone case is pointless if he doesn't use the damn thing. Or, just thoughtless. Yeah, thoughtless, that's him."

More typing. The dog's yellow eye closed; he returned to sleep while the alpha figure spoke, occasionally, in a tone that communicated nothing, but tilted his head when he heard "What the hell?"

Ford's neighbors Rhonda and JoAnn, who lived aboard an old Chris-Craft, *Tiger Lilly*, had sent an email, subject: *Man of the Year*. There were photos of Tomlinson, naked on a bed, posing with three topless women—two large-breasted blondes, the other dark-haired, younger and attractive, despite cat whiskers painted on her face. Little tufts of horns on her temples, too, which caused her to resemble a woodland creature with teeth.

Ford was no prude but closed the photo after reading Rhonda's note:

Copied from Facebook just now before they took it down. 726 likes. Capt. Quirk went back to Key West?

Relief, is what he felt at first. A foursome negated the chances of radiation poisoning or a bullet. Yet, something about one of the blondes tugged at his subconscious. He opened the photo again . . . had to zoom in tight to avoid the distraction of her Teutonic breasts. Tomlinson's boney thighs, thank god, vanished, too. Ford removed his glasses, cleaned them, and focused on a necklace the blonde wore: a silver shield transected by a tiny ornate sword. Atop the sword's hilt was a star.

"Jesus H. Christ." Ford pushed his chair back as the dog's head bounced to attention.

"He has no idea what he's gotten himself into. I'll call Rhonda. It might help to know when this was posted."

The dog didn't bother to stretch, trotted to his side, while Ford, talking to himself, picked up the phone and muttered, "That woman, she's with the goddamn KGB."

Actually, the FSB—Russian Federal Security Service. No reason to explain to a dog that only the name had been changed.

MOORED BETWEEN PILINGS beneath the stilthouse was his boat: a 26-foot rigid hull inflatable purchased through friends at the Special Ops base in Tampa—a confiscated cocaine boat, supposedly, but he knew otherwise. It tugged at its lines on this night of calm and stars, no moon, no clouds, no wind or waves.

Weather blew through the tropics with the indifference of airplanes passing overhead.

Ford found the light switch. Mullet scattered; shadows of big fish drifted under the dock until the dog vaulted after them.

"Damn it. Now I'll have to get a towel for the truck."

Instead, he stepped aboard. The deck, mounted on hydraulic shocks, absorbed his weight without listing.

Couldn't hurt to check a few things, although he was a fastidious man who obsessed over his tools, from microscopes to fly rods, dive gear, and weapons.

Boats received special attention. This one was made by Brunswick Tactical in Edgewater, Florida. It had all the high-tech frills: a radar tower aft, a cavernous console, and an electronics suite above the wheel. The hull was Kevlar encircled by tubes of black carbon fiber that looked bulletproof—and maybe were, considering the agency that had commissioned it. To minimize radar signature, the boat was built low to the water with few right angles or vertical surfaces, and had a bow hood made of neoprene polymer sheeting that was radar-absorbent. When opened, the hood covered the bow like a tent.

For power: twin Merc 250s, top speed over sixty, a range of four hundred miles—almost to Cuba and back, or almost to the Yucatán.

Almost being the operative word.

Ford checked fuel, oil, and plugged in the charger even though all four batteries were new.

At Jensen's Marina on Captiva he had stored a fifty-gallon gas bladder, thinking he would never need it. He told the dog, "Let's hope I don't."

FROM HIS TRUCK, he phoned Scottsdale, Arizona, Colorado Springs, and an unnamed city in Maryland.

The process was so complicated it resembled ceremony. Six calls, five recordings, and, finally, one human voice: Hal Harrington, an old associate who still owed Ford a big favor, but the conversation did not go well.

Harrington saying, "You dropped out. What do you want me to do?"

Irritating, the bland way he spoke. Before getting in his truck, Ford had sent the man an encrypted note, part of a text he had received from his pilot friend Dan Futch. Implicit was Ford's request for help:

"Mexico such a shithole via Bahamas only safe route. Most likely San Andros, clear customs, use Bethells as residence. Approach from east at night, low altitude, fifty feet max, use mountains to obscure Fat Albert, and hope no boats in the area when we land."

They were directions, a seaplane ingress that could be to only one place, Cuba, although the island wasn't mentioned. Something else not mentioned was that the charter company, Tampa to Havana, would not accept firearms as baggage. Even if they did, the next flight wasn't until Sunday. Neither option would get him to Cuba before Tomlinson arrived the next night or Friday morning, depending on the wind.

Ford attempted patience with his former boss. "I sent you something fifteen minutes ago. Maybe you didn't get it."

"Really? Guess not."

Harrington was lying.

Ford said, "Didn't we learn a technique called communiqué by omission? I'm reluctant to spell it out. Hal?"—he tried to soften this into a request—"Don't make me."

"Is that a threat?"

"You know better. Maybe if you check your emails again? In the note's first line, there's a mention of Mexico."

After a couple of seconds, Harrington said, "I'll be damned. A little confusing the way it's worded, but it helps. You should have referenced this in the first place."

"I'm a little rusty, I guess." The dog, with his nose out the window, ears flapping in the wind, sneezed.

"Gesundheit," Harrington said.

"Thank you," Ford replied. "I wouldn't jump the ladder if I didn't think this was serious."

"Does that mean you're interested in coming back?"

Ford resorted to a lie. "It's that obvious? I never thought I'd get tired of sitting on my butt in air-conditioning, but, yeah, I sort of miss the old days."

"You've always been a sentimental guy, Doc." A hint of sarcasm there. "Well . . . I guess I could do some checking around. As a friend—not as a contracted deal, of course. Keep that in mind. What I'm still unclear about is—"

Ford pushed the phone away from his ear, thinking, *I might as well hang up right now.* That happened a few minutes later when he lost patience and said, "I don't give a damn, Hal, if it's protocol or not."

Harrington was a trigger-puller, the real deal, but, through necessity, had developed the polish of a politician. "I know," the man replied. "Any wonder your special phone doesn't ring anymore?"

FORD HAD INTENDED to buy extra dog food at the 7-Eleven. Instead, he headed for Jensen's Twin Palm on Captiva, which was across Blind Pass Bridge. Impossible not to slow at Castaways and check the cottage windows. Maggie was there, the same cheap rental in the drive.

"I don't know what's got into me," he said to the dog, thinking the words but sometimes speaking aloud. "This one-night-stand bullshit, it's symptomatic of something. Totally out of character."

The dog wasn't interested.

"If she's awake, I've got a built-in excuse. Those papers stolen from Castro's estate? Didn't find a single damn article. She wasn't lying. Why would she make that up? That tells me something about her possible occupation. Reason enough, I think, to sneak a look at her phone. Now I'm glad I did." Ford noticed car lights behind him and pulled into the grocery parking lot, the store and Sunset Café closed, but the Flamingo still open if he was hungry.

Maybe later.

"On the other hand, if I ask, she might have to reveal

something about herself. Next, we'd be trading numbers and I don't want that. Know why?" With the truck running, he focused on Maggie's cottage, hoping the screen door would open, also hoping it wouldn't.

It didn't.

On the road again, he finally admitted, *Because Maggie's married, that's why.* Pissed at himself because he'd known from the start. You can remove a ring, but not a tan line. Breaking a personal rule was taboo, but lying to himself was worse.

That wasn't his only lie.

At Jensen's Marina, by the docks, palm trees framed a vast darkness where navigation lights blinked, red, white, and green. Ford let the dog out, walked to the bait tanks, and stared. To the northeast, across six miles of water and muted by mangroves, a milky dot marked the fishing village of Sulphur Wells. A woman lived there. An unusually good woman; smart, independent, and solid. Captain Hannah Smith was also a first-rate fishing guide.

They had dated, but it was more than that; now they were done.

Ford touched the phone in his pocket . . . hesitated, still staring, and sent a telepathic message: *I'll call you when I get back.*

The fifty-gallon fuel bladder, stored beside the office, was empty, so it was easy enough to load. It took longer to unlock the fuel pump at Dinkin's Bay, where Mack complained, "Working the graveyard shift now, are we? What's up?" It was almost midnight.

Ford contrived a story about Ridley turtles and camping on Shark River, south of Naples.

Hours later, in darkness, with engines synched, he threaded the cutoff Lighthouse Beach and pointed his boat toward Key West.

Key West Cemetery is nineteen acres of ship-
wrights, cigarmakers, gunrunners, wreckers,
sailors, and others who would have been happier drowned at sea. Not a cheery place at night, especially after an hour spent searching for a missing
shortstop. No flashlight, only a lighter to flick, after
tripping over several tombstones, one of which turned
out to be the grave of an old friend.

Tomlinson felt a descending melancholy. He sat with
his back against the stone and tested a happier theory.

"Hell, Shine . . . maybe I'm imagining this entire
goat fest. Is that why you called this meeting?"

From beneath the stone Captain Kermit "Shine"

Forbes responded, *Boy, get off your dead butt an' go find that li'l Cuban.*

Tomlinson obeyed. He was striding toward Passover Lane when he noticed blue flashers to the south and sirens. Experience told him to flee north, but he maintained control and crept toward the lights anyway. When he was close enough, he stopped behind a tree and listened as two cops questioned a man who, even seated on the grass, was the size of a grizzly bear.

"We got anyone on the force who speaks Russian? Harry, try Spanish and see what you get."

Harry wasn't as loud. The bear-sized man, who was Russian, mumbled. Tomlinson crawled on hands and knees to the next tombstone so he could hear better.

". . . That's all I could understand. He says their attacker was a Cuban guy."

"In this town?" Cop laughter. "He'll have to do better than that. Jesus Christ, the guy's huge, huh? Over three hundred pounds, I bet."

More questions, more mumbling. Then Harry, sounding surprised, said, "Christ, he claims his buddy is dead. Somewhere around here, beaten to death. Or half dead. And says he—this guy—that he tripped over something and maybe hit his head. That's why he got away."

"The Cuban, you mean?"

"Yeah, the assailant—if it really happened."

"Bullshit. Where's the body? I don't see blood on the guy's clothes or anywhere else. I think he's wasted."

"We'll have to see what he blows. Wait . . . Now he claims the guy, the assailant, had . . . what? Say it again . . . Yeah, he says the Cuban had knives on his shoes—'razors,' I think he means. That he used . . . a shoe."

"Used a shoe as a murder weapon? Geezus, what next?"

"I'm just telling you, guy's Spanish sucks."

"He's shitfaced. Meth, maybe. Wait and see, he's a junkie."

"I dunno . . . A guy his size, and more than a thousand euros in his wallet. Notice those white socks and the shirt. He's just a tourist, I think. Call, have dispatch look up the Russian word for 'spikes.' As in track or baseball."

Oh shit . . .

Tomlinson, on his knees, did an about-face and crawled toward the monument to sailors killed on the USS *Maine*, Havana Harbor, 1898.

When it was safe, he ran.

FIGGY WAS INVISIBLE, curled cat-like in the dinghy, until he sat up and asked, "What took you so long? Two hours was plenty for me."

Tomlinson had to cover his mouth, it scared him so badly.

This was around four-thirty a.m., still dark, but the wind was freshening. By dawn, they were aboard *No Más*, south of Sand Key Light, sails taut beneath seabirds that flocked landward. Upon a cobalt sea, shadows spooked fish to flight—comets of silver like dragonflies.

Tomlinson had to make a decision. Return to Sanibel Island or maintain course to Cuba? Tethered high above Cudjoe Key was Fat Albert, a radar balloon that narced innocent boats and planes for a radius of two hundred miles. Nosey pricks, those feds. A sailboat would draw less attention, of course, and the Cubans wouldn't notice until they'd crossed the Straits, but, even so, harboring a murderer as a shipmate invited prying eyes.

This was a decision that couldn't be discussed with the suspect in question, who also happened to be a dope-smoking illegal—two marks in Figgy's favor, but not enough to convince Tomlinson. He would have called Ford for advice—the biologist was an old hand at this sort of ugly business—if his cell phone hadn't drowned. There was always the marine operator via VHF, but the probability of eavesdroppers nixed that idea.

He steered south and, at noon, disengaged the autopilot and changed to a heading of 230 degrees to avoid Havana and negate the relentless flow of the Gulf Stream. *No Más* creaked and groaned, cleaving waves that shattered like crystal and threw spray to salt his first beer of the day.

Figgy, subdued, stuck to bottled water, but did remark, "I'm done with German witches. They give me a headache."

An hour went by before Tomlinson finally asked what he'd been afraid to ask: "What happened to your baseball spikes?"

The Cuban wiggled his bare toes. "I still got one left, but you told me no spikes on the boat."

"I appreciate that. What about the other shoe?"

He expected a lie but sat straighter when Figgy replied, "I used it to beat the *Santero* on the head, then it flew away and disappeared. Makes me sad to talk about. Why don't we put on some music?"

Okay—the Latina enchantress Omara Portuondo singing "Dos Gardenias." Tomlinson turned it up, saying, "You're sad because the guy you beat is a novice priest, yes, I understand. Were you hurt during the fight?"

Just a scrape, which looked more like a puncture wound when the shortstop extended his arm.

"What about the *Santero*?"

"Sure hope I hurt him. All my life, I wanted nice baseball spikes. That son of a bitch, I think he caused my shoe to disappear because I was hitting him hard, brother. Now I've got no American dollars and only one shoe."

Gad. Time to regroup. How to handle this without turning it into an interrogation? One thing Tomlinson knew, Figueroa Casanova was true to his vow not to lie. Or wait . . . In a past conversation, hadn't he allowed himself some wiggle room? *I promised never to lie unless . . .*

Unless what?

Tomlinson was averse to verbal traps because his own innocence had been tested too often. He toned it down by asking, "What happened to the Russian? In the cemetery, I heard him talking to cops. I couldn't tell if he was hurt or not, but he claimed the guy you hit is dead. That you clubbed him to death with your shoe."

"Killed the *Santero*?" Figgy had to think about that. He drifted inward, fingering his necklace, red beads and black spaced with tiny cowrie shells. Returned, saying, "Maybe he only appeared to be dead. Eleguá is famous as a trickster."

"That's the *Santero*'s name?"

"No. Eleguá is my guardian saint. That the kind of shit he does, brings his followers to the crossroad of good and evil. Like, 'Child, *you* decide.' The *Santero*, he's the asshole I mentioned—Vernum Quick. I don't mind being chased, but, man, don't you catch me. Yeah, I beat the shit out of Vernum bad."

"Who you think played dead?"

"Vernum, he don't play at nothing. Some years ago, he murdered three schoolgirls on their way to school. Used a machete out in a cane field, then blamed me. This was after their bones was found, but before he come to my *mu-maw*'s house. He wanted to know where certain items were hidden—only he said 'buried.' Which tells you how dumb even a *Santero* can be."

"Your mother's house?"

"My grandmother who raised me. My *abuela*. What she should of said was, 'Vernum, what kind of fool buries three motorcycles under the ground?' Expensive machines, you know? *Harleys*, with lots of chrome. At the time, of course, she didn't know about them dead girls—or that the Guardia, the police, would come for me later. This was three years ago."

Ms. Omara was singing "Noche Cubana" now, the sweetest of wistful love songs. Tomlinson adjusted the volume and reminded himself, *Don't press, let the man talk.*

Lunchtime. They ate tomatoes pilfered from a garden on Simonton and canned black beans. For seasoning, a key lime. At one p.m., the wind dropped. Tomlinson used the diesel to put twenty miles behind them before he tired of fumes and noise. A little before three, the wind died, but that was okay. He dumped the dinghy over the side, locked the motor to the transom, and re-rigged the towing harness for something to do. At four, *No Más* wallowed in waves while the halyard clinked. From the southeast, a bank of clouds drifted, seeking the warmer water of the Gulf Stream. They descended as fog—not thick, more like tendrils of steam, but dense enough to drip from the sheeting.

"Smoke," Tomlinson smiled. "Don't the clouds remind you of that?" He broke out a hash pipe, which he seldom used—he associated pipes with white-collar stoners, although a bong was okay. Figgy's headache improved after a bowl of homegrown Crystal River. He became talkative.

"It surprised me, seeing that *Santero*. Especially with a Russian. In Cuba, most people hate Russians, hoped they'd never come back, but they did. I was locked up so can't say exactly when this trend began. Not so long, though." He pivoted to look into a misty horizon that had recently cupped the lights of Key West. "Except for them witches and the Russian, I like America. You promise we'll come back?"

Tomlinson noted visibility and felt it safe to nod. "Vernum Quick, huh? That sounds Bahamian, not Cuban."

"It's the same. In way-back times, some men was named for their nature. See? Like how fast they move or their love for women. When the Guardia come, they were already convinced a Casanova took those girls."

"Not just your name, though, right? It was because this dude Vernum lied. The man should be defrocked, if you didn't kill . . . Well, if he's still alive. What did you tell the Cuban cops?"

"The truth, brother. I always tell the truth. That's why the Guardia took me straight to jail."

Tomlinson had been nudging the conversation toward

Gen. Rivera—how had the man learned about the machine guns and hidden Harleys?—but had to back up. "Even though you denied murdering the girls?"

"That's not the way it happened. The lieutenant come to my *mu-maw*'s house and asked why I murdered three innocent people."

"Your *mu* . . . ? Oh, your grandmother."

"Yeah. I told him those people weren't innocent, and I only killed two people, not three—and no way their bodies were found—so why was he bothering us? You see, at the time, I knew nothing about the girls in the cane field."

Tomlinson took a minute to collect himself by pretending a need for the sextant. To the north, cumulus clouds that had once marked the Dry Tortugas were now a curtain of gray. All sorts of things—airplanes, ships, the steady flow of refugees on rafts—often disappeared out here in the Straits. He closed the box of polished teak, saying, "I'm sure you had a damn good reason to do whatever you did."

"That's what I explained to the lieutenant."

"Explained why you had to kill—"

"Yeah. Two men come snooping around at night— big fellas like the one back there"—Figgy motioned— "so I used a baseball bat, a bat I'd carved from a *madera*, which also makes me sad. I packed their bodies on a mule all night and threw that bat off the cliff, too. What choice did I have? If I promise to protect a certain place, man, I *protect* it. Same with the briefcase . . . but only because I didn't know what it contains." The Cuban glowered at the cabin. "General Rivera, next time I see him, I think I'll beat his head with my other shoe."

"You clubbed them with a baseball bat until they were . . ."

"Of course. Isn't that what I just told you?"

Holy Christ. This new shipmate of his was a stone-cold killer. But sitting alone with a felon in the middle of the Gulf Stream was no place to quibble over morality or the outcome of what was, perhaps, one drunken night and a whim.

Tethered off the stern, the dinghy, with its shiny black motor, urged the need for a plan of escape. Instead, Tomlinson forced himself to think about the briefcase. Intuition told him there was a connection between Castro's letters and Figgy. No other way to explain the shortstop's reaction when he saw them. Maybe the letters had been written to a woman in Figgy's village. Possibly even to a relative. Or even Figgy's grandmother, but that was a stretch. No matter—Tomlinson felt confident the Cuban would get to it. He offered support by saying, "Typical cops. Even when you tell the truth, they're pricks."

"Exactly what I said—'Man, I being totally straight, here'—and the lieutenant ask me why didn't I confess earlier? Confess? What a stupid question. Brother, why would I confess to something I never lied about in the first place?"

That made so much sense, Tomlinson wanted to write it down.

The shortstop continued, "I explained to the lieutenant about my vow of honesty. Know what he did? Laughed at me. Laughed right in my face. Said, 'Boy, you are lying or you are crazy.' I told him, '*Cabrón*, I never lie.' For that insult, I knocked him on his *puta* ass—used my left hand, of course, 'cause, you know, I throw with my right."

Listening, Tomlinson exhaled a long breath. "Dude, you're as sane as the day is long. A ballplayer's got to protect his throwing hand."

"Yeah! But they took me to crazy prison anyway. The one on the road to José Martí, right there by the ball field."

Prisión demente is what Figgy called the asylum in Spanish.

"Can you imagine? Sit in the dark, hearing baseball through the walls. You know that sound a bat makes when you hit it good? Hit a ball, I mean, not like the one I used to kill those fellas. Sometimes I cried and cried. Three years, three months, and three days. Got so them guards really believed I was crazy."

A cooler was strapped to the cabin bulkhead. Tomlinson got up. "You know, Figgy—uhh, is it okay if I call you Figgy?"

"That's cool. Although 'Figuerito' is more proper. Three, you understand now why three's my lucky number?" The little Cuban accepted a beer and tossed the cap over the side.

Normally, Tomlinson would have mentioned the handy trash bag but stuck to the thread. "Thing is, Figuerito, on these little cruises of mine strange shit always happens for one reason or another. Nobody's fault, understand. It's God's way of preparing us, I think, for the serious weirdness that awaits if a man outlives his *pinga*."

A nod; a white-toothed smile.

"We've got to stick together, in other words. We're shipmates, right? After last night, I feel like I can call you my very good friend."

"Figgy's okay, too," the shortstop replied. He was interested in something portside, straining to see through the mist while his shoulders danced to Ms. Omara crooning "Pensamiento."

Sensing a lack of focus, Tomlinson cleared his throat. "Being called a pussy in Russian was my first clue. That's a new one even in my world. See where this is going? Amigo, I think we need to read those letters to understand why all this bizarre bullshit's going down." A tangent popped into his head. "Hey . . . how'd you know the Russian word for 'pussy'? Because your father danced ballet?"

The shortstop didn't respond, continued to stare into the mist, eyes widening while he grabbed the boom and pulled himself up. "Wow!" he said. "Is that Havana already?"

No . . . it was a cruise ship, its bow five stories high and cutting a wake that, if Tomlinson didn't get the engine started, would crush *No Más* and drown them.

8

Thursday afternoon on Bahamasair, Key West to Nassau, Vernum Quick looked down at a glittering sea and watched a ship—one of those newlywed and nearly dead cruise liners—disappear into a cloudy mist. The entire flight, he hadn't said a word to his Russian handler, a man so big he'd purchased two seats—same as two days ago when they'd landed in Fort Myers.

Kostikov was the guy's name, supposedly. Who knew? In this strange business, lying was a way of life. It was easier to believe he'd been a super heavyweight way, way back in the day. Boxing or wrestling or weight lifting, Vernum hadn't inquired. The man's bad Spanish demanded a lot of work, as did his Cossack temper. Better to smile and pretend to understand.

One thing for certain: Kostikov was a killer. He could kill a man with his hands—snap his neck, crush him to death, or stick a pencil through his eardrum. Vernum had seen him do this in a grainy KGB video, a self-defense instructional that sacrificed three dumbass prisoners—Afghans, they looked like—who had volunteered. The huge Russian, after each demonstration, would grin as they dragged a body away. A man who had aged since those days but still loved his work.

As a mentor, however, Kostikov was a vicious old socialist. Bitch, bitch, bitch, all the way to the airport, then a final dig about Vernum's cowardice last night because he'd yelled for help, then played dead to save himself from that crazy little bastard with a knife.

Well . . . Vernum had believed the shoe to be a knife, and no wonder: his wounds had required an ambulance ride to the ER. Which is why, aboard this cramped little airplane, he sat alone, his face bandaged and swollen. Thirty-three stitches to close those gashes around his eyes and to mend his lower lip; thirty-three, his unlucky number as of now.

A zombie from Hollywood is what he resembled in the mirror.

Never volunteer, he reminded himself.

Vernum was a thinker, not a fighter.

CUBA STRAITS

• • •

In Nassau, he found a seat far from the steel band so gringos wouldn't gawk at him and opened his new laptop. Did his smiling act when Kostikov made eye contact, then reviewed a file he'd been secretly compiling. They'd told him lies, mostly, but he'd been putting it together on his own by eavesdropping, searching the Internet, or stealing peeks here and there.

"Vernum Quick is *quick*, man" was something he liked to brag.

The puzzle was taking shape.

A month ago, Cuban Intelligence Service—the DGI—had recovered an aborted listing on eBay that had been removed shortly after it was posted.

Fidel Castro, Love Letters to a Mistress, 1953–63

Seeing that magic year, 1963, had been enough. There was no record of the letters, no hint of what they contained, according to the Russian, but why risk linkage to the assassination of JFK?

Evidence was already out there, of course, but never in Fidel's own hand.

The DGI made inquiries. No response from the seller. The DGI went to work on the seller's passwords. Three weeks ago, for reasons Vernum still didn't understand, the trail brought two special agents to his door-step in the village of Plobacho, western Cuba.

"People say you are respected and feared here, a nov-ice *Santero* who votes the right way. That you've helped police in the past."

This was true.

"You served in air force intelligence until . . . well, an unfortunate incident, but the board's findings might have been hasty. Care to reopen your case?"

Definitely not. This was a blackmail visit, the way the system worked. How much did they want? Vernum had posed that question. As a Santería novice, he had a little cash, but not much.

Both agents smiled. They didn't want money, but there was a price. They named it by asking, "Do you know the Casanova family?"

Why . . . yes, he did—if you could call an old woman recluse and her retarded, murdering grandson a "fam-ily."

The agents had liked that, or pretended to.

Was he aware that Figueroa Casanova had escaped from Havana Psychiatric?

Vernum played along. "The one by the airport, José Martí? I'll help you catch the bastard if it's true."

It couldn't be true. Criminals didn't escape from that prison—not without a scar on their forehead or in a cof-fin. Vernum knew this. He stayed current on rumors about Havana Psychiatric for a reason: the place terrified him. Couldn't even look at the building from the road. His fears were grounded in his own dark secret: a demon lived within his brain. Sometimes the demon had to be fed.

Over the years, only two witnesses—Figuerito and a little girl—had survived after learning the truth. This, too, had been a burden, but it was a Santería maxim that finally set him free: *Blame not the heart for demons in your head, nor hungers that torment your soul.*

My hunger—that's the way Vernum thought of the demon now. Instead of an asylum inmate, he'd become a respectable citizen, believed he'd earned pleasure in whatever form it appeared. Like all religions, Santería was quick to forgive, but in a way that was tougher; none of that turn-the-other-cheek bullshit. You want something? Man, go get it. Prayer was okay, but potions and powders and the ancient spells were faster.

Another aspect of Santería that attracted Vernum was its reliance on blood sacrifice to appease the gods and bring good luck. The ceremony was so strict in procedure that it absolved even a young *Santero* of guilt. Coconut rind cut in four pieces represented the four corners of the Earth. A papaya freshly sliced resembled the undefiled chasteness of a girl. Turpentine, bluestone, ground cowrie shells. The knife must be clean, specially sharpened. The neck of the victim must be gently shaved before the first sure stroke, then tilted just so to fill a ceremonial gourd. All the while chanting *Oggún shoro shoro . . . Oggún shoro shoro . . .*

Say those words with passion, they assumed the rhythm of a beating heart.

Vernum's favorite song.

Entering the priesthood was the smartest move he'd made. True believers were eager to reward even a novice *Santero* who produced results, which is why he had respect, women, and a little money—but never enough, it seemed to him.

The Cuban DGI agents didn't care about Santería. What they cared about was the deal they offered the next day after driving Vernum to Havana.

"If we close the files on that unfortunate incident, would you be willing to help us?"

Hell yes, but Vernum didn't want to appear too eager. He knew they thought he was just a dumb peasant who could be used as a mule or fall guy . . . *something* that now, sitting in Nassau, he was still ferreting out.

Kill Figueroa Casanova is what they wanted but didn't admit. Said they wanted the little man detained and interrogated about a stolen briefcase (no mention of the letters) before he was sent back to Havana Psychiatric. A special drug, they had instructed Vernum, would provide the needed interrogation time.

That was another key to this puzzle. To store his new laptop, they'd given him a shoulder bag. Inside was a shiny silver Montblanc fountain pen. *Use it like a needle,* he'd been instructed. *Just a scratch is enough and the defector will be cooperative for a week, possibly ten days.*

There had been no demonstration. In fact, the DGI agents had behaved as if even the shoulder bag was dangerous. Nor did they touch the pen, which was oddly heavy as if lined with lead and stored in a metal case.

It was something a dumb peasant wouldn't have noticed.

Vernum Quick did.

This was a once-in-a-lifetime opportunity, as he was aware. But success required that he make some behavioral changes. As village *Santero*, he had affected aloofness. He had spoken in parables and often began sentences by asking the blessings of Oggún, or hinting that a gift to the High Babalawo would impress the saints. Changó, his guardian saint, was a favorite topic.

But he had dropped all the theatrical bullshit the day he'd met the Russian.

The Russian . . . The man was now returning from the corridor, where tourists scattered to make way. Vernum closed the laptop, stored it, and decided to have fun with a little experiment. He stood and offered the bag to Kostikov, saying, "You mind holding this while I piss?"

"No talk now!" the man hissed, and stepped back—a familiar reaction.

Poison, yes, he'd been right about the fountain pen—a type of poison that required a lead case.

Vernum had researched that, too.

After using the men's room, he ate some jerked pork and ruminated over a new puzzle: the saints had delivered Figuerito into his hands, no doubt. But how could he keep that little psycho alive long enough to get rich— and without getting killed himself?

THEY FINALLY SPOKE on the government flight to Havana, safe now unless this shitty old Tupolev, with two propellers and a broken door, fell from the sky.

"Comrade, how you like that jerked pork?" Vernum asked. Interested because he'd added a few drops of special oil when he'd added more sauce.

"Ummm," Kostikov grunted. "Ummm-huh." The man chewed with his mouth open, red sauce all over his chin. "I tell you plan now."

Vernum had been wondering about this return to Havana but preferred to look out the window while the man explained. Figuerito had escaped from Key West in a sailboat, the Russian told him. They knew the boat's name: *No More.*

"*No Más?*"

The Russian nodded. "Scarecrow man we saw last night is captain. I still laugh the way he talk so tough. Hah! This hippie boy-girl threatening me, *Kostikov.*"

Maybe that really was the big guy's name. It was

painful to smile with thirty-three stitches, but Vernum managed. "Yeah, he's nuts. That's what I was thinking at the time. But if they're in a boat, why didn't we just rent a faster boat and catch them?"

"You question orders?"

Orders? Vernum hadn't heard any orders. "No, man," he said, "just asking."

"The scarecrow likes hear himself talk to women, tells them everything. Don't worry, we have plan." The Russian balled up his napkin and lobbed it forward, where a woman sat alone behind the pilot, one of the blondes Vernum recognized from last night. She was lighting a cigarette in a noisy plane that had a rattling door and wasn't pressurized.

Vernum said, "I didn't realize there was a connection, but—" He stopped himself before inquiring how the Russian had found time to locate her. At the ER, they'd wasted two hours, counting the cops and the stitches.

"Many sources," Kostikov said. "Now you go home and wait. That's all now." He turned around, his big butt taking up two seats.

Huh? Vernum slipped across the aisle. "*Whoa!* man. You mean my job is done? You haven't interrogated Casanova yet. And what about the briefcase?"

The Russian had more hair on his eyebrows than his head, so looking him in the face was like confronting two cornered animals. Lots of vodka and violence and ruptured veins stared back. "You claim used device on defector, yes?"

The Montblanc pen, he meant. Yes, Vernum had tried to use that bad boy, but said, "Well, I think so, but, man, we was punching the hell out of each other. You know how that goes. Those two probably left for a day sail and they're back in Key West right now."

The Russian motioned to the overhead bin. "You still have device?"

Uh-oh. He hadn't expected that but stayed cool, got to his feet and bluffed, saying, "Of course. Issued by my government. I'll get it for you."

"No!" The big man didn't relax until Vernum was seated again. "We have many sources. Information no need for so many people to share. You understand meaning?"

Yes and no—the Russian was a pig and couldn't speak Spanish but apparently knew where Figuerito and the hippie were headed.

"Sorry I doubted you."

"No, is good you want this defector so strongly. I see this in you even after so much stupid coward shit you do last night. But"—Kostikov pushed closer—"I think you be fast at learning this trade. You would like?"

Had the Russian attempted a fatherly tone?

"Yeah," Vernum replied, "I'll do whatever it takes, man."

"Oh?"

"An opportunity to serve my country, of course."

"A patriot, eh?" The Russian's tone said *Bullshit*. "I am told you are criminal. A deviant who buys girls with opium of religion. As patriot, you have read Karl Marx, yes?"

"Uh . . . I'd have to think back. What do you mean?"

"God, all your gods, are shit. That was truth Comrade Marx wrote. Your Santería is more shit than even Papist shit."

Vernum thought, *Dude, you are playing with fire*, but changed his approach. "Man, you'd have to experience where I live. It's all dirt roads and oxcarts, the same tired village women every goddamn day. So I—"

"Your women are superstitious fools," the Russian said. "They fear stupid fears—even a devil in the cane fields, I hear. Is true?"

Vernum shrugged, thinking, *Uh-oh*.

"Your DGI say some hide their children, or defect on rafts, because of you. See? Religion total shit. Is large difference between devils and a man who is deviant, huh?"

That question, in an odd way, disapproved of superstition but not deviants. Vernum felt a tad better. "As long as you understand what I'm dealing with. Think what you want, but, as a respected *Santero*, I've gotta, well"—he risked a man-to-man wink—"restrain my interests in things that Havana, Key West—name any city—can offer men like us."

Two bloodshot eyes stared through him, then swiveled toward the blonde or the pilot, who wore a headset and was also smoking. The Russian looked out the window— blue ocean a mile below—then asked, "You have phone with camera?"

DGI agents had given Vernum a cheap one, but what did that have to do with anything?

The Russian used a finger to wag him closer, then leaned his nose an inch from Vernum's face. "No more your coward bullshit. I give order, you obey. I say truth, you obey. You want learn trade, you obey. Is clear?"

This was more than Kostikov had spoken in three days. "Sure . . . yeah, never question your orders. Damn clear . . . comrade."

"Come. I want you take video." The plane listed slightly when the Russian stood and he pulled himself seat to seat past the German blonde to the pilot, who he tapped on the shoulder, the pilot not surprised, more like *I'm ready when you are, sir.* Then put out his cigarette and fastened his shoulder harness.

Vernum, standing in the aisle with his phone ready, noticed and thought, *We're either landing or he's trying to scare the shit out of me.*

He looked out the window—nothing but water down there, José Martí International still twenty minutes away.

The Russian turned and spoke to the blonde, not loud enough to hear but congenial in manner. The blonde had been subdued but suddenly smiled and said, with her grating accent, "Yah. I have camera. Anything, comrade, for you." Unsnapped her seat belt and stood, the cigarette in her mouth, and dangled her white breasts when she leaned to dig through her purse.

Why did Kostikov need both of their cameras?

Vernum thought, *Fat pig, he's screwing with me*, and was sure of it when the Russian laced a wrist through some cargo netting near the door and ordered, "Come, hit video button. You ready?"

It was the way Kostikov grinned that warned what was coming—his assassin's grin from the KGB video— but Vernum was so goddamn scared, he crept a few seats closer anyway and watched it happen through the viewfinder.

Kostikov saying to the blonde, "Ah . . . such beauty, your necklace," which she took as a compliment to her tits. She smiled, aiming her camera, but used a free hand to tease her blouse open, just a flash of nipple, before scolding him, "You are very, very bad man."

That grin again. "Yah. Bad." Kostikov reached as if to touch her tits but ripped the necklace off.

The way the blonde's face paled, from sunburned to dead white, Vernum found himself breathing heavier, hungry, very hungry, the demon inside him demanding to be fed. He called to the Russian, "Wait . . . let me change angles," and ducked in two rows behind the woman, swung his legs over an armrest for a better view, which Kostikov confirmed, before he forced the door open and lifted the woman by her hair while wind roared, debris scattering as if they'd flown into a sandstorm.

"Don't stop," the Russian ordered, "use camera!"

Vernum, deafened by the noise, realized those orders were for the blonde, who already looked dead, her eyes so wide and still, but rallied and did exactly as she'd been told while Kostikov looked into her lens and spoke Russian as if addressing future KGB agents.

"Obey always me," he told the woman. "Keep doing."

Hopeful, the expression on her face until he swung her out the door, held her there while the airstream ripped at her clothing, but, by god, she didn't drop that phone.

Vernum thought, *I would marry her*, and then leaped to his feet when the Russian signaled *Come closer*.

"How's this?"

"*Nyet*, coward, here."

Mother of hell, this was a test, he realized, and so far only the blonde was passing. He shuffled his feet, video rolling, while he brachiated from seat to seat. The opening was no wider than Vernum's shoulders, but a universe of screaming reality out there when he was at the door. A mile down, miles above, nothing but blue.

"Is angle good?" The assassin showing his artistic side while the blonde clawed at his wrist, her shoes gone, her blouse shredding like a flag.

Through the viewfinder, Vernum managed eye contact with the woman and fell in love with her face, a perfect blend of horror and pain that fired his deepest needs within. *I would give anything,* he thought, *to trade places with that pig. Why isn't he laughing?*

Kostikov was more concerned with his lesson for today. Yelled a phrase of Russian at the lens, barked something else to the woman, his manner stern, and that was it—he dropped her with a *Good riddance* swipe of the hands, didn't even watch her body rocket downward, tumbling, although Vernum captured it on HDV.

My god. *Ecstasy.* Even without reviewing footage, he knew this was something he would watch over and over a thousand times, at night, alone—or with that right special someone just before he ate her soul.

"SECRECY," THE RUSSIAN SAID when they were seated again, "is first rule of importance. Here, I show you." A satellite phone was produced. On it a Facebook photo: the scarecrow hippie and two female German agents, all naked, but only one of them wearing the KGB necklace that now dangled from Kostikov's pocket.

Vernum, for a change, spoke with respect. "Comrade, this is the work I have searched for all my life. Please give me another chance to—"

"Shut your talk" was the reply. "Obey orders, that second rule of importance. Tell truth to superiors, that third." The Russian was slow on his feet, but his hand grabbed Vernum's chin before he could react. Pulled him across the aisle until they were nose to nose. "Fourth rule: I am your only superior. Is clear?"

Yes.

"Above all others."

Oh, yes!

"Is true you are sex deviant?"

A trick question. Vernum was screwed either way, so he tried a broader truth. "I like . . . killing."

"Good."

Really?

Yes, the Russian approved. "Is okay with women or girls, even boys. Bugger ten dead goats, what I care? But do not lie to Kostikov." A pause. "I tell you something— just us. Your DGI agents are idiots. Your government is shit. What you think of that?"

Vernum could only nod.

"I tell you use device or take gun, shoot all Cuban generals, what then?"

"Follow orders, comrade" was the correct response.

The Russian released him. "Okay. I want briefcase. Just me. Same with defector of name Casanova. Just me. You will help."

Vernum, close enough to smell the man's breath, said, "Of course," but had to wonder, *Is this another test?*

"In DGI debrief, you will confirm whatever I say. No mention of German whore"—the man was fishing something from his pocket—"or video that you now make for me copy. What this called in Spanish?"

"A memory stick," Vernum replied. He glanced forward and, for the first time, realized their pilot was Russian. My god, it was true, he was being recruited by the KGB. "Right away," he said. "I'll make a copy before we land, then delete it from my phone."

Smart—that was Kostikov's reaction. He appeared to relax a little, settled back and gave Vernum permission to watch the footage first.

Hunched over his phone, hunger is what he felt.

"You enjoy?"

Oh my god, yes. Twice he played it, always pausing when the blonde made eye contact, and knew he could never bring himself to delete the footage.

Kostikov sat back, hands laced behind his head. Taking it easy now that the job was done. "Is important to have hobby. Like me. I have hobby."

Vernum's attention zoomed. "More videos like this?"

"No, a hobby is for amusement. That is question I have for you. About your village, I hear story of time before Fidel. You know this story? I think was 1958."

Even now, speaking Fidel's name was dangerous, but that isn't why Vernum evaded. "A story about . . . ?"

"Motorcycles," the Russian said. "Do you know story?"

Vernum was too frightened not to tell the truth. "I do. Three Harley-Davidsons. I know where they're hidden, but not *exactly* where. But that traitor Figgy Casanova, he knows."

The Russian's tongue circled his lips. "Story contains stupid game, baseball. Three fascists during Cold War—"

That's as far as he got. The man burped, touched a hand to his belly, and his thoughts turned inward while jerked chicken filled the air. Burped again, looked out the window. "Must shit," he muttered and called something to the pilot that might have been *Hurry up and land.*

9

Ford topped his tanks at the Chevron pier, Key West, and was south of Sand Key Light when the electronics suite bonged with a special alert to mariners. Alerts weren't rare, but this one was synched to his GPS, so he paid attention.

Between 13:30 and 14:00 hours EST, the U.S. Coast Guard received three reports of near collisions with a cruise ship or freighter, registry unknown, and one report of debris, possibly from a raft or sailing vessel but unconfirmed. Conditions: light to medium fog, seas near calm. Coast Guard has dispatched assets to investigate. Advise all vessels in shipping lanes south of Key West to be on alert . . .

Exact GPS coordinates followed.

Ford considered how this might impact his crossing. He didn't want to be seen by the Coast Guard, especially in international waters. On the positive side, cutters and helicopters were likely to collect in one small search area.

A stroke of luck, he decided.

Even in fog, collisions at sea were uncommon, but only because the sea is so damn big. A rogue freighter, is what it sounded like, one of those mega-ton robots with a sloppy crew who didn't bother to stand watch when on autopilot. Ford pictured a raft full of refugees, or novices in a sailboat screaming, waving their arms to get the attention of an empty helm while the monster plowed them down.

Tomlinson was too good a sailor not to stay on his toes in the shipping lanes.

It was nearly three-thirty—15:30 hours. Ford switched his radar to a wider grid and steered a 230 heading, which was his best guess at the line Tomlinson would plot to Havana, or Marina Hemingway, fifteen miles west.

His friend hadn't shared particulars. This was another guess. But he had told Ford why he was sailing to Cuba: *A woman's love letters are sacred, so I'm going to return them.*

That simple, but only because Ford had condensed his pal's diatribe into a simple declarative sentence. Tomlinson was a romantic idealist, ruled by emotion yet smart enough to rationalize even the dumbest of choices. Less so in this case, but seldom so passionate. He had used phrases such as *Internet flesh peddlers, political ping-pong gawkers,* and *soul merchants.* The moral imperative, he'd said, trumped all: we have a duty to right wrongs if it is within our power. "I don't give two hoots in hell who wrote the letters, the sentiments belong to only one heart, a woman's heart. Those letters are her last linkage, for christ's sake, to the days when she was young and full of hope. Screw world voyeurism, man. I want to strike a blow for human privacy."

The grand gesture. Tomlinson seldom missed an opportunity, although, in this case, nostalgia and his leftist idealism probably played a role.

Ford had made the mistake of asking, "What if Castro's mistress is dead?"

That mystic journey could not be summarized in a sentence.

Ahead were clouds separated by miles of water, the surface lucent, punctuated by coral heads and banks of white sand until the Earth ruptured into canyons below. There, a line of cobalt marked the color change.

"No bottom" was the old mariner's term.

Flying is how it felt to Ford when he tapped the throttles up to 4000 rpm and let the boat settle into the slow rise and fall of the Florida Straits. He checked gauges—oil, water, fuel, amps—all good. Looked astern—the simplest of safety precautions that amateurs often failed to do. Went through his list while frigate birds searched the sky for thermals: safety harness with EPIRB where it belonged . . . kill switch attached to belt . . . enough water and MREs for a week stowed with emergency gear; tactical mace, a survival knife, and his old Sig P226, plus the mini Sig Sauer he'd taken, along with an ankle holster, from the cable installer. Two hundred rounds of 9mm were in a waterproof sleeve fitted *inside* the chemical toilet's flush tank.

Ingenious, the agency that had designed this boat.

For purposes of deception: fishing rods with gold International reels in plain sight, four radar decoy buoys, a false passport, ten thousand in dollars and euros, a field kit that could only belong to a biologist, and a letter of introduction confirming he was doing important research on sea turtles.

The letter was signed with a flourish and the personal seal of Gen. Juan Simón Rivera, former president of Masagua. Even if Ford caught up with *No Más* and convinced Tomlinson to turn around, he would need the equipment because he'd made up his mind to continue on to Cuba.

Check. Check. Check. Like the pilot of an airliner, he went through the list, stayed busy until he'd reached the equivalent of cruising altitude.

Flying. To Ford, that's how it felt to point a good boat at the horizon and leave the world behind.

RADAR SHOWED a gathering of vessels ten miles ahead, close enough that Ford caught glimpses of a Coast Guard cutter's tower, so he adjusted his course eastward, where clouds descended into the warm Gulf Stream. Rain most likely. Fog was rare this late in the afternoon.

A helicopter appeared, one of the big ones with all the electronics. The best hope of avoiding attention was to steer toward it. He did, maintained course, while the chopper drifted away in a methodical search pattern.

Maybe it was true: a robot ship had hit a smaller vessel and dumped people into the water. It was the sort of diversion he needed, yet his mood took a hit. *Poor bastards,* he thought. "Good luck." Said it aloud and meant it. Even on a bright, calm day, the odds of finding a person adrift were not good. In rain or fog? Or if the wind freshened? Forget it. Technology had yet to match the enormity of the open sea.

For no good reason, the image of *No Más* popped into his head. Earlier, he'd tried to raise Tomlinson on VHF radio. He tried again on the four channels commonly used in Dinkin's Bay.

No response.

He'd already done the mental arithmetic but reviewed anyway: two boats with different departure times, traveling unequal distances at greatly different speeds, *might* intersect, give or take a few hours, on a large acreage of Gulf Stream.

In the electronics suite, the GPS chart suggested that *No Más* should be within radio range—fifteen to twenty miles. On a sailboat, antennas are mounted atop the mast, and Ford's boat had a communications system unavailable to civilians. No surprise that Tomlinson didn't answer his cell, but his radio? The man was a VHF whore when it came to local gossip.

Unless . . . he had the damn stereo booming. Yes, that was probably it. The refugee shortstop wouldn't have been fool enough to climb on a boat to Cuba, so Tomlinson was alone and drowning his solitude with Hendrix or Buffett.

Ford was unconvinced, and remained subdued. Focused less on his destination and more on the water around him. Soon, tendrils of fog swept past the boat at forty knots. He slowed to thirty on the pretense of saving fuel.

Not a chance in hell they're looking for Tomlinson, he told himself. Even so, he activated the boat's thermal imaging system. A lens overhead scanned the surface and translated temperature into colors on a screen. Lobster buoys and floating litter were gray. The sea was cool blue. A person adrift would appear as a speck of fiery red. It was the same imaging system used by the helicopter, so what was the point?

He asked himself that and pursued the logical thread. What if you do find wreckage? Or even a survivor? You'll have to involve the Coast Guard. Then you and Tomlinson are both screwed. So get back to speed and stop this nonsense.

Ford was unaware that he often argued with himself. Part of him believed that emotion was a useless tie to the Stone Age. Not unlike the nub of prehensile tail at the end of his spine. He liked people, though, couldn't help it, so empathy was his most consistent opponent.

To be adrift out here, alone, in a thousand feet of water, would be hell . . .

That kept going through his mind.

In the distance, he saw what might be a box someone had thrown overboard. Dusky gray on the thermal screen. More objects bobbing nearby—a pod of flotsam that might be wreckage. He backed the throttles, his eyes moving from the water to the electronics suite. A bag of garbage surfaced momentarily, then submerged.

Ford stood—something bothered him about the bag. He dropped the boat off plane and focused on the spot, because plastic bags don't sink. Didn't blink until the bag appeared again a boat length away, but this time resembling the back of a turtle. He checked the screen, saw a blob of orange heat, and knew then it wasn't a bag or a turtle. It was a person, either dead or almost dead, the body losing heat fast. He killed the engines, dumped what he could from his pockets, and went over the side.

A corpse . . . that's what he found. It was obvious when he snatched a pale wrist, did a reverse thrust with his legs, and exposed what was left of the body. Nothing identifiable. A male, possibly, wearing ragged shorts, no shoe on his only foot, and no right arm to offer tattoos or prints as an ID.

Going through the dead man's pockets could wait. Ford sculled backwards to create distance.

Sharks had been feeding on the body, which was still warm. Obvious. Just as obvious: sharks from a quarter mile below, and miles around, were not done feeding.

"Dumbass." Said this to himself aloud, not because he'd rushed to the rescue but because he hadn't bothered to grab a safety line before jumping overboard. His feet had kicked the boat away. Now instead of a few yards, he had to swim the length of a pool.

He started out with a breaststroke but, looking down into the black maw of the Gulf Stream, invented shadows that cruised beneath him. The elementary backstroke was more distressing: a dorsal fin breached the surface to his right and pirouetted to investigate.

Hammerhead, Ford, the biologist, decided. The damn fin was as tall as his arm.

The shark submerged with a swirl that spun chunks of Styrofoam and other wreckage into a whirlpool while a pair of big remoras cruised past. Bad sign. They were shark suckers in search of a larger, more productive host.

Ford, the biologist, wondered, *Why don't they glom*

onto me? then stiffened when he realized *Because there's something a hell of a lot bigger nearby.*

A few strokes later, his head collided with a chunk of debris—bamboo lashed to plywood. This evoked enough nervous laughter that he was disgusted with himself.

Just swim to the damn boat and get it over with.

Over many years and several oceans, he had swam a lot of open water, so no big deal—until he stood on the transom and looked down. There were so many sharks— one the size of a canoe—that the giddy sense of relief he felt was replaced by a new empathy: if there were survivors adrift out here, they wouldn't survive long.

ON THE BOAT NOW, he reached down, grabbed the corpse's belt, and noticed a shadow. Water exploded. He fell back with a pair of ragged shorts in his hand, that's all. The dead man, if it was a man, was gone. Ford leaned over to confirm: below, far below, in shafts of angling light, only shadows and a sprinkling detritus remained.

He thought: There can't be anyone else alive.

In the shorts, he found a wad of pesos, all worthless Cuban scrip. Folded within was the prize: a twenty-dollar bill, American. A wallet in the back pocket contained a photo ID, laminated: Alex Molera, Department of Sanitation, village of Cojimar, plus the equivalent of a Social Security number. A final treasure hidden under a flap: an antique cameo, the photo obliterated, on a necklace of beads and cowrie shells.

Santería, the unofficial religion of Cuba.

At idle speed, Ford did a slow circle of what had been a homemade raft: oil drums for outriggers, bamboo lashed to blocks of Styrofoam. Small; no engine, but a rigging pole suggested they had improvised a sail. Fewer than five people, he guessed, but no telling. In Cuba, desperation spawned crazy optimism. They would choose a secret spot and bet their dreams on vessels they constructed of wood, tar, inner tubes, and hope. Every year, thousands succeeded. Every year, unknown hundreds died.

Something else: on this raft, a child had been aboard, a girl. He shifted to neutral and retrieved a plastic doll with nylon hair and a bright red dress. Floating nearby was a Tupperware canister. It contained family photos, an address book, and the girl's medical records. Rosa Molera, age four, had been in good health when she, her father Alex, and her mother had been crushed by a cruise ship or freighter, registry unknown or yet to be reported.

Ford stowed the items beneath the deck but couldn't let it go after that.

Maybe a second raft had been hit.

He switched the radio to 83-Alpha, used exclusively by Coast Guard personnel, and followed a spattering of debris as he listened. The cloud bank lifted, creating a white dome that drifted with him at idle speed. He could no longer hear the helicopter, but it was visible on radar from thirteen miles away, distinctive because of its speed. From what the radar told him, and what he heard on VHF, at least one other vessel had been hit by the robot ship. The Coast Guard had clustered its assets, boats and a chopper, working one small section of water to the southwest. They had found wreckage, too.

Ford turned northeast.

Fifteen minutes, he told himself. *Then I'm gone.*

Twenty minutes later, he spotted a wooden pallet. Nothing strange about that. He'd already seen a couple, probably dumped by passing ships. This pallet, however, was industrial-sized and covered with what looked like plastic bottles, hundreds of them, draped under shrimp net.

Check thermal imaging: a shapeless heat signature that, probably, was plastic warmed by the sun.

Trash. For a millennium, mariners had used the ocean as a dumping ground, but now, unlike the mariners, their garbage was impervious to the centuries.

Ford veered away and shifted to neutral to prepare for the sixty miles of open water that lay ahead. The boat's T-top and the electronics tower folded forward to reduce radar signature. Another stealthy touch was the neoprene spray hood coated with radar-absorbent paint. He pulled it taut, secured the cover with carabineers, then re-coiled the safety line he'd readied just in case he had to go into the water again.

Dumbass, he reminded himself. At sea, when alone, never lose contact with your vessel. A cardinal rule.

Port side on his boat, a door opened into a storage area beneath the helm. It was a large space, enough room for a chemical toilet, a handheld shower, and an electrically cooled Igloo. He ducked inside to grab a Diet Coke and a bag of peanuts. Or would a sandwich be better? He was deciding when he heard a radio transmission: a girl's voice that warned *"¡Silencio! Va a atraer a los tiburones."*

Ford translated without giving it much thought: Be quiet! You are attracting sharks.

Odd, though. Why was a child transmitting on a channel used exclusively by the Coast Guard?

Then, again in Spanish, he heard, "I'm tired of paddling with my hands, you brat, and you are not my boss."

Not the same voice . . . And it wasn't coming from the radio.

The console door was small. Ford banged his head going out. He idled closer to the pallet.

It took some cajoling. Soon, the pile of bottles stirred, netting parted, and two frightened girls appeared, both in flowered dresses, the oldest no more than thirteen.

No . . . only one was frightened. The younger was pissed. "You can't arrest me," she hollered in Spanish, "because I'll swim."

Ford didn't speak down to children, believed it was

demeaning to both. "That's foolish. It's better to get on my boat while we wait for the Coast Guard. Are you thirsty?"

"So *they* can arrest us," the girl countered. "Fascists in uniforms. It's a lie, and I won't be tricked by a gringo fascist. I'm warning you, stay away."

"No one's going to arrest you. I have water and sandwiches; peanuts, if you want. Key West is thirty miles. Can you swim thirty miles? Even if you can, you'll need to eat something for energy."

"To hell with Key West, I want to go home. I'll swim home if you try to make me go to Gringolandia."

The older girl was less agitated. He spoke to her. "How long have you been adrift? You need water and medical attention. Please explain this to . . . Is she your sister?"

A nod, the older girl saying, "She's mad because she didn't want to come to America. Then this happened. She gets mad a lot."

"How many people were on your raft?"

The sisters bickered for a moment, the older one finally saying, "Three—five, counting us—but a large ship hit us and that was the last we saw of the others."

Ford assumed their parents were dead, so Cuba and Tomlinson would have to wait. He spoke more gently. "I'm a fisherman, not the Coast Guard. No uniform, no gun, see?" He extended his hands for inspection and smiled. "You're safe with me, I promise. No one will force you to do anything. I promise that, too. You'll be more comfortable on my boat while we talk. Have a look, then decide." He started the engines.

That's all it took. The youngest girl launched herself into the water while her sister yelled warnings about sharks.

Ford did it again—went over the side without a safety line.

THEIR NAMES were Maribel and Sabina Esteban, ages thirteen and ten, no relation to the Alex Molera family, but they had been paying customers aboard the same raft. In recent years, more and more parents had sent their children alone in the hopes of a better life in *Norteamérica*.

He gave them bananas and peanut butter on bread, which they ate, but they refused Gatorade and even a can of cold condensed milk, which Ford thought might be good for children. The pallet that had saved their lives was loaded with bottles that had been filled for the long trip, so they weren't dehydrated, nor were they sunburned. A few careful questions confirmed they needed no crème for rashes, no medicine for sickness, and their disinterest when he demonstrated the toilet calmed his concerns about diarrhea.

Even so, he had only two options: contact the Coast Guard or take them to Key West. That would require some convincing, especially ten-year-old Sabina, who was a fireball, smart and perceptive, and suspicious of Ford's every move.

When he put the boat in neutral and broke out the fishing rods, he noticed her eye the GPS. "I know which way is north," she warned.

Her sister Maribel replied, "Of course. You know everything. That's the way she is."

"I know you can't fish without bait. This man has no bait, only plastic things with hooks. The liar claims to be a fisherman. You're an idiot, Maribel, to believe him."

Ford said, "I'm going to troll a couple of lines while we talk. If we're not fishing, the Coast Guard will wonder what I'm doing out here. You're wrong about them, they're very nice people, but this will give us some time."

"Where are they? Are there cameras?" The girl in her flowered dress was on her toes, scanning the misty horizon.

"They have radar screens, too," he said. "Later, I'll show you how it works, but after we discuss what's best for you two."

"No."

"What do you mean? If you've already figured out the GPS, learning to use radar won't be a problem for a smart girl like you."

"He promised us," Sabina said to her sister. "He promised to take us home to Cuba. I knew he was lying.

I told you, but you didn't believe me. You never do, you brat."

Repressing a smile, Ford said, "What I promised was that you and your sister would be safe and you are. I didn't say I would—"

"Yes, you did! You promised not to force us to do anything I don't want to do. If the Guardia comes, they will send us to Guantánamo Bay, or put us in buses with strangers in Miami. Isn't that true?"

Ford's smile faded. "Well . . ."

"*See?* It is true."

To Maribel, Ford said, "If your sister didn't want to come to America, why did your parents send her? And what about you, Maribel? What do you want?"

The teenager, frightened again, looked away.

"She can't tell you," Sabina chided. "Mama made her promise not to talk about it. But I didn't promise. Mama didn't know I was listening, so—"

"Shut up, just shut," the older girl said and began to cry.

Ford wondered if he should pat her on the back or something but only said, "Once we're moving, I'd like to talk about a few things, Maribel. But only when you're ready."

He rigged a privacy curtain forward and placed cushions under the spray hood so the girls had a space of their own. Beneath the console, he heard the toilet flush, then the sump of the shower as he idled toward the Coast Guard vessels, ten miles away, his fishing lines out. It had been a while since he'd tried hailing Tomlinson. He had the mic in his hand when ten-year-old Sabina appeared and approached in a sneaky, tiptoe sort of way.

"We'll wait for your sister," Ford said.

"Not if you want to know why Mama sent us away," the girl shot back. She looked at the GPS. "Why are you driving west? Cuba is south. Are you lost?"

Ford patted the seat next to him. "Hop up, I could use a good navigator."

"Only if you keep your promise to take us home."

"Sabina, if your mother and father were here, what would they—?"

"No father," she interrupted, "so keep him out of this. I never wanted to meet him anyway."

Ford tried a different approach. "Okay . . . what would your mother want you to do? She paid money to get you to America and you're so close. Only thirty miles. I can't go against your mother's wishes without a good reason."

A dramatic sigh of impatience before the girl climbed into the seat next to him, neatened the dress over her knees, then waited until she had Ford's full attention. "Mama didn't want us to leave. We had to leave. Mama was scared we would be killed because of what Maribel saw."

"Oh?" Ford didn't give it too much.

"Something very bad. At night, sometimes, Maribel still has dreams. That's why Mama made her promise not to speak about it to anyone."

On the console was a box of cheese crackers. He offered them to the girl. Watched her arm, no thicker than a sapling, disappear into the box, then reappear with a handful. "This sounds serious," he said. "It happened recently?"

"No, I was only nine then. After that, Mama was too afraid to sleep—but she and Maribel are always afraid of something. Then a man said he would drive us to Florida in a big boat, but he lied. It was a very small boat with a motor, and that night, our first night, he made us get on the raft with Mr. Molera. I didn't like Mr. Molera, but his wife was worse. She spanked me, called me a spoiled little nag, and made us sleep on the front of the raft."

The girl popped a cracker into her mouth and chewed while Ford said, "I wouldn't worry about them now. I'm more concerned about your mother. If she was afraid, why didn't she come with you?"

"The man who lied about his big boat charged so much money, Mama had to borrow the rest and said she would come later. She didn't *want* us to go, understand?"

Ford, although he believed himself to be open-minded, seldom changed his mind, but this situation was beginning to realign itself. A mother, unaware she was being conned, had spent her last cent and stayed behind rather than risk harm to her daughters.

"That's why you must take us home—like you promised. If the bad man comes looking for Maribel, what will Mama do in the house all alone?"

Ford asked, "The man who lied about his boat?"

No, this was a different man, which the child explained, a Santería priest who pulled three girls into a cane field and stabbed one to death, then did something worse, although the ten-year-old in the flowered dress didn't think that was possible.

"But Maribel knows," Sabina said, "because that's what she saw before she ran from the cane field and hid."

10

Before dawn, meteorites showered seaward over clouds from the south, but the clouds weren't clouds, Tomlinson realized. It was Cuba.

Maybe Figgy was right, he thought. Maybe I'm not dead.

It wasn't the first time God had taken His cuts and missed.

He'd been dozing on the foredeck, a space reserved for the dinghy, but the dinghy was gone. Same with a lot of other gear swept overboard when that freight train wake hit them, a wave the sailboat had surfed in the wildest ride ever until the bow buried and they'd pitchpoled.

Figueroa had been swept over, too.

After that, events were fuzzy and very, very wet. There remained, however, the memory of the little shortstop saying, *Brother, you are unconscious. It would be wise, I think, to wear a helmet if we make this trip again.* Later, another lucid vision: Figgy, a wrench in his hand, saying, *That* puta *Vernum Quick is the cause of all this. Him and his magic. I will beat that* Santero *when we meet in hell.*

Around midnight, Tomlinson's brain had rebooted sufficiently to take stock. The boat's cabin resembled a trailer park after a tornado, but a few true valuables had survived: his vinyl records, a little brass Buddha, three baggies of heirloom grass, his baseball bag, and a minor miracle: the leather briefcase, the initials *F.A.C.* barely damp.

A sign, Tomlinson decided. In a day ripe with omens and harbingers, the message was clear: continue south, but *carefully.* No more of this blind hipster bullshit, blundering into the unknown. After that, all planning was prefaced by a simple rule: stop being creative, and try to think like Doc Ford.

It was five-fifteen a.m. For more than an hour, *No Más* had been allowed free rein to drift and settle low in the water while a mild Bahamas breeze did its work. Tomlinson stood and stretched. Cuba, yes. A few twinkling lights up there in the hills, a whiff of woodsmoke beneath a cavern of stars. More convincing was the knot on his head.

Better luck next time, big fella. Guess I'll hop back on Your crazy carousel.

He climbed aft over the broken mast and a tangle of cables, tangs, and turnbuckles that he'd done his best to secure. *No Más*'s little diesel, still warm after twelve hours of constant work, started at the touch of a button. Almost no fuel in the tank, however, thus the wisdom of drifting.

After a glance astern—no dinghy there either—Tomlinson throttled toward land, and then a distant navigation tower that, hopefully, marked the entrance to a fishing village, but certainly wasn't Havana.

When the gunboats stop me, he thought, I'll know for sure.

THE CUBAN MILITARY was ever on alert for vessels that strayed within the twelve-mile limit, yet *No Más*, waddling like an injured duck, went unchallenged as Tomlinson rounded a point and motored into one of the prettiest little harbors he'd ever seen. No yachts or crotch rockets here, just a few fishing dories beached amid garbage, and a guard tower built in the time of the Conquistadors. Bougainvillea, hibiscus, and roofs of red tile. Dogs yapped; people stared, then looked away.

Weird, Tomlinson thought. Almost like they're expecting me. Or maybe they're always afraid.

On the other hand, maybe it was because he was naked except for a red bandana tied around his head. He was surprised when he realized that.

Damn—a couple of cops watching, too, and someone else inside a car parked with one door open. A woman in uniform, it looked like.

Well . . . shit-oh-dear.

He swung down into the cabin and reappeared wearing jeans and a tank top that were sodden and stunk of diesel fuel. Ahead was a cement pier, but most of it had collapsed. The only other place to tie up was built over the water, an ornate structure with French doors that might have once been a restaurant or, with luck, might still be a restaurant.

Was that coffee he smelled?

Yes, it was. Twenty minutes later, he sat at the bar of La Terraza with an espresso, a cold Cristal beer, and a papaya he'd bought from a vendor in the street. No food available from the kitchen at seven-thirty a.m., but the manager seemed eager to have the tall gringo stick around.

Interesting.

Tomlinson's suspicions were confirmed when the two cops he'd seen arrived with a woman from the customs department; the woman in a uniform of blue, the cops in gray.

"We've heard reports of this incident you described," the woman said after listening to his story. "Did you see the name of the vessel, any identifying marks? Or, perhaps, it all happened too fast."

What Tomlinson had seen were military goons laughing down at them from the cruise ship's fantail, but the way the woman glanced at the cops put him on alert. She had intentionally provided him with an out. Why? Or was this a subtle warning?

Possibly. Figueroa had identified the goons by their Russian uniforms—something the Cuban government wouldn't want confirmed by an eyewitness.

"It's hard for me to think straight," he replied, "so I'm glad you speak English." He lifted the bandana to show the knot on his head, then straightened it and smiled at her necklace of white and blue beads. "I'm just getting into Santería. Those colors, they honor Yemayá, correct? Goddess of the sea and sensuality. Wasn't she Changó the war god's first lover?"

A slight nod from the woman as she tugged at her collar. "Please answer the question."

"It's all a blur," he replied, because that's what she wanted to hear.

No Más's documents, along with his passport, were in a waterproof bag, which she opened and went through one by one while the cops stood at the door and glowered. The woman asked several more questions: Did he have money? How much? Could he arrange for more money if allowed to stay while his boat was repaired?

A small van arrived. A team of four clomped down the steps to the quay. "They're going to search everything," the woman said. "Experts, the best at what they do. Is there anything else you want to tell me?"

Another warning.

That goddamn Russian grizzly narced us out, Tomlinson thought. Figgy was right about him.

He said, "Yes. They'll find two baggies of very good ganja. And something else—it's hard to talk about. I didn't mention there was someone traveling with me."

The relief on the woman's face was visible. She gentled him along, saying, "Better me than a judge in Havana. Where is this person?"

"Swept overboard. Yesterday by that ship or freighter or whatever it was. I was knocked unconscious, so maybe I dreamed that he survived, that he somehow got back to the boat and helped me. I want to believe that, but when I woke up—this was before sunrise—I knew he was gone."

"Drowned," the woman said. "That's the last you saw of this person? When the wave knocked you both into the water."

Tomlinson sniffed and looked through the amber bottle in his hand. "On my boat, you won't find his papers. He told me he didn't even have a birth certificate. Last night, that really got to me for some reason. Like he'd never been born, so I searched through all that mess wondering if I'd imagined the whole damn thing. But I didn't. Kind of a strange little guy but a hell of a shortstop. His name was Figueroa Casanova."

The woman, who was stocky but had a good face and warm eyes, recognized the name but tried to pretend otherwise. "Are you sure he didn't wait until you were close to shore, then jumped?"

Tomlinson had to smile at that. "He couldn't swim. Even if he could, all your people will find is his shoe, a baseball shoe. You know, spikes? That was enough for me."

"To you, this shoe proves he existed? Or that he's dead?"

"A size eight," Tomlinson replied, "take your pick. You saw me on the boat naked, so it sure as hell doesn't belong to me."

HE HAD LANDED in the village of Cojimar, a name that was familiar, but he didn't remember why until a man with curly hair and a beard entered and sat at the bar. Ordered a demitasse, black, lit a cigarette, and struck up a conversation about photos on the wall. There were many: portraits of leathered fishermen, close-ups of their hands, a cast net beaded with sunlight, and fish, blue marlin and sharks, all black-and-white gothics from the 1950s.

"The great photographer Raúl Corrales made these images," the man said. "He lived here, if you're interested in that sort of thing."

Tomlinson, browsing as if in a museum, listened for a

while. "These are timeless. None of this photoshopped, digital crap. Yeah . . . a true artist. Did you know him?"

"Very well, before he died. I'm Raúl Corrales Junior."

Tomlinson grinned and shook the man's hand. "Buy you a beer?"

It was almost noon.

"Another coffee," Raúl said. This time, he spooned in raw sugar, the granules big and brown like salt. "There are images you haven't seen in the next room. One in particular that Americans like—a giant shark we still call *El Monstruo*."

The Monster of Cojimar, Tomlinson realized.

In 1945, four local fishermen, drifting outside the harbor, caught the largest great white shark in history, which took hours to land, and several more hours to tow home. The entire village turned out, an event captured in black-and-white and framed on the wall: men, women, children sitting atop a shark that was twenty-one feet long and weighed seven thousand pounds.

"The Monster had been stealing blue marlin and swordfish from their lines, so our fishermen had to do something or go broke," Corrales explained.

They returned to the bar and talked about photography, then Florida. Every Cuban has a relative within driving distance of Miami. Raúl's daughter lived in Orlando. Tomlinson said, "I'll call her when I get back . . .

if I get back," and began to relax by ordering another beer.

He had been fidgety, a little nervous, before Raúl showed up, but now didn't feel so alone. The customs cops, who were finally gone, had found only the two bags of grass, but not the third bag, which was hidden, and not the briefcase, which had gone over the side with Figuerito, its faithful guardian. Tomlinson had been through too many customs shakedowns to admit how much cash he was carrying, but that's not what worried him. Would the woman, whose name was Berta, return with official permission to stay until *No Más* was seaworthy? He was screwed if she didn't because the cops had confiscated his passport.

There were other concerns. He had to find a safe place to moor his sailboat. Were there hauling tracks in this little bay? More pressing was his need for a map and private transportation.

The shortstop and Castro's love letters were central to this issue.

Raúl had inherited his father's perceptive eye. "I'm curious about the ring you're wearing. I've seen that symbol before."

From his pinky finger, right hand, Tomlinson removed a small gold ring and said carefully, "I bought it in the East—the pyramid is so old, you can barely see it."

"José Martí, our national hero, belonged to the same fraternity," Corrales said and handed the ring back.

It was not the reply Tomlinson had hoped to hear.

"There's another thing I'm curious about. Do you mind? We don't get many visitors here."

"Fire away, man. The customs agent, her name's Berta something, she's supposed to be back in an hour or so, hopefully with my visa. Until then, I'm all dressed up with time on my hands."

The man smiled but was already ahead of him. "No visa. I thought so. Other damaged boats have tried this harbor—not many, but a few—and you're the first they didn't take to Havana for questioning. It's none of my business, but are you famous? A former athlete, perhaps?"

"Well . . . I wrote a book a while back. There's still the occasional groupie, thank god, but, no, I've been wondering myself why the cops left me at a bar. Figured the local economy needed"—Tomlinson paused to think—"I look like an athlete to you?" He swiveled his chair around. "Raúl, I appreciate the compliment, but let's put our cards on the table here. If you were sent to spy on me, far out. We all have to eat. So ask what you need to know, then we can get back to discussing these amazing photos."

Corrales chuckled over his coffee while his eyes confirmed they were alone. "So plainspoken, gringos from the States. A spy? Hardly that. I asked because I heard they found baseball equipment on your boat."

Word traveled fast in this village; probably true of the whole island. The Coconut Telegraph, Buffett called it.

Tomlinson spoke as if sharing a confidence. "It has to be tough to keep a low profile in a place like this, huh? I thought my equipment went overboard when this goddamn cruise ship swamped me in the Gulf Stream."

Corrales had heard about that, too, but stuck with baseball. "Do you play? Every afternoon, at the top of the hill, the village has a game. Men, and a few boys who are good enough."

A surge of serotonin brightened the room. "Play, hell yes. I pitch a little and can steal a base; a slap hitter, unless the ball's in my wheelhouse. Think they'd let me? Wait . . . you're saying they need gloves and bats more than players?" He touched his forehead. "I'm a little slow today. Okay, no problem. When I leave, everything I've got stays with your village team."

The refugee problem, Tomlinson suspected, is what the man actually wanted to discuss. It was in what came next: a polite vagueness with much hidden between the lines.

"That's quite a large boat you have. Is the hull damaged or just the rigging? Either way, there's a wooden bridge at the mouth of the river. If you can get under the bridge, fishermen here can fix just about anything."

"You know someone who can help?"

"Me—if the proper officials give permission. There's no crane, of course. We still wait for low tide and careen sailboats like in old times. Slower, but the results are the same."

"Screw technology," Tomlinson replied. "It's turned good sailors into video drones. The mast needs to be stepped and the stays re-anchored, but I've got all the hardware. Three or four days would get it done." He hesitated, made eye contact. "You're right, my boat's too big for one person. Plenty of room for friends of yours, if they'd like to go for a ride."

Corrales didn't wince, exactly, but came close. "That's not what I had in mind." He took his wallet out, removed a few pesos, and something else—a business card, possibly. "My flat's next door, down the steps, on the water. We shouldn't talk again unless they issue you a visa. You see, there's a reason I laughed at your remark about spies: my father was Fidel's official photographer during the Revolution."

"For real?"

"His work is in museums. The famous image of Che Guevara in his beret, the *campesinos* on horseback with flags? Everyone knows those images. Which is why everyone knows me. I'd be a poor choice to spy on anyone."

"My god," Tomlinson said. That's why Cojimar had sounded familiar: Castro's photographer and the monster shark. "Is your family still—"

"That is a question you shouldn't ask. Something happened after the Revolution—I don't know what, but that hasn't changed my faith in the government. Understand?"

No, but Tomlinson nodded anyway.

"If you are granted a visa, stop by. I have more photographs. Boxes and boxes full"—a pause for emphasis—"that you might like to see."

Boxes of photos. Was that what they were discussing? If so, things were still in the probing stage. Corrales placed his hand on the bar, the business card beneath it. "Do you have a good memory?"

"Photographic"—Tomlinson smiled—"as long as you've got something to write with."

On the card was a Masonic pyramid and a Havana address for something called the Sons of José Martí.

HE WAS BEING WATCHED: soldiers in a jeep made rounds every half hour; an old black Mercedes with tinted windows parked and re-parked, but no one got out. Finally, the Mercedes left.

Around noon, Berta delivered the visa, then dropped him at the top of the hill to watch the villagers play baseball. T-shirts and a few ragged uniforms, one catcher's mask, no shin guards, and only a couple of baseballs, both wrapped with tape. Tomlinson headed back to his boat at a jog until a girl on a tractor offered him a lift. She waited and returned him to the field, where the game stopped while he sorted through his equipment bag. Teams consisted of a dozen men, the rest teenagers or younger, one of them a lanky girl. Rather than risk embarrassing the adults, Tomlinson called the girl and boys closer.

"My boat's being repaired, so I've got no use for these things," he said. "Would you mind taking care of them?" On the ground were four baseball gloves, a dozen balls, yet the bag still bulged with equipment. He had played every position on the field but catcher and believed in arriving prepared.

"Is he a wealthy fascist?" a boy asked.

Tomlinson had to battle a tear when he heard that. "Little comrade"—he smiled—"you give me hope for the world. No . . . there are still a few of us who are simpatico. What position do you play?"

"*Premira* and *lanzador*," the boy answered, "and sometimes in the garden, too"—first base, pitcher, and occasionally the outfield, which had a sweeter name in Cuba.

Tomlinson slipped his hand into a Wilson A2000 first baseman's glove, popped it a few times. "Are you left-handed?"

"Of course." The boy's indignation inquired *Don't you know anything about this game?*

After that, Tomlinson would have adopted the kid, would have given him anything—money, his bicycle, even his boat—but was required, philosophically, to spread the wealth. He tossed him the glove, saying, "From now on, you're in charge of this, but you have to share with your teammates. Understand?"

"For how long?"

"How long can you keep it? When you're too old to play, ask me then."

Christmas morning. It was in the kid's eyes until he put the glove on. "Mother of God—it's soaked. Why did you leave this in the rain? It needs oil. I will oil the glove and sleep with it until it forgets such shitty treatment."

Adopt him, hell, Tomlinson thought. I'll steal the kid and take him home if he doesn't have parents.

When the equipment bag was empty, he pitched a couple of innings, then struck up a conversation with a fisherman, who asked about the condition of *No Más*.

Tomlinson went through the list of repairs. "Can you help? I know it's Friday, but I'm eager to get started."

"For a man who gives baseballs to children, of course. My grandfather taught me how to fix anything that floats, and a few things that shouldn't." He was Gregorio Fuentes, Hemingway's fishing captain.

Cuba was like that, a time warp linked to the 1950s.

"I'm honored," Tomlinson said. "The difficulty is, I lost my dinghy. No way to get back and forth from shore."

"I have a skiff with a motor you can use."

"That's very kind, but"—Tomlinson lowered his voice—"I don't want to get you into trouble. I'm being watched. They would know the skiff belongs to you. Even at night if I wanted to go somewhere . . . well, let's say, leave the harbor for some reason . . . they would hear the motor."

The fisherman confirmed his understanding with an exchange of looks, then a shrug. "You plan to search for your missing dinghy. I would do the same."

"Exactly," Tomlinson said. "And the funny thing is? That happens to be true."

The fisherman didn't believe him. "The less you say, the better. Come with me."

Twenty minutes later, a little before two, they were standing in mangroves near a bridge that separated Cojimar Bay from the river where fishermen kept their boats. "Would this work?"

Hidden in the bushes was a dugout canoe and a paddle, hand-carved.

"Perfect," Tomlinson said. "Now . . . I don't suppose you'd be willing to draw me a little chart? In case I get restless and, you know, decide to look for my dinghy."

Thursday afternoon, after landing at José Martí International, the Russian drove Vernum Quick to a party on a ship recently docked in Mariel. Vodka-crazed men in uniforms and *chingas* from the bowels of Havana. The *chingas* only made Vernum hungrier because his damaged face disgusted even them. So he drank too much and passed out in Kostikov's old Mercedes that, the next morning, delivered him to the farming village of Plobacho.

Home: fifty square kilometers of even smaller villages, bananas, thatched huts, tobacco, valleys between cliffs, cane fields, dull women, and roads dotted with oxen shit.

I can't survive here much longer, Vernum thought—

not for the first time. For five years, rumors about a demon in the cane fields had been spreading.

At two p.m., Kostikov texted via a satellite phone he had provided Vernum—but not in Spanish, of course. Translation required an old textbook from the *Fidelista* days.

The pizdă *arrived Cojimar, told police defector dead. Briefcase drowned. Stay your home.*

Figuerito Casanova was the defector, so *pizdă* had to mean "hippie"—or did it? Nor was it likely a briefcase could drown.

Vernum pumped cold water over his head, then drove his 1972 Russian Lada past the wooden baseball stadium to the square, where chickens scratched under tamarind trees. In the park, three old men sat on the rim of a fountain that hadn't worked in years, a marble bust of José Martí nearby.

"Pizdă?" Vernum inquired as he approached. "You speak Russian. What does it mean?"

"'Kiss my ass,'" one of the men replied, then tried to ignore him.

"That's the translation? 'Kiss my ass'?"

The men laughed, but one grumbled, "Leave us in peace, you evil turd. If a Russian called you a pussy, he's smarter than most of those savages."

Pizdă—it made sense, then, but a *Santero* couldn't ignore an insult like that, even from an old pig who still wore his medals from the Angola war. "Do you know what this is, Oleg?" Vernum produced a leather pouch from under his white guayabera. "It's what will be left of your balls if you don't apologize to the saints, especially Changó . . . Oh, and an offering of twenty pesos for my trouble."

Oleg just grinned. "*Pizdá*—I bet Vernum swallowed the Russian's cigar to earn a name so sweet. Look at how his face was beaten when they made hot oil."

More laughter. The men returned to their gossip while sweat beaded on Vernum's forehead. From the pouch, he mixed a gram of powdered bluestone with turpentine gum and coconut, indifferent to their discussion until he heard the name Marta Esteban, then something about Marta's daughters. To which Oleg insisted, "They returned early this morning, but it can't be true. No *Americano* would do a good deed, then disappear. Set cats on fire to burn our fields, the CIA, yes. *Then* leave in a fast boat—but not after rescuing children."

Vernum looked up, wanted to ask *Rescued the daughters from what?* but decided it was better to wait.

Nothing more to be learned, though, when the men realized he was eavesdropping, so he carried his act through: dabbed a pigeon feather in the goo and placed it on the head of José Martí with the quill pointed at Oleg. "In the morning, your *pinga* will be soft like an oyster and your piss will burn. I warn you for the last time . . ."

"Tell me something I don't know," Oleg roared. "Vernum must have watched through my toilet window. I thought he only peeped at schoolgirls."

Hilarious.

"*Vernum-ita*, instead of defacing General Martí, why not stick that feather up your ass?"

It went on like that, the three men trading jokes, each trying to top the other, while Vernum stalked away. One option was to go to his room and return with the last drop or two of poison he'd harvested from the Montblanc pen. Instead, he relied on Kostikov's bad temper and sent a text: *A gossip saw me in your car. Russian savage, he called you. I want to kill him.*

The response was in Spanish, thank god: *He suspects?*

Vernum typed: *Old man, big mouth.*

Response: *Close mouth, do not kill.*

Vernum felt a glow in his abdomen. He approached Oleg from behind, snatched his cane, and broke it over his shoulder, then hammered him in the face when he was on the ground. Lots of blood, and teeth scattered among the tamarind leaves, as well as a war medal that had pulled free of its ribbon.

Vernum retrieved the medal and lobbed it toward the old man's legs. "If anyone asks, a savage Russian ordered me to punish you," he said, and left in his '72 Lada, with its dents and broken antenna, red paint peeling.

ON HIS WAY out of town, opposite the baseball stadium, was a mansion with boarded-up windows that was mossy with age and neglect. The last of the Casanovas lived there, a scary old shrew of a woman whose only grandchild was that mental midget Figuerito. She was a recluse, did nothing, yet lived alone in that huge place, which proved she had political connections. Vernum despised her for it. Staring at the house, he stopped and configured his fingers into devil's horns, touched the bandage over his eye, then continued on his way.

Hopefully, it was true the fool was dead. One eyewitness down, one to go.

He sometimes saw Marta Esteban in the village but didn't know exactly where she lived. Somewhere in the country. Twice he had to detour and ask directions. *I hear she has some small problem,* Vernum, the *Santero,* explained each time.

Unlike Oleg and a few other old fools, people in the countryside were believers. Women especially. This was how he learned that Marta had sent her daughters on a raft to America. It was a dangerous secret, an insult to the government. Such an act stigmatized family members who stayed behind, but it was safe to confess to a *Santero* dressed in white, even if his face was swollen with stitches.

"No wonder Marta has been in hiding," a neighbor said. "She lives alone, you know. Her husband ran off, so it was just her and those girls. Maribel and Sabina . . . Sabina, even as a baby, she had a snake for a tongue. Even so, Marta must be out of her mind with worry."

"Marta Esteban didn't satisfy her husband?" Vernum

asked. Peasant women enjoyed flirting with a *Santero*, but he didn't overdo it. "Perhaps a love obeah, or a dab of salt oil, for this wife who can't keep a man happy. What do you think?"

Giggle—these scrawny peasants always covered their mouths rather than show their bad teeth. From the pouch, he gifted the neighbor with a cowrie shell, eyes painted on it. "Eleguá," he promised, "will bring steel to your bed tonight."

More giggling, more talk, before he said, "I'm confused. In the village, I heard a rumor that the daughters returned this morning. Something about an *Americano*. Is this true?"

"My husband met the same drunken fisherman. He claimed he saw a fancy boat before sunrise and only *Americanos* can afford such things. But how can it be? Three, four days ago, perhaps more, those girls left forever. I think it is good that Marta has reached out to the saints for help. There are so many liars and gossips who care nothing for the pain of others."

It was good for Vernum, too. Why would a mother send her daughters away unless she had reason to hide them? It was a large province with bad roads, and even a *Santero* couldn't keep track of every peasant girl under the age of thirteen.

And if the daughters had returned? He would deal with it.

Marta's house was on a hillside around a curve and

beyond a wooden bridge that crossed a river. Almost fifteen kilometers by road from the village with a small school nearby, so no wonder he seldom saw the Esteban family in town. Marta, with her Indio eyes and body, had caught his attention almost two years before, but she'd been frosty, almost threatening, the way she referenced a husband in the military. No different a year later when Vernum followed the woman out of town but lost her on the moonless night. This was before he'd bought a car that was faster than a bicycle, so his hunger had sent him hunting near the school, where cane grew tall along the road. There was a playground there. Luck, or Changó, was with him, and three restless girls had appeared, out for a walk beneath the stars. One girl had escaped through the darkness. The others did not.

Maribel and Sabina, the neighbor had said. It had to be one of them.

Vernum, when he saw the Esteban shack from the road, thought, *Got you*.

HE HAD PLANNED to knock on the door and use his authority as a *Santero* to charm Marta when she answered.

Not now.

He took his time, scanned for nosey neighbors, then parked in a shady place that couldn't be seen from the bridge. The river was dark and deep here, not wide, but walled with vegetation. Where the river turned seaward was a path, a few fishing boats tied up, but no one around on this hot morning, with dragonflies and mosquitoes. When he was opposite the shack, he climbed the embankment. Foliage provided cover until he was so close he could smell beans cooking, and see into a window with curtains that were actually feed sacks but neatly pressed.

He moved to get a better view. Marta kept the yard swept, too. There was a chicken coop with fat white hens; mangoes and sour orange trees; and clothes hanging in sunlight: towels, sheets, a woman's panties . . . and two flowered dresses that only young girls could wear.

Vernum felt a slow pounding in his chest, and sat back, thinking, *It's true.* Somehow, the daughters had been returned—as a good deed by an unknown American, according to Oleg, a CIA agent possibly, but Oleg was an old fool whose brain still lived in the time of the *Fidelistas.*

How the girls had been returned didn't matter. Nor did it matter which daughter had escaped the cane field. With Figuerito dead, killing the girls—Marta, too, if he was lucky—would feed his hunger for a month or more, and also eliminate the last living witness.

Vernum circled the shack. Marta's bicycle was under the rain cistern, but no sounds or signs of movement inside. Those beans smelled good, though, and peasants couldn't afford to waste a meal. If they weren't here, they would return soon to eat.

He kept moving while his mind worked. Did the house have a telephone? No . . . there was no phone line, only electric, which, in this region, seldom worked.

The windows beckoned. Even as a teen he'd liked to watch females who didn't know they were being watched. But was a few minutes of pleasure worth the risk? No . . . it was wiser to come back tonight. After five minutes, though, he lost patience and moved to get a better angle, dodged his way through a jungle of banana leaves, then froze before exiting into the yard.

A girl was there, stood with her back to him, busy feeding a chicken or some kind of animal in a cage. She was tall, shapeless, had ribbons in her hair, and wore coveralls and cheap tennis shoes, which was typical of girls nearing thirteen. And too focused on the cage to hear the bushes rustling, so Vernum crouched and watched, thinking, *Thirteen . . . the age is about right.*

It wasn't a chicken, it was a rabbit she was feeding, and humming a song, too, a gringo tune. Clipped to the bib of her coveralls was a tube of bug spray, or something similar, that also suggested contact with an American. So maybe Oleg wasn't such a fool after all. When Vernum had the girl to himself, she would tell him fast enough, and that would be very soon.

First, though, where were the mother and the other

daughter? Better to wait rather than ruin what, so far, had been an afternoon gifted by Changó.

Or was it?

Vernum's good sense battled the fever building inside his head and argued both sides.

They're in the house, fool. Grab the girl while you can.

No . . . sweeter tonight when the three are alone. No witnesses left. You can take your time, man, and do it all.

As the battle raged, the door of the shack opened and Marta appeared, calling, "Come eat or I will throw it away!"

The girl replied, "Yes, Mama," and ran like a deer across the yard and disappeared inside.

"Dumbass." Vernum retreated, muttering to himself. "Damn Russian is right—I'm a *pizdă*, a weakling pussy, to miss such a chance."

He stumbled through the banana patch so mad he thought he was hearing things when a child's voice ordered, "Stop your swearing or you'll burn in hell. Who are you?"

Vernum spun around. It was an identically dressed girl, but a different girl, this one short, not tall, with legs like saplings, and barefoot, which was typical of younger children. She was on a footpath, the two of them shielded from the house, here in the shadows alone. A stalk of raw sugar protruded from the girl's pocket—a treat stolen from the nearby cane field, he guessed.

"Changó." Vernum smiled. "I will give you something nice for this, man."

The girl had a fierce little face with nostrils that flared. "Who are you? You don't belong here." She drew the cane stalk in a threatening manner and placed a hand on the tiny canister clipped to her coveralls.

He knelt, laughing, so they were eye to eye. "Don't be afraid, child. I bet you like chocolate. Do you like chocolate?" The girl backed a step when he extended his hand. "My car is near the river. Come with—"

"You're a trespasser," the girl interrupted, "or a thief. If you've come to steal our stuff, I'll . . ." She raised the stalk, then lowered it. "What happened to your face?"

The stitches. He'd forgotten. "Some evil fool attacked me. I don't like evil men, that's why you're safe with me. It'll just take a minute to walk to my car." Again he offered his hand while the girl stared, puzzled by the stitches in his mouth and eyebrows or as if making up her mind about the chocolate.

No . . . she was making up her mind about him. "You have a snake's face and mean eyes," she said. "Go away or I'll hit you with this." Raising the cane stalk, she stepped back and, for some reason, unsnapped the little canister from her coveralls.

Vernum's expression changed. "You arrogant little *puta*. Someone should teach you manners."

"Stop your damn swearing," the girl said. "Don't come near me or I'll—"

Vernum lunged, slapped her to the ground. That's when Sabina, looking up, used the canister of mace, aimed for the eyes, just as Marion Ford had taught her.

12

riday morning, after cleaning branches, leaves, and other river debris from his boat, Ford paid cash for a slip at Marina Hemingway, west of Havana, then sat in the shade reading until customs agents were done with their search.

Dr. Archie Carr's *The Windward Road*, a book about sea turtles, meshed with what agents found aboard, so he was soon able to make a bed on the casting platform. Cozy there beneath the bow shield. He paid 750 euros for a hundred gallons of fuel, ate roast chicken at El Aljibe in the embassy district, then again fell asleep to the rhythm of marimbas and waves.

Government offices opened at nine. He took a cab to

a complex near the University of Havana and applied for research permits as Marion D. North, Ph.D., the name on his fake passport. Receipts for the permits, stamped on official letterhead, would be enough to satisfy the coastal cops. Even so, he couldn't rationalize another stop at the home of Marta Esteban—not while the sun was up. To associate with an American was dangerous in itself, which is why he'd done only a quick stop-and-drop that morning after navigating two miles of river, hadn't spoken to the mother, and was gone before sunrise.

Ford told himself, *The girls will be able to explain*, yet the subject nagged at him. Maribel had witnessed a murder, but it was not a typical crime. A serial killer was on the loose in her rural district, and gossip about the girls returning would travel fast through the countryside. Was Marta Esteban savvy enough to understand why he had given her daughters money and the name of a hotel—the Hotel Plaza in the old city—and instructed them to book rooms for a few nights? Or would she fear a setup?

No way to contact Marta. Like many homes in rural areas, there was no phone.

Ten-year-old Sabina, with her fierce temper and tongue, was the focus of Ford's worries. That puzzled him because Maribel was the obvious target. It was irrational.

Intuition, Tomlinson would have said.

AT AN AFTERNOON GAME, near the bull pen in Havana's Grand Stadium, Gen. Rivera said to Ford, "That is a dangerous subject here. Even now. Every Cuban has heard the same rumor, but few believe because, well, they don't want to believe." After relighting a cigar, he amended, "Every Cuban born before the days of JFK, anyway."

What Ford had said was "Some myths die hard," an oblique reference to a fact: Fidel Castro had never played baseball. Not even high school baseball. Yet, the legend he had been offered a contract by the Pittsburgh Pirates and Washington Senators was still parroted by U.S. writers, broadcasters, even historians.

Ford replied, "The world doesn't know or care about old lies—not that it matters now. You were talking about an incident, something about Americans who played here in 1959—"

"It matters," the general insisted, but kept his voice down.

"To a few crazies, maybe, but not the rest of the world." Ford was taking in the spectacle. There were a thousand people or so in the stands, cops patrolling every section. Nice field; the scoreboard missing some lights, but he liked that. "Big egos a long time ago when baseball was important," he said. "I can see why it pisses off someone like you, but let it go, General."

"Latinos aren't gringos," he snapped. "It will always matter to the movement, to Fidel's legacy, and to the new government that is already going to hell. Never underestimate the power of superstition and baseball in Cuba."

Ford, who had just arrived, wanted to push through the pleasantries, end this talk of sports and find out what was important. Any news about Tomlinson? The Castro letters—how had Rivera gotten them? More importantly, who wanted them? But the *generalissimo* was a stubborn man. "Juan, you see things from a different aspect. Here, particularly, I know it's better to talk in generalities. Being offered a major league contract"—Ford smiled at the thought—"he wasn't the first man to lie about that."

"If you knew history as I do, you wouldn't take it so lightly. The Revolution interrupted the most important baseball series of that era: the Havana Sugar Kings against the Minneapolis Millers, champions of the American minor leagues. Cubans were furious. To hell with politics, why were these games canceled? National pride, even racial pride, was at stake. There were riots that threatened the Revolution. So Fidel became an instant champion of the game, created his own team, The Bearded Ones, while his propaganda people spread a lie—a brilliant lie that U.S. magazines printed. The world still believes Fidel sacrificed a major league career to save Cuba. That's why the subject is dangerous to discuss. There is an old saying: *Disprove one nail in the cross and religion becomes mere fairy tale*. I was once a believer," Rivera said. "No more."

Ford looked around before warning him, "Yes. Dangerous, as you said, to use certain names."

The general ignored him. Nodded toward the field where the Industríales—the equivalent of Cuba's New York Yankees—and Pinar del Río were tied in the fifth inning, playing before a good crowd that seemed sparse in a stadium that seated seventy thousand. Rivera started to say, "Havana's Sugar Kings were a Triple-A team for Cincinnati in those years . . ." but his attention shifted to a group of men coming through the nearest tunnel. They were noisy, with drunken, florid faces, among them a giant who was older but looked fit, yet had to weigh over three hundred pounds. A former athlete, fluid in his movements, but with a sour attitude; indifferent to the men he was with.

"Russians," Rivera said, suddenly uneasy. "Do you recognize the large one? His name's Kostikov."

Ford knew a great deal about Anatol Kostikov, was surprised to see the man here, but asked, "What about him?"

"I expect to be followed, but it's never been like this. We shouldn't meet for a couple of days." Rivera attempted to stand but sat back when Ford pinned his arm.

"General, don't make it so obvious. Maybe he came

to see the game. But"—Ford had to think for a moment—"just in case, let's get the important stuff out of the way. Do you know if Tomlinson is here?"

A nod. "Don't contact him, he's being watched. Friends say he arrived in Cojimar, but without the briefcase. That might be the problem. Figuerito drowned. Something about a freighter hitting them, but his sailboat survived."

"Geezus. The shortstop? Why the hell would he—"

Rivera pulled his arm free. "Not now. On the Prado, in the old city, there's a restaurant not far from the seawall, La Científico, an old mansion with apartments downstairs. We can meet there tonight for drinks if—"

"What about Tomlinson?"

"Yes, yes, he's fine. I'll tell you later."

"What are you afraid of, Juan? You'll only attract attention if you leave now."

"Don't be ridiculous." The man pretended to watch a hitter for the Industríales take a called third strike. "Curve ball," he said, but his smile was forced. "Almost as good as mine."

Ford focused on the big Russian who was scanning the bleachers while the younger men filed toward seats. "You've been smuggling Cuban ballplayers and selling contraband on the Internet. The Russians are back. You're surprised they're interested?"

"If he was sent to find me, yes. Kostikov was KGB, now the FSB—Federal Security Service—but you know about that. A very high-level talent, if you understand my meaning. Ruthless. You're sure you've never heard the name?"

Ford waited while the Russian's eyes swept past them, no hint of interest, before the man turned and exited. "It's okay, old buddy. You can breathe again."

Rivera dismissed that with a laugh and settled back with his cigar and seemed to relax in the noise of a thousand cheering, stomping fans. Two hitters later, he spoke again, but without turning his head. "We'll discuss Tomlinson and the briefcase at the place I mentioned. La Científico. A great scientist once lived there—Cuba's second president."

"You *are* scared."

"Only careful, until I figure out what is happening. My contacts here, even the powerful ones, are behaving oddly."

"How long since your last visit?"

"Three weeks, almost four."

"Did you actually bribe the warden to get the short-stop out of jail? Or did you help him escape?"

"What does it matter? No one cares about Figuerito. Something else has happened. Something important enough to change how an important person like me is treated. That's what I don't understand."

Ford, looking at the Russians, who were drunk, said, "I wonder what." He asked about Rivera's friend, the woman who had been hospitalized with uranium poison. She was dead. He asked for specifics. How was this trip different? Then brought it back around, saying, "You've spent your career reading powerful men. What's your best guess?"

"It might have to do with the briefcase," Rivera conceded. "And what we were talking about—the year of the Revolution."

"What do a bunch of personal letters have to do with the Revolution? I can't imagine them—you know who I mean—writing to a mistress about political secrets or—"

"Hear me out," Rivera said. "The winter of the Revolution, the Sugar Kings were one game away from beating the Americans in what was called the True World Series, but Fidel's army put an end to it. Do you understand? After decades of being treated as inferiors, this was Cuba's first chance to prove its team was as good as any team in the major leagues."

Ford asked, "The games were played here?"

"All but the fourth game and the final seventh, which was under way, and tied in extra innings, in Pinar del Río. The Minneapolis Millers had great players, such as Carl Yastrzemski and Orlando Cepeda. The Kings had American players, too, from Cincinnati's farm system. Lou Klein broke the Latin League home run record; Luis Tiant was rookie of the year, plus the three American pitchers I told you about. A great deal of pride was at stake."

"And money," Ford said. "Are you sure about those names?" The timing seemed a little off.

"No, but the money, yes. Havana's casinos were run by Meyer Lansky and other Mafiosos. The betting was international. Batista knew he was losing control of the country. He would have paid any amount to have won that game."

Ford said, "And stayed in power," but was thinking, *Rivera is after more than just motorcycles and machine guns. What the hell is in those letters?*

The general signaled a passing vendor and bought two empanadas, which he shared. "As an example, take Nicaragua's last revolution. Nineteen eighty . . . was it eighty-four? No, nineteen eighty-five. When Daniel Ortega came to power, the first thing he did was order the execution of the former dictator's best pitchers and his cleanup hitter. That was—what?—only thirty years ago. To most Americans that would seem absurd, but you know it's true. Personally, I understand the demands of politics, but to do such a wasteful thing shows contempt for the game."

Ford nodded because it was true. "Better to draft them into your army," he suggested.

"*Exactly.* Same with lying about a contract offer from the major leagues. Contemptible. Three perfect games I have pitched and many no-hitters, yet I have never shown disrespect for the scouts who didn't have the balls to sign me." Rivera ate the last of his empanada. "They were biased fascists, of course."

"Intimidated by your stature, more likely."

"No doubt, but I never asked a scout to lie for a story in *Sports Illustrated*, unlike . . ." Rivera touched his chin, meaning "The Bearded One." "There is a book written by a Yale professor—"

"*The Pride of Havana*. I read it." Ford knew where this was going.

"The professor searched every box score in every Cuban newspaper published during Fidel's teens and twenties and found only one mention—a softball game when he was in law school. That man was my hero. You know that. Yet, you now ask why it is important?"

Ford glanced over while the *generalissimo* stared into space. "I'm surprised you let yourself believe something in a book."

"I didn't until I checked with certain sources. I got drunk the night I learned it was all true. Shitty softball, not even the real game. Fidel pitched, his only appearance on a Cuban mound, and *he lost*. My god"—Rivera tossed the empanada wrapper into the aisle—"I would prefer a bullet in the ass to losing a slow-pitch softball game. That book is banned here, of course, because the legend must be protected. Especially now. As you say, people wouldn't believe it anyway, and proof died with one lying baseball scout. No . . . Cubans would never believe the truth. Cubans would have to hear the truth from Fidel's own dead lips."

Rivera festered over that—a man whose political and baseball careers had been lost in the shadow of the Castros—but paid attention when Ford said, "Lips . . . I thought that's what you were worried about. A lip-reader."

The general's reaction: *Huh?*

Ford shielded his mouth with a hand. "I thought that's why you got upset when I brought up the subject. In the press box—someone with binoculars. They're watching us. I assumed you knew."

Rivera said, *"Pendejos,"* and made a show of searching for something at his feet. "Is it Kostikov?"

Ford, getting up, said, "Don't say the name of the restaurant again. I know the place. Are you staying there?"

Rivera's head moved imperceptibly. "Come around ten. You'll have time to check into your hotel. Marion— make sure you're not followed."

FORD DIDN'T LEAVE. He waited inside the stadium, drifting among fans, where meat sizzled on makeshift grills mixed with tobacco smoke, a cavern noisy with maracas and guitars, until Kostikov appeared, a foot taller than Cubans who parted to create a path. Kostikov with a liter bottle of beer in his hand; rude, not making eye contact with those he brushed aside, on his way somewhere, no interest in the game.

Ford followed, but, first, pulled on a green baseball cap he'd just purchased. He had seen photos of the Russian as far back as . . . ten, fifteen years ago. Had the Russian seen photos of him, an American who sometimes went by the name Marion North?

Better to find out here than later on a dark street.

He had bought the hat at a kiosk that sold diapers and aspirin—typical in a stadium that served many government needs. Ford had played ball here years ago, remembered exiting the field into a room of young mothers, some nursing babies, while a doctor lectured on hygiene and birth control.

"Wrong door," the doctor had said, as if she'd said it a thousand times to men wearing spikes. She probably had.

Through another wrong door: people wove mats while a man read to them from the works of José Martí.

Bizarre. The Grand Stadium—Estadio Latinoamericano, the official name—was a catacomb of tunnels and disjointed intent. But Anatol Kostikov seemed to know where he was going, plowed a straight furrow while people scattered, even a cop who looked away when an old man stumbled into a domino collision that tripped him and two others to the floor, both children, who got up fast, but not the old man.

A cane of oiled wood lay nearby, and his hat. Ford

retrieved both and got a hand under one bony arm, saying, "Let me help you, *patrón*." *Patrón*, a noun that granted respect and deference to a man who hadn't had either for a while, judging from his clothes. His temper, however, hadn't aged.

"Clumsy hippo," he hollered after the Russian. "Come back here—I'll teach you manners."

Kostikov, if he heard, didn't slow, pushed onward while people stared, but not the cop. The cop recognized authority without being told, so he went the other way, but only after warning the old man with a glare.

Ford asked, "Are you hurt?"

"That coward. Twenty years ago, I would have boxed his ears. I would have"—the man looked more carefully at his cane—"Damn . . . he broke the tip off. That dickless snake. Do you still see him?"

Kostikov's head was melon-sized. Far down the corridor, he turned toward a sign that read HOMBRES. A bathroom stop. It gave Ford some time. "Take it easy, *patrón*. You seem to be standing okay. How's your balance?"

"To hell with my balance. I hate stupid questions as much as I hate stupid people."

Ford smiled, noting the man's hands—a fighter's hands, all knuckles and gnarled fingers—and asked his name, which was Lázaro. Made him repeat it—Lázaro Junco—hoping he would calm down.

Lázaro had a temper. "Call the Guardia, I want that tourist scum arrested. Was he Italian? The motherless goat dildo. Where did he go?"

"He's Russian," Ford said.

Some fire went out of the man. "Shit. I assumed he was an *Americano* but didn't want to offend you. No wonder Omar snuck away."

Ford handed him his baseball cap, which was old-style, red felt with a Cuban *C* above the brim. "Who's Omar?"

"The security guard."

"Not the police?"

"He pretends to be. I work here, have to see that *maricón* every day. He is a spineless *puta* who masturbates with animals. I will never offer Omar a coffee again."

Ford, watching Kostikov enter the restroom, said, "You have a gift for profanity. What do you do here?"

"Mind my own damn business," the man replied. "Or do you mean my job?" He pointed to a sign over double doors that read STORAGE / ENTRY FORBIDDEN. "I'm in charge of all things useless. I sleep there as well. More than forty years, yet guards allow me to be assaulted by any fat son of a *chinga* who can afford a ticket." With a hand, he used Ford's shoulder to steady himself. "That filthy *baló*. I'll stick this broken tip up his ass."

Baló—Cuban slang likening Russians to beach balls, round and soft.

"You can always buy another cane."

"Not like this. I carved it for my grandfather from a bat broken on this field years ago. My father, the old cock, he used it after an accident, then my legs went to hell. See this?" A shepherd's crook handle was screwed into the knob. "I stole an umbrella from the Hotel Nacional. Meyer Lansky's umbrella, possibly, but it would be a lie to say I am certain." The old man lifted his head, still searching. "Where'd that elephant go? He would need a circus tent to disappear."

Ford hefted the cane, gauged the strength of the ornate handle, the wood dense, solid, despite the splintered tip. A dangerous idea was assembling in his head. "You were a boy when you made this?"

The man was too angry to hear. "Russians are always drunk. I bet he's pissing, so I'll surprise him from behind." He tried to pull away, but Ford took his arm and steered him toward the storage room while he protested, "Gringo . . . I am not a cripple. Where are you taking me?"

"Do you have keys to that room?"

"The storage room? Can't you hear? I live there, for christ's sake."

"Is there a back way out?"

"Not if I don't invite you in, there isn't."

"Then there is. I just thought of something. If the

Russian stays in the *baño* more than a minute or two, that means he's in one of the stalls. I want to borrow this."

"My cane? You've been helpful, but I'm not giving you my goddamn cane."

"How much do you think it's worth? The Russian might agree to pay for repairs. No guarantees, but there's a chance."

"Hah. If you ask him nicely, I suppose."

"I didn't say anything about being nice."

"Force him to pay? You don't know much about Russians."

Ford, looking at the old man, said, *"Patrón*, you know less about me. *Rude men need to be taught manners.* Your own words."

Lázaro focused on Ford's face for the first time. "You're not drunk, I would smell it. Who are you?"

"Wait inside," Ford told him, "and watch for me when I come back. I might be in a hurry."

IN THE LAST STALL, visible beneath the door, slacks piled on size-fifteen loafers proved his timing was just about right. Not perfect, but close; only a couple of guys standing at a steel trough along the wall that served as a communal urinal. Posh by Cuban standards. Anyplace tourists weren't herded, there would be a hole in a cement slab, possibly an indentation for the feet, but nothing for support but fear of what lay below.

Ford entered the adjacent stall carefully so that Kostikov wouldn't see his shoes. No toilet seat, no toilet paper. He left, found a newspaper in the trash, soaked it under a faucet, and crumpled it into a heavy ball. By the time he'd returned, the room was empty but for a bald guy who, Ford guessed, had a bad case of stadium bladder.

He bolted the door, bent to confirm the Russian's pants were around his ankles, then waited, but the place had the acoustics of a locker room. Too much crowd noise outside to hear anyone leave or arriving, so Ford thought *What the hell*, and made his move. He got to his knees, flushed the toilet, and, in Spanish, hollered, "Keep your head down!" Then he lobbed the wad of paper over the wall into the next stall.

Kostikov would look up—a brief window of opportunity. Ford used the cane, hooked the man's pants near the crotch, and heaved mightily as if gaffing a fish. The Russian's butt banged hard on the floor and his legs wedged under the metal divider. The man was so stunned, Ford had ripped off one shoe and was leveraging the other when the violent kicking began.

Control a man's legs, you control the man—it was the wrestling mantra of a great high school wrestling coach, Gary Freis. Ford had lived that sport five days a week for years. In this case, ankles, not legs, which was better because Kostikov couldn't see who had attacked him, or even the hands that stripped his pants off while he bellowed and dented the partition with his fists.

A final touch: Kostikov's own belt looped around one ankle, then knotted to his other ankle with a quick half hitch.

Ford exited the stall with pants and cane tucked under his arm like a football. Didn't run, although the bald guy with a bladder problem was now washing his hands—no clue that he would soon be confronted by a naked Russian giant.

Outside, Ford slipped into the flow of milling fans and kept moving while he searched Kostikov's pockets. He kept a fat leather billfold, an odd little pistol with Soviet markings, and a satellite phone. Underwear, cigars, lighter, loose change, then his own green baseball cap, went into separate trash cans, all jettisoned discreetly. After some thought, he also dumped the satellite phone. Too risky because of the GPS.

Ford didn't look back until the old man, Lázaro Junco, ushered him into the storage room, saying, "Hurry—are they after you?" Then saw what Ford carried under his arm. "Jesus Christ . . . you stole the man's *pants*?"

Near the food vendors, military cops in green uniforms were rushing through a gate, a half dozen, who turned toward the HOMBRES sign far down the corridor.

"You stole Meyer Lansky's umbrella," Ford replied. "My advice is to lock the door."

When Sabina sprayed Vernum Quick with mace, he was blinded but managed not to scream. Arms wide, he lunged for her . . . Lunged again at a blurry shape that was, in fact, a tree. He hit face-first, a collision that jarred air from his lungs and put him on the ground.

The girl pursued him like a hornet, used the mace again, chiding, "When my gringo friend hears this, he will steal your money and drown you in the river. Marion does whatever I tell him." Only then did she run.

Or did she? Maybe the little *mocosa*—"the brat"—was waiting for him to open his eyes.

Vernum couldn't see but knew the river was downhill. He covered his face and rolled into the weeds where the hill sloped abruptly. Kept rolling faster, thinking, *Marion? Who's Marion?* and soon collided with another tree.

"*¡Puta la madre, puta la hija!*" he yelled, a profane version of "Like mother, like daughter."

He listened for a moment, stood and clawed at his eyes, then got smart and removed his linen shirt, folding and refolding it to wipe the spray away. Soon, he could see from one eye, but, damn, that stuff burned. His skin, the lacerations on his face, were on fire.

At the river, he threw himself in. Water helped. So did the mud he washed himself with, but he didn't waste time. Marta couldn't call for help—no telephone. If he hurried, he might intercept them before they got away. He scrambled up the hill to the road, confirmed it was empty, then angled toward a dirt lane that led to the house. No one there either, and Marta's bicycle was by the cistern, where he'd last seen it.

Had they fled on foot?

I'll find them. When I do, that damn little wasp bitch will suffer first and be the last to die.

Rage. It flooded his head and darkened the sky. He fixated on specifics, what he would do to Marta while her daughters watched. Delicious, when he visualized details, nuances of whimpering and skin color of a woman crazed with fear. He drew on past experience, a catalog of images stored away for nights when he was alone and hunger-driven. Never, though, had he been favored with an opportunity like this.

Run, *chicas*, run until you collapse. I love the taste of a woman's sweat.

At the edge of the yard, Vernum stopped and focused his hearing. My god . . . the fools, they were still inside.

From the house came the garbled chimes of girls arguing, their voices interrupted by the bell notes of a woman who was getting impatient. Marta Esteban . . . the woman who had snubbed him for years.

A quick prayer to Changó: *I'll buy you the best damn bottle of rum and light a box of candles. Anything, man, if you let this happen.*

Vernum's head swiveled. No one around. He sprinted to a tamarind tree only a few meters from what he guessed to be the kitchen window, the window open, sweet with the scent of beans. He crouched and turned sideways. The trunk of the tree shielded him while he sorted out three distinct voices, the most piercing of which was that vicious little girl wasp.

"I didn't start this, you brat. No one in this house believes a word I say. Perhaps I will go live with the nuns. They'll shave my head. Probably beat me and force me to eat fish until I die of starvation. No one in this house gives a damn."

"Sabina! Do you want me to soap your mouth?"

"Didn't I tell you, Mama? She swears constantly and

makes up stories to scare me. Sometimes I believe she is possessed by demons, I truly do—"

"Shut up, Maribel. Let the zombie cut your throat. That's what he threatened to do to me. And he would have cut my throat if I hadn't knocked him down—"

"You? Hit a zombie? Mama, she's lying again."

"I didn't say that! I'm the only one in this house not afraid of her own shadow. That's why you hate me. Even my own mother sent me to live with fascists."

"Enough, Sabina. My darling"—Marta's voice softened—"there is no such thing as a zombie. At least admit that part of your story is, well, not a lie, exactly—"

"I'm not lying! His lips were sewn, one of his eyes was sewn, he was ugly and bawled like a pig when I squirted his face. If that's not a zombie, I don't know what the hell is."

The older sister taunted, "Such language!" while Vernum winced and thought, *Lying little puta*. He was back in control of the situation, though, and continued to listen, but not as closely. He'd already made up his mind. Take the axe he'd seen in the woodpile, break down the door if Marta wouldn't let him in. The older girl, Maribel, had to be the one who had escaped from the cane field. With her, he would . . .

Do what?

Damn that brat. It was impossible to think with her incessant talking. He tried to tune the girl out until he heard her say, "The gringo fascist will believe me. He promised he would be back . . . Probably on his way right now. You'll see who is the brave one in this family."

That grabbed Vernum's attention. He searched the yard and refocused while the girl chattered on. "Do you really think I would waste my canister of pepper juice? It fit so nicely on my blouse, a gift from *him*, yet I chose to protect my coward sister."

Marta spoke: "It is true, she used most of her spray. Maribel . . . don't walk away until we decide. What did the man look like?"

"I told you, he was a monster, not a man. Do I have to repeat every word? The rich gringo gave us money for a hotel. That's where we should be, a place that's safe and has a swimming pool—"

"We don't accept money from strangers. Now, stop your whining. How would we get there? Ride bicycles all the way to Havana?"

"Sabina wants to stay in a hotel, Mama. That's what this is about."

"You're the liar! When my friend Marion hears I have run away to live with nuns who beat me, he'll come. He'll buy me something . . . something nice—and drown that ugly bastard."

Mother of God, now the little *mocosa* was crying.

"Make sure the doors are locked, Maribel. Where is the machete? And the axe . . . Oh my god, the axe is outside. Sabina, are you sure the *Americano* said he would come this afternoon?"

"What does it matter what I say? You won't believe me."

"Darling, calm yourself. Check all the windows. I'll be right back."

Vernum stiffened for a moment, then peeked around the tree into the kitchen.

Shit. Staring back at him was that vicious little wasp of a girl. He ducked, then sprinted for cover, expecting to hear a scream, but the girl didn't scream.

Why not? She had seen him. He was certain.

Possessed by demons, the older girl had claimed. Perhaps it was true.

From the bushes, Vernum watched Marta cross the yard to the woodpile, her eyes darting this way and that, until she had the axe in her hand. Still nervous, she took a last look from the porch and closed the door.

Marion. Earlier, the brat had used that name as a threat. But it was a name for women, not men. Was the girl possessed or just crazy?

Either way, Vernum felt his confidence draining. He pictured himself inside the house, facing Marta, who was holding an axe—worse, that devil brat with a machete in her hand. Another scenario: a gringo with a woman's name—a CIA agent, according to old Oleg, the war hero—who might attack him from behind.

Better to wait here until dark, Vernum decided. Do it right, enjoy myself.

Stay positive. That was important in Santería. As everyone knew, the gods were fickle. They were prone to heap misery on the miserable more quickly than shower the confident with good fortune. He tried to make himself comfortable while mosquitoes whined and his mind wandered.

The devil brat. Why didn't she call for help, or scream, or do . . . something?

That bothered him. It was spooky. He had confronted girls who were older—a dozen, perhaps—and they had all surrendered, some in tears, most frozen by fear, but not one had fought back, let alone chased him to ground.

She's crazy. More likely, she didn't see me from the window.

Vernum couldn't let it go. Demons existed; they roamed the island in search of humans to inhabit. That was also part of Santería teachings. He himself had performed several exorcisms. Usually on hysterical women and men who had boiled their brains with cheap *aguardiente*. Only one, however, for a girl, but her madness was caused by her first menstruation. The devil child was no more than eleven.

Fool—she is four feet tall and, at most, weighs fifty pounds. You're afraid of a tiny girl?

No, Vernum feared the demon inside the child, until he remembered *The demon in me will eat her alive.*

DARKNESS DRIFTED UP from the river before the sun was gone. Soon, frogs, screaming insects, overwhelmed the sky's last light and coaxed a slow assemblage of stars—bedtime in the countryside of western Cuba.

Inside the house, Marta appeared at her bedroom window, lit a kerosene lamp, pulled the curtains, and began to undress. The ripeness of her body cast a nippled silhouette. Two windows away, a candle floated, carried by a girl in a thin gown.

Vernum wet his lips.

He heard the devil brat's shrill voice: "Where's the water bucket? How am I supposed to flush if there is no water bucket?"

Marta untied her hair and fanned it over her shoulders. "Maribel? Did you hear your sister?"

"Mama, she used it last."

"I did not!"

"You did. You were too busy making up stories and left it outside."

Marta's hands moved to her face. "Don't leave this house. Sabina . . . Don't you dare leave this house. Do you hear me?"

"But what about—"

"You can flush in the morning. It's not important. In fact, I want you girls to sleep with me tonight. Sabina . . . have you gone deaf?"

"All right! But don't blame me if we all die in our sleep and strangers come and see we don't bother to flush."

A smile tightened the stitches in Vernum's lips, a joyous pain. He had gone to his car and returned wearing a dark shirt and carrying a coil of wire, tape, matches, and a knife. He opened the knife now.

"Mama, she's trying to scare me."

"Talk louder. The zombie's probably outside right now, listening."

"Mama!"

"Come to bed, Maribel. Sabina? *Sabina.* You, too."

"I'm not finished yet! I needed the water bucket for when I *am* done, but I'm *not* done. And what if the gringo arrives and sees no lights? That's very rude."

"Five minutes, young lady. Do you hear?"

More bickering. Marta extended her arms toward the ceiling, a baggy gown cascaded down to veil her body, emphasizing the slope of her breasts, the angle of her chin.

Sometimes—not often—Vernum preferred women to girls.

SABINA KNEW her mother's weaknesses and strengths. Books were a weakness. A request to read by candlelight was seldom denied.

"As long as you sit in the chair outside my door—and just a chapter. Is that clear?"

"Yes, Mother."

"And no more sad poetry. It gives you dreams."

"Promise, Mother. I'll choose a book with pictures. Is that okay?"

Pictures—hah! Sabina hated idiotic children's stories. Instead, she sat in the hall near a window with a book of poems by Dulce María Borrero. It was a thin volume beyond her understanding, or so a teacher had warned. Being told she could not do something only guaranteed Sabina would do it anyway, and she had fallen in love with Señorita Borrero's melancholy verse, although it was true she didn't always understand. The poems were short, though, seldom more than three lines, but it was a photo of the writer, who had brooding, dark eyes, that spoke to the girl. Those eyes told of pain and loss and injustices suffered by all Cuban woman before Fidel—and after.

> *In the gardens of silence, sister,*
> *I will plant roses of harmony*
> *And fertilize them with my cold sorrow*

Those words thumped at Sabina's chest like hammers.

My cold sorrow . . .

She knew exactly how Señorita Borrero had felt. Same with poems about an unfaithful husband, which is why

Sabina had vowed never to marry, and about celibacy and death, and one about the Cuban flag, which ended "Our parents are stained."

Try living with my mother, Sabina thought. Yours, at least, didn't put you on a raft to Gringolandia. My next visit to Havana, I will put flowers on your grave in my favorite cemetery and we will weep together. And if the fascist gringo didn't lie to me, perhaps stay in a nice hotel with a swimming pool.

She turned a page, aware that Maribel had been partly right about selfish motives. Sabina liked Havana, but truly loved Colon Cemetery, which was a few kilometers west of the grand baseball stadium. Acres of ornate mausoleums, a forest of marble with statues so lovely it pained her heart to leave. She had seen *The Wizard of Oz*, but the majesty of the Emerald City did not compare to the mystery and magic of Cuba's greatest cemetery. Of course she wanted to go—especially if the trip was paid for by a wealthy gringo. When would such an opportunity ever come again?

> *In a woman's life*
> *All is fragile, all is brief*
> *As the moon's reflection*

That was never truer than today.

Señorita Borrero, I want to be buried next to you.

When my mother and cowardly sister visit us with flowers, perhaps then they'll understand the pain of being ignored.

Sniffling, the girl closed the book, reached to snuff out the candle and realized her mother was asleep. Maribel—nothing woke her. You could pound on the bathroom door for hours, that brat wouldn't notice.

All is brief as the moon's reflection . . .

Not if you were waiting on Maribel, it wasn't.

Sabina went to the window to see if the moon was up, but the tamarind tree blocked her view. She could see the pump, though, and . . . Damn it to hell, her sister had been right about that bucket. Sabina had left it out there. In the morning, Maribel would nag and gloat unless the bucket was found somewhere else.

An idea popped into her head—what if the bucket was discovered in Maribel's bedroom?

That will teach her to doubt me.

Cupping the candle, she went through the kitchen, unlocked the back door, and peered out. There was wind in the trees, no one around, and dark. She closed the door, then backtracked. When she stepped out onto the porch, she carried the candle in one hand, a machete in the other, and the mace canister was clipped to her pink-and-white pajamas, even though the canister felt empty.

There has to be a little left, Sabina reasoned.

The pump was midway between the rabbit hutch and the tamarind tree, the bucket in the sand nearby. When she stooped to get it, she dropped the machete. Then a gust of wind put the candle out. At the same instant, a strange, dizzying sensation swept over her. It caused her nostrils to flair, and she knew without knowing that someone was coming toward her, a man who had been hiding behind the tree.

"Don't scream," his voice warned.

Sabina couldn't scream. It wasn't like that afternoon, when she'd been angry. She had no air, couldn't breathe, but managed to whisper, "What will you do if I run?"

"You mean after I catch you?" the man replied. "That's what I want you to see."

14

Ford didn't get to the Hotel Plaza until late afternoon because he'd spent more time than expected in the stadium storage room. At least an hour waiting for the military cops to leave, then another hour listening to the old man.

Lázaro Junco had been talkative. He had stories to tell about a room crammed with boxes and bins he called junk but that actually cataloged the history of Cuban baseball.

As Ford discovered, the storage room wasn't just the old man's home, it was his prison.

An interesting day, though—and profitable. In the hotel lobby, Ford overtipped key staff members and paid cash in advance for a room. All in euros, compliments of Anatol Kostikov.

At the desk, he asked if Marta Esteban and daughters had checked in. "No," the clerk said, but answered "Yes" to Ford's other inquiries and requests.

Suite 216, marble floor and ceiling fans, was up the stairs to the right. He wedged a chair under the doorknob, showered and changed, then carried Kostikov's billfold to the balcony, where he snapped on surgical gloves. Driver's license, credit cards, and a complicated ID in Russian, with a photo, a thumbprint, and a hologram, and another in Spanish, a third in Arabic.

Ford created two piles: items of interest, items that were not.

Under the billfold's flap was emergency money: two five-hundred-euro bills. In another, a blister pack of Viagra tablets, a condom, and an address written on a napkin in a woman's hand. Using Hotel Plaza stationery, Ford copied the address, before flipping through a stack of cards that included memberships in a cigar club in London and the International Association of Harley-Davidson Riders.

Amusing. Even professional killers had hobbies.

Hmm . . . Did the card suggest a link to the motorcycles from 1959?

There was another potential link: contact information for a man who lived in the same rural province as

Marta Esteban and the girls. Vernum Quick was the name, *Noviate Santero* written in a Cuban hand, and a phone number.

A coincidence?

Ford made notes. It would have been easier to photograph each item, but his phone would be the first thing confiscated if there was trouble. Paper was safer in this age of electronic spoor. When he was done, he wiped everything clean, and soon the billfold was exactly as he'd found it, including the hidden emergency money, but minus a wad of bills too obvious for a common thief not to find. More than two thousand in euros and pesos.

The old man had refused to accept all of the money despite his bitterness toward Russians and the sad turn his life had taken. Lázaro hadn't been a boxer, as Ford had guessed. He'd been one of Cuba's best baseball players, a catcher and third baseman for the Havana Sugar Kings, but his dreams of a major league contract had ended with the Revolution.

A scrapbook and Lázaro's broken fingers proved it.

Junco's RBI Beats U.S. Champs, Series Tied. The old man had beamed when he'd flipped to the headline. Easy after that to discuss the events of 1959 and the True World Series. Ford was eager but kept the questions light. It paid off. Lázaro, who had played in that final, unfinished game, knew details that few others could know, let alone discuss, including the three American pitchers who had ridden off on their Harleys rather than return to Havana.

"Excellent teammates, but I admit some of us felt a certain resentment. We, the Cubans, were paid shit, while the gringo stars were treated like gods, yet it was difficult not to like those three. One, he was from New York, I think. Even in the shower, he smoked a cigar and had this trick—I don't know how he did it—of making smoke come out of his ass. The others were big, like well-fed farm bulls. They would ride to the countryside and speak of growing corn and wheat instead of cane. Simpatico, you understand? With the peasants who got their hands dirty. They didn't care if they had money bulging from their pockets or not, but those men, hah! They loved Cuban women and their shiny Harleys."

Lázaro had shared a secret then. "I will tell you something few know. Those beautiful motorcycles never left Cuba." He had paused for effect. "And I know where they are."

Ford said, "I hope you're not foolish enough to tell anyone. Including me."

"Why not? I'm not allowed to leave this goddamn place. Why not entrust what I know to a partner?"

It was the first hint that the stadium was the old man's prison. Ford had offered to help but reminded the man they were both thieves, which got a toothless smile.

"They're hidden in a mausoleum in a cemetery west

of here," Lázaro said. "A beautiful place, but I must admit this to you if we become partners: I'm not sure which mausoleum. And that cemetery is ten kilometers by ten kilometers, thousands of places those Harleys might be. True, I've heard of others who have searched without success. But I am a catcher, señor"—he had tapped a finger to his head—"Brains, that's what makes us different. Oh, if I could spend some time in that place, I would soon figure it out."

Fun talking to the old guy, despite the military cops outside searching. If nothing else, Ford had learned that the story about the three Americans was widely known, which suggested that Rivera had been taken in by another treasure-hunting cliché.

For an hour, Lázaro Junco's bitterness was displaced by his memories until Ford mentioned Fidel.

"Sooner or later," he'd said, "I should have known. Every tourist asks the same goddamn questions. Which is why I avoid the stupid bastards. I hoped you might be different."

"I didn't say I believed the story," Ford replied. "There must be a few players alive who actually saw him throw or swing a bat. I've even heard there are films that prove he never played the game."

"Films?" A cynical grunt mimicking laughter. "There are no films. And if there were, they would have been destroyed long ago."

Ford took a gamble. "That's not what I've been told."

That suspicious look again: *Who are you?*

The old man also took a chance. "Do you know what would happen if a player, even a great infielder, whispered the truth about Fidel?" With wizened hands, a gesture to a room filled with boxes, a sink, and his cot. "He would spend the rest of his life in this shithole—but banned from ever walking on that field again . . . or leaving through the gate."

GO TO COJIMAR? Or drive west to check on the girls if they didn't arrive at the hotel soon?

Thinking about that, Ford went out on the balcony of his room. It overlooked a park that separated Old Havana from Chinatown and the squalor of a city that, for half a century, had been trapped in a vacuum and was still waiting to breathe. Lots of traffic—vintage cars and exhaust fumes—buildings painted in pastels now bleached to bone by a sun that was just setting.

A black Mercedes-Benz with dark windows was an anomaly in a place like this. Ford noticed the car, watched it circle the park while pedestrians averted their eyes. A Mercedes symbolized power.

On the east side of the park was a police vehicle that resembled an ambulance. The Mercedes pulled alongside and stopped. A back door opened, a man with his hands cuffed behind him was ejected, followed by two military cops in green.

Ford went to the railing for a better view. The man in handcuffs was bald, wearing jeans . . . *Christ*, it was the same guy he'd seen washing his hands after robbing Kostikov. But now, along with prostate problems, his face had been beaten crooked, then bandaged. They'd done a sloppy job.

Ford winced. *I should've warned him, goddamn it.*

Maybe so. But nothing he could do now but watch and wonder who was at the wheel of the Mercedes. A massive shape within the tinted glass. The Russian, possibly, but the car pulled away, while one of the military cops led his prisoner to the sidewalk, not the ambulance. Not yet anyway. First, the cop pointed to a series of buildings, his hand moving clockwise while he lectured.

Hotels, Ford realized, that's what he was pointing out. Police were going to force the poor bastard to help search room to room for the man he'd seen exiting the toilet, a gringo wearing a green cap.

Ford retreated and closed the doors. The baseball cap was in a stadium trash can, but he wasn't going to wait around. There were hundreds of hotels in Havana. By midnight, when he was done meeting with Rivera, it might be safe to return—but only after checking with the Plaza security captain he'd overtipped, a smiling man named William.

In a canvas briefcase, he packed everything but the clothes he wore: khaki slacks and a gray guayabera shirt that passed for formal wear in Cuba. He didn't care about fashion. Guns were illegal in Cuba, so he wore the guayabera like a smock to hide the 9mm pistol holstered inside the back of his slacks. In an ankle holster was the mini 9mm Sig Sauer.

He hadn't made up his mind yet about the Soviet pistol. It lay on the counter, where he had fieldstripped and reassembled the odd-looking thing—a miniature stainless barrel with an oversized magazine. The grips were polished bronze like a 1960s cigarette case. Inside were six brass cartridges that looked more like tubes than 8mm bullets. The magazine had confirmed what he suspected—this was no ordinary pistol.

Something else he realized: he was in a lot more trouble than he'd anticipated.

During the Cold War, a Soviet armorer had designed a silent bullet, a slug propelled by an internal piston and lethal up to fifty meters. Building a gun to fit the odd cartridge came later and this was the newest version—a PSS Vul, with a six-round magazine.

The Vul was truly soundless—or so Ford had read—hugely expensive to produce, and among the rarest weapons in the world.

The Russians won't stop until they get this back. Unless Kostikov is too embarrassed to admit he was pantsed in a public toilet. Or . . . unless he dies before the theft is reported.

Both were attractive possibilities. Ego was the commonest of silent killers.

Once again, he removed the magazine, shucked the slide, and tested the trigger—too much slack, then crisp at the end with a short reset. He did this a few times and experimented with the hammer, cocking and uncocking. When he felt comfortable, he seated the magazine but didn't chamber a round. The Vul's holster was wallet-sized, the trigger unprotected, so easily snagged. If the gun went off accidentally, how would he know unless he felt the impact and saw blood?

Before leaving, he wrote a note to Marta on hotel stationery, then a second note on blank paper, both in Spanish:

> *Seeking Señor Anatol Kostikov. A wallet containing cash and credit cards was found in the parking lot of the Grand Stadium after the game between Pinar del Río and the Industriales. Please apply in person with proof of ownership at* [he left a blank space]. *A small reward is not necessary but would be appreciated.*

Ford put the note in an envelope.

Later, if he found a suitable ambush spot, and if the timing felt right, he would add the location.

IN THE LOBBY, he asked William, the security captain, "Where's the dining room?" which gave them time alone in a corridor, where he slipped the man an envelope addressed to M. Esteban, plus another fifty euros. After whispering instructions, Ford exited through a side door.

Havana at dusk: shod horses on asphalt, frangipani blossoms, diesel fumes. Never take the first cab. Or the second. He walked south on Paseo del Prado, a boulevard built for lovers and parades. Benches beneath trees, streetlights dimmed or broken, villas converted into tenements, where, high above, baby diapers, towels, hung from balustrades designed for debutantes and politicos.

It was seven-fifteen. Almost three hours before he was to meet Rivera at a restaurant that was on the same street but closer to the sea. Ford considered returning to the stadium to check on the old man but knew, before deciding, that he would take a cab to Cojimar.

Tomlinson is being watched, the general had warned.

That was okay. Ford would do some watching of his own. And if he happened to see a black Mercedes . . . well, he would play that by ear. Send the cab away, pretend to be a tourist who was lost and didn't know the language. Or a drunk looking for a good time with money to burn. There were many ways to convince a stranger, even a high-level assassin like Kostikov, to roll down a window or open a car door.

If it didn't happen, he would check on Tomlinson, then find Sabina, Maribel, and their mother. Hopefully, they were on their way to the hotel. If not, he would hire a cab, or take his boat and from a distance confirm they were safe.

The name on the card in Kostikov's wallet still bothered him: Vernum Quick. Coincidence and random intersectants were common, but less so if three links hinted at a possible triangle. The man lived in Plobacho, the village not far from where the girls lived. But how far?

Ford crossed the Prado and stopped under a lamp. There were no detailed maps of Cuba available—the government didn't allow it—so he had come prepared. From his bag he selected a print from Google Earth that showed the mountainous coastal region west of Havana. Tiny Plobacho wasn't visible, but he found the Espinar River to the west. He used a knuckle to measure. By road, the village was about three miles from the remote hillside where Marta Esteban lived. A comforting distance, but she and her daughters no doubt frequented the village *tiendas*. Also, Vernum Quick was a *Noviate Santero*—a "Novice Priest." That increased the odds of interaction.

He did some other calculations. By boat, as he knew, the mouth of the river was a little over twenty miles from Marina Hemingway. By taxi, Plobacho, which was inland and a mile east of the river, was—he used his knuckle again—a hell of a lot farther because there were so few roads in the region, most of them unpaved. Say . . . an extra fifteen miles.

Ford put the maps away and continued south toward the sea. In his right pocket, the Vul silent pistol was an uncertain asset. He'd never fired the damn thing, and Russia wasn't known for quality control. That was okay, too. He had the Sig P226, which had never failed him, and a threaded sound suppressor in the briefcase—a Maxpedition tactical bag designed for quick weapon access. On his ankle, the little 9mm Sig pocket pistol.

Surprise was on his side.

On the street, an antique Chrysler slowed to a stop—exactly the kind of car a tourist would choose. "Are you interested in a tour of Havana?" the driver asked. "I'm a licensed guide. Or a beautiful woman? I know a place that has food and music and the most beautiful women in the Caribbean."

Ford negotiated a price to Cojimar and got in the back.

The driver said the trip would take an hour or less, but twenty minutes later they were still on the Prado, stuck in traffic, with no way to turn around.

"There must have been an accident, señor."

Ford felt a welling uneasiness. They were only a block or two from the place he was supposed to meet Rivera, an old mansion with a restaurant and apartments. "I don't see police lights."

"Sometimes that is the way in Havana, señor."

"Do you have a phone? A radio, maybe? A friend of mine lives not far from here and, well, his health isn't good. Would an ambulance use flashing lights?"

"You are worried."

"A little. He's an old friend."

"What is the name of this place?"

"La Científico," Ford replied, "but that might be the name of the restaurant, not the apartment building."

"It is the same, señor." The driver put the Chrysler in park. "When traffic is like this, it is better to shut off the engine and relax. I will check for you. Would you like a beer?"

They both got out and weaved their way through traffic while horns blared, no cars moving in either direction. Ahead, a crowd had gathered outside a four-story building of marble and stone, a house befitting Cuba's second president. On the balcony were tables and a patio bar—the restaurant. People had gathered at the railing. Ford knew from the way they reacted when they looked down that a body, or someone badly injured, was on the sidewalk below.

The driver said, "Wait here, please," and pushed his way through the crowd. Seconds later, he was back. "Police have ordered people to disperse. And not just any police. They are wearing suits, not uniforms. We should leave."

"What happened?"

"An important man fell off the roof, I think. Or jumped. It is not something I can ask." The driver cleared his throat, oddly emotional.

"Do you know who it is?"

"I think this man would have chosen a taller building if he had wanted to die. Yes, I am sure of it. We must go to another place for beer, señor."

"I'll look for myself," Ford told him, and threaded his way through a wall of gawkers.

General Juan Simón Rivera, revolutionary and former dictator, was beneath a tarp, his shoes and his face not yet covered, hair and beard as black as the blood in which he lay. Perhaps he had been shot or stabbed—no way to know—but the man's head rested at an angle so grotesque that his neck had to be broken. Ford was sure of it, just as he suspected that Rivera hadn't died from the fall. The skull was intact, no lacerated scalp, no pressure-bloated eyes. The general—a barroom brawler, a heavyweight in the ring—had been murdered by someone bigger, faster, stronger, unless there were wounds hidden by the tarp.

Anatol Kostikov, Ford thought. You son of a bitch.

He stood there, not blinking. Death had a weight to it, and a silence that drowned out street noise, and, for an instant—a single, solitary tick of the clock—Ford was in a rainforest at Juan Rivera's side once again. The moment passed, and with it more than a decade of revolution, death, baseball, drunken nights, and small confidences—all gone.

He wanted to ask questions and eavesdrop. He wanted to observe the behavior of cops working the scene, and pry information from people around him, but that was foolish. Instead, he returned to the street, where the driver was still getting his emotions under control.

"I hope it is not your friend, señor. If he was, you should be proud, and my condolences. But you must leave right away. Soon, they will begin questioning people who appear overly interested."

Ford peeled off a few bills. "Why would I be interested? I've got to find another cab."

15

In the village of Cojimar there was no hotel, so Tomlinson rigged a hammock aboard *No Más*. At sunset, he sat in the bar of La Terraza and enjoyed Cuban baseball on a TV with an antenna made of aluminum foil.

It was the end of a busy day that wasn't done yet. After giving so much baseball gear away, everyone recognized him on sight—not good. He'd felt uneasy paddling the canoe back to *No Más*. Next, it was down the steps for a visit with Raúl Corrales, who invited him to stay for dinner, but he had refused, thinking, *If things go wrong tonight, they'll think he knows about the letters.*

Tomlinson liked Raúl a lot.

So here he was, sitting alone with two old friends—

cold beer and baseball—watching a TV from the days of Barney Fife and the Beav. That was fitting. Nostalgia dulled his anxiety. Yeah . . . sort of like time-traveling back to Mayberry. No traffic in the streets through the open doors, and dark out there in a country that rationed electricity. With cash and his new visa, there was no need for a passport, but he would have felt fidgety traveling without the thing—by car or in a cab.

A dugout canoe was a different story.

Tomlinson now had a hand-drawn chart of the area, thanks to the grandson of Hemingway's guide, plus a lot of detailed advice about landmarks and tides. He had told the fisherman the truth—a partial truth anyway. Tonight he was going to search for his missing dinghy.

"Think I'll turn in early," he announced to the bartender. Got up, stretched, and yawned, while the bartender informed him that, in Cojimar, seven-fifteen was considered late.

Tomlinson doubled the man's tip, went to his boat, and putted into deeper, safer water with the canoe in tow. He had memorized the chart, no need even to look at the thing. Near the wooden bridge, he dropped two anchors, set them with the engine, then secured everything aboard. Old habit. In strange harbors, expect sunshine but be prepared for kimchi to hit the fan.

As a final precaution, he tied the canoe portside so it couldn't be seen from shore, then switched off the lights.

Being watched by cops in a military jeep was bad enough, but the black Mercedes had really spooked him. The vehicle had left before noon, returned around five, then vanished before sunset. No cognitive proof of who was at the wheel, but his extrasensory powers warned of sinister shit and mucho bad juju.

A restless half hour later, Tomlinson was gone. He was in the canoe, paddling like hell, hugging the shoreline for almost two miles before he saw the towering trees he'd been told about, and then campfires of a village. Beyond was the mouth of a creek. All exactly as marked on the chart.

The opening into the creek was guarded by shoals on both sides. Using the paddle as a rudder, he banged over some oysters, then entered the creek, thinking, *Be there . . . Please be there . . .*

After five minutes of hanging moss and shadows, that mantra changed to *Where the hell is that bonehead?*

Tomlinson wasn't telecommunicating with his lost dinghy.

No moon out, but the stars were bright. The creek narrowed, and on the western bank was a little clearing with a path through the trees. It was the sort of path boys make when they aren't playing baseball. He beached the canoe, stumbled up the bank, and whispered his fears out loud: "That little dumbass gave me bogus directions."

Nearby, a pile of banana leaves exploded, and Figueroa Casanova scared the hell out of him again. Sat up, asking, "Brother, what took you so long?"

CASTRO'S BRIEFCASE was in a white burlap sack with a shoulder strap. "A cane-cutter bag," Figuerito explained. "That's why I'm short, 'cause I planted so much cane before I went to crazy prison. A boy carry all that weight, how's he gonna grow? In Cuba, no *campesino* with brains would steal a cane-cutter bag."

Tomlinson had to ask, "Where'd you get it?"

"Stole it," Figgy replied. "Same with this . . ." A machete, the length of a sword, which he used to signal *Follow me.*

It was nine-fifteen. Figgy led the way through trees, past barking dogs and hovels of cement where people slept behind bars. Stopped and waited for Tomlinson to catch up before he placed the bag on the ground and made a sweeping gesture. "This is it. Been twenty years since I was a youth here and this is where I played."

"Played what?"

"You don't see any hoops, do you? What do you think?"

It was a rock-strewn clearing, chicken wire for a backstop. In right field, a fifty-gallon drum smoldered with trash. Tomlinson took it all in before saying, "Looks like a good spot for a dental clinic. Why are we here?"

"To show you, why else? Oh yeah, lots of bad hops. An infielder lose his teeth if he don't have good hands on a field with this shit." Barefoot, he kicked a stone away. "These little *putas*, there is a bad hop in every single one. How is your head, brother? You're still talking sort of strange."

Tomlinson touched the spot where the boom or something heavy had hit him just before *No Más* had pitchpoled. "One of God's little love taps. All pain is illusory, man. Then you die. The question is, do we have transportation?"

"After we dead? Of course. Everyone knows that."

"No, amigo, tonight. Did you find us some wheels?"

Before dawn that morning, the last thing Tomlinson had done before Figgy rocketed off in the dinghy was remind him, *We need a car and fuel. But nothing fancy, because we want to blend in.*

"Same answer," the shortstop said. "Only better 'cause we're still alive."

In an alley where chickens roosted was an old station wagon with dents—a 1955 Buick, but now with a Ford engine—and no tailgate because racks of cages had replaced all but the front seats. Figuerito had leased the car from a woman who sold eggs but couldn't drive. He got behind the wheel, turned the key, and said over the noise, "Eighty dollars U.S. Think that's a fair price?"

"How long can we keep it?"

"Long as we want, I guess. Isn't that what *lease*

means? The woman, she didn't know either." He switched the engine off and closed the door.

"Did she recognize you?"

"Nobody remembers I lived here and they stopped asking questions real quick. I told people I was a ball-player headed for the *Estados Unidos* and would use this"—he hefted the machete—"to chop their damn hands off if they touched my boat, especially my fast engine. Or an arm if they complained to the Guardia about me using a creek that is practically mine, since I damn-near drowned there twice as a youth. See? All true." He smiled, but the smile faded. "I didn't know I was lying when I said I could swim good. You saved my life, brother. Twice you saved me, because it was smart, just like you said, for me to take the dinghy and let you deal with the police."

Tomlinson, preoccupied, watched the streets, worried engine noise had drawn attention. The car had smoked and sputtered like a Nazi Messerschmitt. "The way I remember it, you saved mine. But let's focus. The important thing is, we don't draw attention. Next time—this is only a suggestion, understand—instead of cutting an arm off, maybe tell them something like 'I have faith in your integrity.' You know, lay a guilt trip on them."

"Yeah, guilt," Figgy said. "Now I owe you my life. That's what I'm saying. I've never been in water that deep and, Mother of God, so dark under them waves. If it was shallower like I'm used to, yeah, I can swim pretty good."

"Uh-oh, car lights," Tomlinson said. "Don't look."

The shortstop spun around. "Where?"

At the end of the block a diesel Mercedes crept past, followed by a military jeep. Tomlinson feared the cars would turn, but they didn't. "I saw them in Cojimar earlier. A couple of cops. I don't know who's in the Mercedes."

"It's the Russian," Figgy said.

Tomlinson had started toward the river. "Who?"

"The giant bear-man. Same man who called you a pussy in Key West."

Tomlinson stopped. "You're kidding."

"No, that's what he called you. You forgot already?"

"That's not what I mean. This afternoon, the Russian guy came to me in a clairvoyant flash . . . But hold on a sec. It's dark, the windows are tinted, how do you know it's him?"

"It was sunny this afternoon, so I saw him just fine," Figuerito replied. "He drove by in that nice Mercedes. Didn't even wave, the *maricón*."

"You waved first?"

"Sure. This isn't Miami. In Cuba, you have to be polite to a man with a car like that."

"Hmm. The same Russian guy you assaulted in Key West," Tomlinson mused, then added in a rush, "Quiet . . . I think they're coming back." He gave the shortstop a push toward a trash barrel, where they both hunkered low. "You're sure he saw you this afternoon?"

"If he hadn't, he would've run me over. But he didn't recognize me 'cause I was carrying this sack. Carrying this machete, too. What's a Russian care about a peasant cane cutter? Pissed me off he didn't wave. Made me wonder if maybe that bad *Santero,* Vernum Quick, warned him it was okay to chase me, but not—"

"Shit-oh-dear," Tomlinson whispered, "they're looking for someone. Probably us."

The jeep, lights out, reappeared two blocks away, while the quieter Mercedes approached from the opposite direction. No lights from the Mercedes either. On these dark streets, headlights would have ricocheted off the tin roofs and brightened the sky.

"We've got to move," Tomlinson said. "Only two choices: try to slip past them in that old Buick or run for the boat. What do you think?"

Figuerito, holding the machete, said, "I'd rather kill the Russian and drive his Mercedes. I've never been in a Mercedes before. Maybe if I sneak through the alley . . . Hey, brother, let go of my pants."

Tomlinson had latched onto Figuerito's belt. "We're not killing anyone. Cops have guns. You want to get us shot? Hey—is there a place to hide near here?"

"There's the egg woman, but that house of hers is hardly big enough for her and the chickens."

Tomlinson whispered, "Uh-oh . . . now what?"

A block away, the jeep had stopped, one cop already out, carrying a flashlight, while his partner popped the rear hatch and spoke a command to something inside—a dog. The dog, ears pointed, was wearing a sort of vest. He jumped down onto the street, circled, then hiked his leg to pee.

"Is that a helicopter?" Figuerito asked. "I've always wanted to ride in one of those, too."

"Are you nuts? It's a German shepherd, for christ's sake. Okay, let's go—on our hands and knees. Where does the woman live?" Tomlinson began to crawl toward the nearest shack.

"You gotta get your head checked, brother. That isn't a dog unless dogs can fly."

He heard it then, the whine of a powerful engine, but it was a boat, not a helicopter; the distinctive seesaw roar of a boat negotiating sharp turns, moving fast on the river where he had beached the canoe.

"In my village," Figgy said, "we got a doctor. She'll look at your head. There's something bad wrong if you think a helicopter is a dog. Try closing one eye."

Finally, Tomlinson turned to look. "We are so screwed," he said, because he saw it, a chopper flying low. It was following a searchlight, coming toward them at an incredible speed. Something else: the Mercedes had returned, sat squat in the middle of the street to seal off the block.

"I think we should leave now," Figgy said. He wiped his hands on his shirt, then dropped to his knees. "Are you ready?"

"Oh god, yes."

Single file, they crawled into the next lot, pursued by the ceiling fan *thump-a-thump-a-thump* of the chopper and the squelch of police radios. Houses here were tiny, built shoulder to shoulder amid a poverty of weeds and smoldering trash, each backyard a tangle of clotheslines and scrawny dogs chained to trees.

Figgy talked as they crawled: "I couldn't hurt a dog, but it's different with people. Some anyway. If they come to catch me or rob my *mu-maw*—my *abuela*, you know?—it doesn't bother me. There's a cliff near my village. Or did you forget that, too? It drops straight down to the sea." He looked back. "Are you sure you don't want to steal that Mercedes?"

Tomlinson replied, "Somehow, the timing doesn't feel quite right," but he was thinking, I should have slapped a restraining order on myself years ago. My sorry ass belongs in the insane asylum.

Mostly, he worried about the German shepherd nailing him from behind, until the helicopter screamed past at tree level and, for an instant, blinded Figuerito with the searchlight.

"You shouldn't have waved," Tomlinson said. "Christ, why'd you do that? Not with a machete in your hand. Get down before they circle back."

Figgy, rubbing his eyes, replied, *"Pinche par de pendejos,"* which was profanity that could not be argued.

The helicopter didn't circle. From the safety of some

bushes, they watched it hover over the river. Soon, the jeep sped toward it, followed by the Mercedes, while the helicopter drifted seaward, following something or searching.

"I heard a boat," Tomlinson said. "Fast one, a really big engine. Maybe they're after the boat, not us." But then remembered the canoe and the dinghy. "Yeah, we are totally screwed."

"Never have I seen a light so bright," Figgy remarked, still rubbing his eyes. He made some comparisons—stadium lights, the sun—before asking, "A boat with a motor? A big motor or a big boat?"

"An oversized outboard, yeah. Which way is the woman's house? Let's get out of here."

"That river is too shallow for a big boat—unless the captain is a magician. Well . . . except for the spot with the tire swing where I nearly drowned. In the *Estados Unidos*, what is the brightest light you ever saw?"

They were jogging through backyards, with the river, the helicopter, and cars behind them. Tomlinson didn't respond.

Unless the captain is a magician. The phrase stuck in his head, although he tried to convince himself, Naw. Impossible.

It couldn't be Marion Ford.

FIGGY TOLD the woman who owned chickens but couldn't drive, "If I was going to lie, I would have chosen a happier lie. If the Guardia finds us in your house, they'll arrest you, too. I have no passport or birth certificate, and the gringo is carrying illegal drugs. You should also know that if the helicopter comes to take us away, don't look up or you'll be blinded."

The woman listened to this and more, often glancing at Tomlinson as if to ask *Is he crazy? Or drunk?*

Finally, she posed the question herself. "Why would I let two strangers stay in my house? I have only one bed, and no food. Well . . . eggs, of course, and sometimes a rooster who is too old to screw. Is there something wrong with your head?"

"I'm tired of that question," Figuerito replied. "The judge who sent me to the crazy prison didn't believe me either."

"An insane asylum?" she asked. *Manicomio* was the word in Spanish.

"No," the shortstop replied, "the *prisión demente* near José Martí Airport. Everyone knows the fences and baseball field there. From the outside, it looks nice, but it's not."

The expression on the woman's face—horrified—but then she smiled. "*Whoa!* What a fool I am—you're joking, of course. You are an entertaining pair, you two."

"You can't hear the helicopter? Step outside, walk to the river. There is a bad Russian there the size of a whale. You'll see a Mercedes. I wanted to steal it, but this gringo wouldn't let me."

"A Mercedes . . . in this village?" She was laughing now. "Such an imagination. What you are is a wild boy full of the Ol' Nick. At first, I was sorry I opened the door. Now I'm not."

Figgy replied, "As long as you understand. Our plan is to stay until the Guardia leaves, and we will pay you . . ." He turned to Tomlinson for a dollar amount.

Tomlinson, ducking his head because the ceiling was so low, asked her, "How much is the most beautiful dress in Havana? And shoes to go with it? A woman who lives alone deserves to feel as special as anyone else."

Her name was Olena, a widow in her fifties who had been beaten down by work and loneliness, but still had a spark of Africa in her eyes. In her body, too. It was in the saucy way she said, "There's only one bed, so you crazy boys will have to sleep on the floor . . . or take turns." Then later, with the lights out, doors locked, she asked, "Is it for true you have drugs? What kind?"

"Just ganja," Tomlinson said. "Don't worry, we won't smoke in here."

Olena's response: "You're too selfish to share?"

Figgy, who'd been bouncing off the walls, mellowed after that. In a cluttered room that smelled of incense and chickens, they passed a joint around. The helicopter left, then the jeep and Mercedes made a slow tour of the streets and left, too. They rolled another one and drank *aguardiente*. Olena, who had done more in life than sell eggs, offered Tomlinson advice. "If you don't want the

223

pesquisa to notice you, you've gotta change how you look."

"*¿Pesquisa?*"

"The secret police," she explained. "Clothing is just a costume, and all costumes are a disguise. I know. I was a dancer at the Copacabana before my life went to hell."

Olena could still dance. Tomlinson liked that about her, too. And trusted her enough to wait while she rousted a neighbor, then brought him a change of clothes. A whole new look she created for him.

"This is so me," he said in front of a mirror. "I always wanted to be a Rastafarian. But don't you think my beard should be a little darker? Or braided—that could work, but not too much. I don't want to look like a pirate."

Something else she returned with was local gossip about the cops and the helicopter. The boat Tomlinson had heard was probably Bahamian gangsters from Cay Sal or Miami Cubans up to no good. She hadn't gotten the whole story, but rumor was that the boat had been shot out of the water when it was a mile or two offshore.

"But they often lie about shooting Miami Cubans out of the water," she added.

He and Figgy departed at ten-fifteen in the old Buick, a car Olena said she was too smart to drive, so be careful, don't trust the brakes, and never, ever go fast enough to need third gear.

"Rides good for a station wagon, don't it, brother?"

Figgy had to yell over the roar of a broken muffler and six squabbling chickens caged in back. Already the car was doing fifty and they weren't on the paved road yet.

"Gad . . . how many joints does it take to numb that metabolism of yours? Olena warned us about shifting to third. You didn't hear?"

"No problem. That's why I'm still in second. See?"

Tomlinson didn't look. He kept his hands on the dash, eyes front, because what he saw was a car with its lights off, partially screened by trees. Too late he yelled, "Speed trap, slow down."

No . . . it was the Mercedes.

Figgy, watching the rearview mirror, told him, "Grab my machete from under the seat," and then he did it: shifted into third gear.

The Mercedes held back but at any time could pass with guns blazing or ram them off the road.

16

The girl, Sabina, tried to scream when she saw Vernum step out from the shadows of the tree but only made a chirping noise, she was so scared. Then fumbled the mace canister, dropped the candle, too, which had gone out, and began bawling. Just stood there, a tiny, trembling creature wearing pink-and-white pajamas, and waited for Vernum to take her.

A demon doesn't live inside this brat, he realized. She'll wet her pants and go limp, just like all the others.

After that, well . . . pure pleasure, the euphoria of total control.

When he grabbed the girl, though, she fought back. Somehow found the candle and speared him in the

226

face—hot wax that burned like hell—then bolted down-hill into the woods.

This little *chica* could run. But he was quick, Vernum Quick, and he caught her from behind. She tripped; he stumbled but was still on his feet, until he went over a ledge that wasn't high but angled sharply toward the river. A thicket of bayonet plants grew on the rocks be-low, each blade an elongated thorn. They stopped his fall, but his hands and legs were bleeding by the time he got back to the top of the hill.

The girl was gone.

He swore at himself—*pendejo*—then ran toward the house. He checked the yard, listened for voices and slamming doors. Nothing. No lights on inside, no cries of concern from Marta. He searched the banana grove, circled the property, then returned to where he'd last seen the devil brat. "I know you can hear me," he said, but not loudly. "I won't hurt you . . . but I'll by god hurt your mother and sister if you don't come out."

He zigzagged through the woods, repeating that warning. Behind him, bushes rustled. He reversed course and soon heard a mewing sound from some-where near the ledge, but it stopped the instant he stopped. An animal, perhaps . . . or a whimpering child. He said it again, louder: "I'll torture your mother. Where are you?"

Vernum didn't have a flashlight, but he had dry matches from the car. At the top of the ledge, he lit a match. "Would you rather hear what I do to her? Or your sister scream? What a sick little brat you are not to care." He waited until the match went out. He lit another, then another, and flicked each dying flame toward the bayonet plants. Finally, he'd had enough. "Selfish little *puta*, God will punish you for this." He threw the matchbook. "I'm warning you: I'll kill you if you ever tell a soul."

Near the tamarind tree, Vernum found the girl's machete; picked it up, liked the feel, and decided to use it instead of the knife. On the porch, he tested the door. Unlocked. He opened it just enough to get a whiff of perfumed soap and kerosene, and to confirm all was quiet inside. That silence, the silence of sleeping females, registered in his belly. In his brain, the demon sniffed for warmth.

Vernum turned, looked into the darkness of trees, stars, lightning bugs. The little brat was still out there somewhere. Probably on the road or the path along the river, running to a neighbor for help. Vernum considered his options and weighed the risks. Within a kilometer were fishermen who lived in shacks and fools who cut sugarcane because they weren't smart enough to do anything else.

Peasants, nobodies, the demon in his brain promised. *Do it now. Feed while we can.*

But what if the fishermen had a radio? Or even a car? Vernum cupped his ears, strained to filter a distant silence from the buzz of insects and frogs. Beyond the trees were cattle; a heron squawked . . . and something he hoped not to hear: an engine—motorcycles, possibly—on the road that followed the river to the sea. High-pitched, powerful twin engines, Hondas or Yamahas that were too expensive for Cubans to own. And driving too fast on a single lane of sand that curved with every bend of the river.

A pair of drunken tourists, the demon insisted. *What are you waiting for?*

The hunger in Vernum was taking control. He knew it, recognized the throbbing pressure behind his eyes, so he had to think clearly while he could. He pictured the motorcycles stopping for the girl. Pictured the riders using a cell phone to call police. He pictured . . .

Who cares! The word of a child against a respected *Santero?* Besides . . . there are no motorcycles, you idiot. Do those damn bugs really sound like motorcycles to you?

Could he have imagined it?

Yes . . . maybe. The powerful engines—if he'd actually heard an engine—were suddenly gone, displaced by screaming insects.

With his thumb, Vernum tested the machete's edge. Sharp. But what about the devil brat? Should he hide and hope she came sneaking back? Or go ahead, rush what awaited him in the bedroom, before neighbors could alert police?

He cracked the door again and sniffed: two females inside, breathing, fragile, alone. Their scent severed a last cognitive thread.

The demon moved from Vernum's head into his eyes.

BENEATH THE LEDGE where the zombie man had stood was a hole that opened into a space with a straw mat and a floor neatly swept. It was cramped, but Sabina thought of it as a cave, or sometimes a burrow when she brought rabbits along for tea. She hadn't done that in months, though. Tea parties were for children, not a girl who would soon be eleven. Also, it had been upsetting to kill and clean her furry guests when her mother wanted fried *conejo* for dinner or rabbit fricassee. Some Sunday mornings—the traditional time for butchering—this was where she came after washing off blood, a secret escape where she could rage against life's unfairness and cry her misery dry.

Sabina was crying now but used her hands to silence her mouth while the zombie rained sparks down from the sky. After that, no doubt he was a devil, not human. Then a final warning before he left: *God will punish you for this . . . I'll kill you if you ever tell a soul.*

Chastened by the truth, Sabina's mind had censored the devil's profanities. It was true. She was selfish, she knew it. Only a terrible person would refuse to save her own mother . . . or, at least, run home and call out a warning. Trouble was, fear had done something to her legs and she was dizzy from hyperventilating. What if the zombie man hadn't left? He would grab her, then attack Maribel and her mother anyway.

I hate you, I hate you, I hate that damn devil . . .

She lay curled in a fetal position for what seemed a long time, then crawled to the hole that opened onto bayonet plants and stars in a high black sky. "I'm coming out," she warned. "I have a knife and I'll cut you like a rabbit if you bother me."

On her hands and knees, she exited the hole, and added new threats as she went up the incline to the ledge. "I'll blind you with pepper juice . . . I will order the gringo to tie you with rope and feed you to sharks." Oddly, those threats reshaped Sabina's fear into a tentative boldness. Her imagination took over as she crept toward the house.

I'll bite his finger off and have him arrested. If he hurts Mama or Maribel, God will strike him with lightning . . . I'll push him down the well and bury him where pigs shit—then I'll hide where he can't find me.

False courage got her to the edge of the yard, where she stopped and gulped. No sign of the zombie man, and the house appeared unchanged but for a frightening oddity: the porch door was open wide and a kerosene lamp burned in the kitchen.

Someone was inside.

She began to hyperventilate again, then remembered,

The machete. She had dropped it between the tamarind tree and the pump. With a weapon, even if he had entered the house, she could . . . do what? Sabina tried to think it through but went numb when a dead branch snapped behind her.

She spun around: shadows, lightning bugs, then *pop*—another dead branch. Her thumping heart cloaked a slow, distant rhythm . . . the sound of something big was coming up the hill, moving cautiously so as not to be heard. Then, for an instant, he appeared, a gray shape moving from tree to tree. It was a man—the zombie man—who had tricked her. Not fast but on a straight line, almost as if he could see in the dark.

Sabina lost her nerve then. She sprinted toward the house, screaming, "Mama, he's going to kill us all!"

THE LOOK in the mother's eyes when she heard the little brat scream . . . *Delicious.*

Vernum licked his lips while the demon retreated so he could think. On the floor next to the bed was the teenage daughter, gagged with electrical tape, arms wired behind her. He had taped Marta's mouth, too, although sparingly—such a beautiful Indio face. He hadn't had time to finish wiring her hands or, more importantly, to position her legs as he wanted.

"Don't move," he told her. "I'll kill your daughters first."

Marta's horrified reaction . . . *Exquisite.* He had to force himself out of the room, through the kitchen where the lamp burned, to the door where he stood looking out, the machete in hand. There she was: the devil brat running hard, knees pumping beneath baggy pink-and-white pajamas while her eyes focused on the darkness behind her. It was as if she were being chased. But then turned to holler, "Mama . . . Maribel, wake up!" which is when she saw Vernum and stopped so fast, she sprawled belly-first in the sand. Then was up again, confused, in a panic, and bolted toward the banana grove.

Vernum went after her through the darkness.

Banana plants multiply at the roots; grow in dense thickets, their leaves as wide and long as a man. He used the machete to hack his way through, not because he had to, but for effect. With each swing of the blade, the girl yipped or sobbed or cried out. Easier to track her while she evaded or hid like a rabbit down a hole.

"Why are you running, little *chica*? You are old enough to learn to enjoy yourself. Wouldn't you like that?"

No reply, just her steady sobbing, the crash of foliage, then silence while she attempted to hide again.

This time, Vernum saw her but pretended he didn't. She had wedged herself between two banana stalks, a space too narrow for a snake yet wide enough to cloak all but one tiny foot. Her toes hung there in the shadows like a blossom of bananas, a tempting target for the machete . . . but not yet.

Vernum had some fun. "I give up. This girl is too damn smart. Guess I'll go back to the house and cut off her mother's—"

"Sabina . . . *Sabina*?"

Shit. It was Marta Esteban calling from the porch.

"Where's my daughter, you bastard? Oh my god . . . answer me, Sabina."

Vernum parted the leaves. Marta was on the steps near a kerosene lantern, biting at the wire on her hands, almost free. Behind her, the teenage daughter appeared.

"Maribel, I told you to run. Go—do what I say!"

Christ, it was all falling apart. There were three witnesses now. Well . . . if he couldn't enjoy their bodies, it was better to kill them all and be done with it.

The devil brat's tiny foot hung there, a ripe target, although she began to sob when Marta called her name. Vernum, done with games, pushed his way toward the girl. "You stupid *chinga*, you'll never run from me again." He grabbed her ankle and pulled. Sabina screamed and kicked at his face.

"Go away—I have a knife," she hollered.

He yanked her from the tree and stood over her, a looming darkness as he raised the machete . . . and that's when the girl proved her special powers. A specter materialized from within the foliage, a demon that was gorilla-sized and had one glowing green eye.

Vernum, staring, dropped the machete, reached for his Santería beads, and whispered, *"Bienvenido espíritu santo . . ."* but too late to stop the creature, or the crushing weight that choked him to the ground.

A DEMON, a beast, controlled by a child . . .

Stupid peasant nonsense.

That solitary green eye had shocked Vernum into believing for an instant, but he was conscious now. He had preached the reality of demons and devils so often that part of him accepted it as true. But there was a small, secret voice in his head that reminded him it was all a fairy tale, the same voice that guided his hunger and had for years cloaked his deceptions and kept him alive.

That little *puta* has the power of demons? Bullshit.

A man, not a demon, had abducted him. But who? Until he understood, it was stupid to reveal that he was awake enough to see and hear and think. Better to remain deadweight that could be lifted or rolled or, for the last several minutes, had to be dragged like a plow. Painful. His head banged off rocks. Leaves, dirt, cactus needles abraded his skin. No matter. His only hope was to play dead until an opening presented itself.

Vernum Quick was a survivor.

His abductor had bound his hands and ankles with plastic strips, material that took only a second to cinch tight. Then did the unexpected—pinched Vernum's nose until he had to open his mouth to breathe. This allowed something flat and hard to be inserted, an object that tasted of chemicals but in fact was epoxy. The flat object had immobilized Vernum's tongue when he closed his mouth. The epoxy on his lips had sealed almost instantly.

Super Glue—popular in the United States.

The meaning of it all was terrifying: this man had abducted people before. An expert, he went about his business methodically, no hesitation, and the most frightening thing of all: he didn't speak. Not a word. Like a machine . . . No, like an assassin.

Kostikov. Vernum believed it was the Russian until he risked cracking one eye. Wrong. It was a big man with shoulders, but not a giant. And strong enough to drag him by the feet through the woods, down the hill to the river, where finally he stopped to rest . . . no, to roll his shoulders, then piss.

Vernum's eyes blinked open and he watched. The Cyclops eye was some sort of night vision optic. The man wore boots and dark clothing. He zipped his pants when he was finished and retrieved a bag he'd placed on the ground. Inside were items taken from Vernum's pockets. Each was inspected as if evaluating its worth.

The wallet and satellite phone held the man's interest. He knew how to use the phone, punched buttons, probably checking previous calls and contact information. That was okay. No names had been entered. The man stayed busy for several minutes, long enough to dull Vernum's interest, but then startled him by asking, "How long have you known Anatol Kostikov?"

Christ . . . even with his lips glued shut, he'd almost tried to answer. A trick, Vernum realized. A shrewd bastard who spoke Spanish with a gringo accent. How did he know about the Russian?

"Stop pretending. I don't care if you see me." The man came closer. "You were out for less than a minute. If I'd shut off the blood to your brain much longer, yeah, you'd be in bad shape, but I'm careful about how I do things." The man paused long enough to open the wallet. "Vernum Quick. Is that your real name or do you work for the DGI? Nod if you're with Cuban intelligence."

Vernum felt a boot nudge his thigh while he recalled the old war hero, Oleg, jabbering about a CIA operative who had rescued the girls.

"Former air force, but discharged after only nine months, huh? I'm surprised you're not in jail." Another pause. "You were going to murder those girls and their mother . . . but only after you assaulted them, right? Don't pretend you don't know what I mean by 'assaulted.'" The boot again, harder. "Answer me. A nod means yes, a grunt means you're lying. My rules, and you're running out of time."

Vernum controlled his breathing. If the man lost his temper, he might say something to provide a bit of leverage or do something stupid.

The latch on the bag opened, then closed. "There are a couple of easy field tests I can do to prove you're conscious. You won't like it. This isn't the movies—jab a prisoner with a pin or use a match. A motivated subject wouldn't even flinch, but there is one fail-safe way to find out. I'll take this hypodermic needle, heat it up, then stick it through your eardrum. The freaky types suggest a couple cc's of cold water, but I don't happen to think torture is funny." The man knelt and touched a finger to Vernum's nose—his only source of air—a warning. "Now, open your goddamn eyes."

Vernum did and was surprised to see the LED screen of his own satellite phone, not a needle, only inches from his face. There was a recent text in broken Spanish. The name of the sender, thank god, was not included.

The pizdă *hippie and defector both alive. Will intercept or follow. Contact soonest.*

The time stamp was five minutes ago, nine-nineteen p.m.

"This is from Anatol Kostikov, isn't it? Grunt twice if I'm right."

Vernum attempted to shrug while shaking his head. Weird to look into his abductor's face and see only one dim green eye.

"You're lying, but that's okay. The Russian wouldn't have hired you unless you have something to offer. Usually, it's a special talent, but there's nothing special about a *pederasta* who should have been euthanized long ago. Isn't that true?"

Pederasta. A pedophile. Disgusting. Vernum had never been called that before but nodded anyway, frightened by the tone—detached—a man who asked questions as a test because he already knew the answers.

"That tells me you have something they want. That's good enough for starters. The important thing is, I'm not to going to kill you"—the man touched Vernum's neck with the delicacy of a surgeon and found his jugular—"because you're working for me now. Keep that in mind when you wake up."

An hour later, Ford was hiking up the hill to Marta Esteban's home when the *Santero*'s phone buzzed with a second message: *Why you no contact? They in car red Buick that is with gallineros seated driving west. Police do not know. Watch soon with eyes ready.*

Ford puzzled over that, unsure if Kostikov was writing code or if his Spanish was as bad as Vernum had claimed. Tomlinson and the shortstop were in a car somewhere between here and Cojimar, but the Russian didn't want Cuban authorities involved. That much fit with what Ford already knew and confirmed that Tomlinson was in danger but not immediate danger. But what the hell did *gallineros seated* mean? *Gallinero* was Spanish for "chicken coop."

Gibberish, Ford decided. The *Santero* had become an eager, earnest informant after forty minutes of questioning. The key to breaking a hostile interrogant was plying his ego or tapping into his innermost fears. The man didn't swim well. He was terrified of sharks. Blindfolded, Vernum had believed he was adrift in the Gulf Stream when, in fact, they hadn't left the river.

Ford had a lot of information to sort through. Juan Rivera would have killed for what he had learned tonight. Instead, Juan had fallen victim to something he didn't know.

The pressing issue was Vernum's claim that he hadn't hurt Marta or the girls. It was late; Ford had changed into fishing shorts, a blue chambray shirt, and a ball cap—better to look like a tourist and less like a ninja. But Kostikov's message took precedence. If the Russian had found his phone in the stadium trash, that meant Vernum's phone also contained a GPS chip. He'd assumed as much and was still unsure what to do with the damn thing. Using one finger, he texted a response: *Dropped phone in water. Messages garbled cannot call. Meet you where?* After adding a string of random letters, he hit *Send*.

That would give him some time. Somehow, though, he had to silence the phone's tracking signal. Even if he shut it off, the thing would still transmit. A possible solution was in the systems menu. He found location services and disengaged all links.

Ford crossed through the trees to the drive and jogged the rest of the way. Every window in the Esteban house was alight with candles and lamps. He stopped near the tamarind tree, switched on a flashlight, and called a friendly warning: "Marta . . . it's me, the guy from the United States. Your daughter calls me the gringo fascist."

Lighten the mood on this traumatic evening, is what he wanted to do, the whole time hoping more trauma didn't await.

But it was okay. The porch door flew open and the younger girl, Sabina, came flying out wearing baggy pink-and-white pajamas. "I told them, Marion, I told them both! They didn't believe me—so typical . . ." Then she became shy as she drew nearer and stopped. Behind her, the mother appeared, carrying an oil lamp, a diffident woman with Polynesian hair that hung to the waist of her bathrobe.

Ford moved the flashlight so she could see his face. "Sorry, Mrs. Esteban. I didn't know how to find the place by car, so I waited at the hotel, hoping you'd check in." He squatted to be at eye level with Sabina. "How're you doing, *tiburónita*? Where's Maribel?"

"Little shark"—a nickname—and Maribel was on the porch, one hand clinging to her mother's robe.

Sabina backed a few steps. "You look different."

Ford was counting on it. "I cleaned up at the hotel. Is that so bad?"

242

"You're not as big . . . and your legs are bare. Why are you dressed like a tourist from Canada? Don't lie to me. Everyone thinks I'm stupid, but I'm not."

Smiling, Ford stood and spoke to Marta. "If it's too late, I can come back tomorrow."

"No . . . stay. Please stay, come inside. Maribel, where are your manners? Bring the *patrón* a glass of cold water. Or coffee. Would you like coffee?" The woman's eagerness signaled the shock of what the *Santero* had done. Ford had heard only one side of the story but had decided not to press for details. If Marta wanted to talk, he would listen. The complexities of emotional trauma were outside his field, but he had a bedrock respect for personal privacy.

On the way to the house, the girl looked up. "What did you do to him? The zombie man, he would have murdered Mama and Maribel, then you came. He would have killed me, too, but I fought like hell. Did you see me kick him? I did. Kicked him and tried to bite him."

"A *zombie*?" Ford replied. It took a second to connect that with the stitches in the Cuban's face. He asked Marta, "What's she talking about?"

"You know who I mean," the girl said, then began to second-guess herself as she looked him up and down. "What happened to the thing on your"—she touched her forehead—"and the holster you wore here?" Sabina's hand moved to her side. Puzzled over that, then turned to her mother. "I swear it was true. I told the truth about what happened. A man, a giant with a green eye, he came out of the trees, but maybe it wasn't—"

"Stop pestering our guest," Marta interrupted and focused on Ford while she waved the girl into the house. "Your name is Marion? I'm glad you're here, but I'm so upset, it's hard to think. Something happened tonight."

"Serious?"

"Do you have a car? You've already done so much for us, I hate to ask, but, if you have a car, I think it's dangerous here. We'd like to leave."

Ford, who had the keys to Vernum's old Lada, replied, "That can be arranged. Why don't you tell me about it."

HE DIDN'T SMOKE, but sat at a table with coffee and a cigar he had accepted because the woman was so eager to please. Unlit, it wasn't bad. Tasted of moist leaves with a leather tang. He bit the tip off but refused politely when she lit a match and extended her arm—pretty, her face, the way her hair glistened behind the flame. She blew the match out and turned for an ashtray. A contrail of smoke framed her profile: Aztec nose, chin, and elevated cheeks; an estuary for her eyes, which were volcanic brown, isolated, and private unless she granted contact.

Marta granted eye contact now. She stood, the table

and kerosene lamp separating them. "Coffee keeps some men awake. Are you sure?"

Ford handed her the cup. "A little sugar, if you have it." It would be hours before he'd have a chance to sleep.

"There's bread I baked yesterday, maybe a bit of honey, I'll look. I wish I had more to offer." The lamp, which provided backlight when she walked to the kitchen, verified that Marta Esteban had a great deal more to offer: a sturdy body, lean-waisted, with breasts that moved beneath the robe.

Mr. Esteban, Ford decided, wherever he was, had either died happy or was a fool.

She made herself busy in the kitchen. "I used to work at the cigar factory in Plobacho. I was a girl. They started me with cheroots—sort of like cigarettes. By the time I was fifteen, they trusted me to do Cohibas—only the best leaves, the best fillers, and each layer had to be cut and wrapped perfectly. Very, very tight." Marta did sort of a rolling, chopping ceremony with her hands. "I'm sorry you don't like the cigar."

"You made this?"

"No, but I *could*." For the first time, she smiled. The haunted eyes softened. "You don't smoke? If you like something milder, I could make that, too. Whatever you wanted."

Ford nodded his thanks. "Tell me about the cigar factory."

"They had a man read to us—twenty women in a room on benches with a fan but no radio. He would read for an hour, take a ten-minute break, then come back and read some more. There was a microphone at the front of the room on a tall desk that wasn't really a desk. He read José Martí and Ernest Hemingway, anything that was approved by . . . well, I don't know who approves these things. That's how I fell in love with books."

They had been discussing Sabina. She and Maribel were pretending to be asleep in the big bed in the next room, door closed, which is why the adults kept their voices down and, so far, the subject matter light. Earlier, when Marta had started to describe the attack, it was out of fear for Vernum Quick—yes, she'd recognized him—and a sense of urgency, so Ford had taken her aside and said, "He's not coming back."

The woman had almost broken down when she heard that but battled through to spare her daughters. She had yet to ask the obvious question.

Later, on the porch, with the lamp turned low, she did. "Sabina was right, wasn't she? She saw you do something to that . . . I won't say his name. Then you both disappeared."

"I don't know what she saw, and I've learned not to argue with her. On the raft, when I found your daughters, she not only threatened to swim to Cuba, she actually tried. That girl's a fire-breather, Mrs. Esteban."

246

"Marta," she corrected. "I shouldn't have asked, it was rude. You must be tired. I didn't see car lights. Did you come by boat?"

Ford confirmed that with a look.

"The girls said fantastic things about your boat. How fast it is, with lights that blink like a spaceship. Funny . . . I believed very little of what they told me about you. But tonight, I would believe anything." She reached for the lamp and inspected his face as a nurse might. "You're tired . . . or worried. I'd like you to sleep here . . . in the girls' room, of course. Or there's a hammock—"

"I have to meet someone," Ford said. "But I need to ask a few things before I go."

"Questions about the—"

"No, not about that. About the village, things only a local would know." Ford turned east toward Plobacho, not far as the crow flies, but so small there were no lights above a tree line dominated by stars. "You grew up here?"

"My grandparents, too, but I don't understand. You told me we're safe and I want to believe you, but the girls will be afraid. It's so dark out there on the water, and you could rest and have a good breakfast. Are you in trouble?"

"A friend of mine might be. That's who I have to meet."

Marta broke eye contact. She placed the lamp on the railing near the ashtray and picked up the cigar because that's what her fingers had been trained to do. "I had no right to ask that. What would you like to know?"

"My friend, he's looking for . . . well, looking for something and I want to be there when he finds it. I'll explain when we have more time. I have the location narrowed down, but I don't know the area. Here, have a look." He opened his bag and handed her a page from his notebook—a map he'd sketched while interrogating Vernum.

"It's soaking wet," she said.

"I slipped coming up the riverbank. Didn't the girls mention I'm clumsy? I'm not much of an artist either." The smile in his tone was intentional. He scooted his chair close enough to touch the map. "Here's the village square. And this is an old baseball stadium, I was told. And the X—I circled it. Do you know the house?"

"A large green house with . . . I don't know the word . . . *towers* on each side . . . or *gables*?"

"Maybe."

"If it's the same, a wealthy man built it years ago. Very, very rich, before the Revolution, and his only daughter still lives there. Hector Casanova was the man's name. His daughter is old now. Imelda Casanova. *La Viuda*—the Dowager—is what she's called. She's a recluse. My grandmother was a maid in her house, but only for a few years."

This was an unexpected bit of luck. Ford had questions about the Dowager but wanted to orient himself first. Marta had watched games at the baseball stadium but didn't know much about the place. She confirmed the location of a few other landmarks but was puzzled when he asked, "Why does a village as small as Plobacho have such a large cemetery?"

"What do you mean? The nearest cemetery is twenty kilometers from here in Artemisa. Or, if the family has a little money, they choose the Cementerio de Caimito. These are simple places, not large."

Vernum had been caught in his first lie—or the shortstop Figueroa Casanova had lied to Vernum.

"I pictured something more elaborate. Nothing closer? With mausoleums, sepulchres, a lot of them, I was told."

Marta glanced inside, where her daughters pretended to be asleep. "West of Havana, there is the magnificent Cementerio de Colón."

Ford thought, *Maybe Lázaro is right*, while the woman continued. "Members of the elite can be buried there, but not people like us. Sabina thinks it more beautiful than photographs of Disney World." A wistful smile faded while she thought it through. "Although . . . there was once a burial field near the river. Not far from here"—she nodded in the direction of the village— "unless you go by car. It was called the Pauper Cólera, but bulldozers came many years ago and covered it.

Most of it. There are still some ruins of buildings. That was after Fidel and the Revolution but before I was born."

"There was a cholera epidemic?"

"I suppose so. Or because it was a swampy area that flooded. Cholera, malaria, black bowel fever. In those days they were called pauper diseases because peasants were considered unclean. Some say the bodies were dumped and covered with cement. Others say they were burned. It was to protect our water supply, so no one argued, but you know how old people are. They still believe diseases come out of the ground there."

Marta, the cigar in her hand, reconsidered the map, which consisted of stick drawings and cryptic abbreviations. "This is the public garbage dump, not a cemetery."

"Is it close to the place you're talking about?"

She noted his interest and looked beyond the river, northeast. "No. As I said, the Pauper Cólera is beyond those trees. Not far on foot, much longer by road. I've never been. Why would I?" She put the map aside. "Is it rude to ask what your friend is looking for? Perhaps I can help."

"My source of information has mixed in lies with the truth. I think it has something to do with Imelda Casanova. I'm not certain yet. Or her grandson. Something he knows, or something he did."

"You are speaking of Figueroa."

"Yes."

"There's not much I can tell you."

Ford took a stab. "Is he really her grandson?"

Marta fidgeted while her fingers graded the quality of the cigar, then placed it in the ashtray. Nervous, Ford decided, reluctant to discuss the secrets of a family that had once been powerful, then fell from grace—or so Vernum had claimed.

That wasn't it. She turned to him. "Figuerito has the brain of a child, that's true. But if he was guilty of murdering children, explain why the same murderer attacked us tonight? Other girls from the countryside have been attacked or just disappeared, *poof*"—she illustrated with her hands—"even though Figuerito was locked away. Now you tell me my daughters are safe, but the fear I've lived with for two years—more than two years—praying every night, worried all day that . . ." Marta cleared her throat, too emotional to put it into words because words provoked mental images. "To allow my babies to fall into the hands of that monster . . . I couldn't. So I made a decision that broke my heart, to send them away. That's why I'm asking you . . . why I must know if . . ."

Ford waited for her to finish, a little impatient—he had to get moving—but soon realized she was crying. He hesitated, then placed a hand on her arm. Just as he'd feared, she jumped as if startled but felt better when she leaned against him and sobbed. It didn't last. A moment later, she pulled away, saying, "Don't . . . I haven't bathed. This is like a terrible dream. Please understand something: when I said I wanted you to sleep here tonight, I didn't mean—"

"Of course you didn't. In the girls' room or the hammock, you made that clear."

"I know, but before the words were out of my mouth I realized it sounded so cheap. A man like you, a man of character, would never . . ."

Never? Ford was easily undone by tears. He wanted to tell her that recent one-night stands within twenty-four hours with a stranger didn't constitute a man of character. Instead, he spoke in soothing tones as he searched the porch, hoping to see a handkerchief or a towel. "Calm down . . . try to breathe . . . I'll be back with something so you can blow your nose."

She was still crying when he returned empty-handed. "Marta?" he said. Then more firmly: *"Marta."*

It was a while before she could look at him. "Don't you understand? I'm disgusted with myself. You gave us money for a hotel. Sabina begged and begged and I should have listened. But I swear, what you think happened tonight didn't happen. It's my daughters I'm worried about."

Heartbreaking. Why did good women, no matter how smart, how solid, blame themselves for the cruelty of predators who viewed victims as faceless objects? Ford chose his words with care. "No matter what happened, you and the girls aren't at fault. *You* are not at fault, Marta. So if you're worried I think you're somehow tarnished, trust me, that's not why I have to go. Anyone who blames you is a damn idiot. Do you understand?" While she sniffed and nodded, he took her hands and helped her stand so they were facing. "Sabina will be okay. I can tell. What, Maribel?"

She didn't speak until he tilted her chin with a finger. "That . . . person didn't touch her. Well, he tied her hands and feet, but he wanted me first, I think. Then he heard Sabina and ran outside."

The relief Ford felt didn't rival the anger that had been building all evening.

"Marion"—she spoke his name for the first time, but in a whisper—"did you kill him? I hope you did. I wouldn't tell anyone ever. If you killed him, then I'll know we're safe."

Ford couldn't risk the truth—Vernum Quick was bound, gagged, and cabled to a tree, still alive—so he pulled Marta into his arms and held her because what the hell else could he do but pretend to be kind and caring and worthy of this woman's misplaced respect? "You'll never see him again," he said. "That's all I can say. Do you believe me?"

Her head bobbed up and down against his chest.

"But you're still afraid."

Another nod but more emphatic.

"Okay . . . let me ask you something." He was thinking of the little palm-sized 9mm Sig Sauer that was now in his briefcase. "Have you ever fired a pistol before?"

18

Vernum, trussed in the trunk of his own car, said to Ford, "*Jefe* . . . why don't you talk? I hate it when you do this. That's why, huh? Mind games. I've had training, man. My KGB handler, the one we want to kill, he does educational videos. That we want to neutralize, I mean. I'm more valuable than you think, *Jefe*. Give me a chance, you'll see."

Jefe, pronounced "HEF-fay." Eager to please, the *Santero* was addressing him as "Chief" because he was scared shitless.

Ford didn't bother with Super Glue and a tongue depressor. If he needed an answer fast, applying solvent took too much time. "I'm going to make two stops," he said. "If you lied to me, I'll set your car on fire and walk away. Think before answering. Vernum . . . is there any-thing you left out?"

Yes . . . several minor details that weren't minor, but he had an excuse. "How many times have you shut off the blood to my brain, man? *Jefe*, please, if you don't think that affects my . . ."

Ford found the man's jugular vein—end of explana-tion. He balled cotton into Vernum's mouth and used duct tape.

The Lada had a bad clutch. It needed a ring job and the starboard headlight was out. No big deal in Cuba. In Havana at eleven-twenty, there would be a few cars and donkey carts, but sparse. In the countryside, even on main highways, no matter the time of day, there was no traffic. Just the occasional transiting of a Chinese bus that stunk of propane, a Russian half-track hauling cane, a car or two on wobbly tires, then long spaces of silence and wind over asphalt that had been engineered for the future but led to nowhere but the past.

The bombs of the Cold War had never been deployed—except here where they had detonated in spirit. Their mushroom gloom had emptied the highways in a slow-motion panic that joined two centuries yet isolated the young, the hopeful. Instead of aspiring, instead of cov-eting their first success, they sold tamarinds and man-goes by the roadside in the silence of asphalt, unaware they were the newest casualties of a long-gone war.

Ford drove to the main road and, after a few miles, turned left toward Vista del Mar, then another left on a rutted lane toward Plobacho. Didn't see another car, not one, only the sparks of candles and kerosene poverty through trees, while, on the highest hillside, a satellite tower strobed a single red warning to pilots from the north.

That reminded him to check Vernum's satellite phone. He had to hold it away to see the screen . . . but nothing new to read.

Kostikov hadn't responded. That could mean only one thing: the Russian knew something was amiss. His next move would be to find Vernum. Right now he would be in his Mercedes, somewhere between Cojimar and Plobacho, watching a laptop or meter locked onto Vernum's phone. *This* phone.

WHAT MARTA had called Pauper Cólera Vernum called Campo Muerto—"the field of the dead." He said a leper colony had burned to the ground here in 1917, but they continued to bury the poor and diseased until the Department of Health had sent in bulldozers fifty-some years ago and changed the name.

"Peasants are superstitious," he explained. "It's better not to frighten them, but no one comes here anyway. I told you, man, I knew the perfect spot." Vernum, with his legs free, no longer gagged, was talkative, full of attitude even with his hands cuffed behind him. "But"—he paused to stress the importance of what came next— "this is between us. A covert action, right? I can't wait to see the look on that fat Russian's face when we bring him here."

They wouldn't have to bring the Russian if they didn't hurry. Kostikov would find the place by himself.

Ford said, "He should be in a hospital by now, if what you told me is true. You screwed it up somehow. Or were exaggerating."

"*Jefe*, how many times have I explained? You know more about the Russians and uranium poisoning than I do, man."

What Ford knew was that Vladimir Putin, a former KGB hit man, now president, sometimes ordered agents to use polonium-210 to murder his enemies. A dose the size of a grain of sand, if pure, was so lethal that even if it was immersed in an ounce of water, the victim would die in agony within a week. To Putin, an additional benefit was that his agent would die, too, just from handling the stuff.

Plausible deniability.

But the effects of polonium were dose-dependent. If enough wasn't ingested or injected, or if the dosage was diluted, the symptoms—diarrhea, vomiting—might linger for months. There was no antidote, but the victim would recover.

According to Vernum, he'd been smart enough to realize what was in the fountain pen, so he had drained the contents into a vial. To the vial, he'd added olive oil. "To make it taste good," he said. "I put a few drops on his jerked chicken sandwich. The man has had the shits ever since, so I know it's working."

Vernum also claimed he'd cut Figueroa with a blade contaminated with the stuff, but was less sure about that. Rather than listen to it all again, Ford gave him a push and said, "Shut up and walk."

They were on acreage that had been cleared years ago but had gone wild with weeds and wetland vines that thinned as they ascended a hillock that had been piled high by a dredge or contoured by earthmoving machines. Columns of brick sprouted from the bushes in a random pattern, like stalagmites in a roofless cave . . . then a brick wall with holes punched through. On the river side, viewed from the top of the hill where Ford stopped, was the husk of a building with a towering chimney or cupola, no roof, and only three walls.

"Is that where you dumped the bodies?" he asked.

Vernum had admitted killing only two girls, but then imagined himself locked in the trunk of his 1972 Lada while the car burned. After that, he had upped the number to five but insisted, "As a *Santero*, I took an oath to weed out the bad ones. You know, possessed by evil. Hey—it's true. There's a ceremony, man, very strict the way every detail has to be prepared. The purest turpentine, a coconut rind sliced in fourths with a knife that's been cleaned and sharpened. I can't, you know, share all the secrets, but it's about purification. It's about feeding certain spirits what their hunger craves. Life must feed on life. I don't expect you to understand, but how else you gonna deal with something so bad?"

Until then, Ford had refused to be baited. "The Esteban girls are evil? Maribel hardly says a word. And the mother, don't blame some bullshit ceremony on what you planned to do to her."

Vernum was immune to insult. "How many times I say this? Man, I don't expect gringos from the *Estados Unidos* to believe, but it's true."

"Good. I'd have to tape your mouth again."

"All I'm saying is, your religion doesn't train you—"

"Keep moving," Ford warned, and started down the hill.

Vernum hustled to catch up. "It doesn't train you to recognize the signs. The evil ones, they get more powerful as adults. Are you Catholic? Catholics understand that demons are real, man. We can't see them, of course. They're like parasites. They move at night like a worm seeking, what do you call it, fertile ground. But, *Jefe*, when a demon finds the right person—a child with a bad disposition, say—they slip in through the mouth or nose. Pretty soon, you're dealing with a devil who's a total maniac. See? Now you understand why I do what I have to do. As I told the Russian, I'm well suited for this type of work."

Ford's jaw flexed. He checked his watch. They were almost to the brick shell of what had once been a sanitarium run by nuns—a leprosarium.

Vernum couldn't stop talking. "When a demon roots inside the brain of a kid, it's actually a kindness. You know, end their misery before it gets worse. That youngest girl—what's her name?—the brat squirted acid in my eyes and laughed, she threatened to bite my fingers. *A goddamn child.*"

Ford had to smile, but only because he could picture Sabina doing it. Vernum was ballsy—hands cuffed, struggling to keep up, his face a mosaic of stitches, yet still preaching in his superior, street-hip way. No . . . he was justifying his own crimes.

"My KGB handler, for instance. Sometimes the things I do, things you do in your profession—I think you'll agree—it's necessary for the good of others. You saw the video I shot. That's how the Russian dealt with that German traitor."

Some, but not all, of the video. Ford, in a remote part of his brain, had critiqued the way Kostikov had played Vernum, the aspiring spy, against the German agent—a blonde he recognized from Tomlinson's brief stardom on Facebook. His methods worked but were heavy-handed. A truly gifted operator would have manipulated the scenario so that when the woman went out the door, even the pilot would have believed it was accidental.

Anatol Kostikov of the KGB: low marks for creativity. Zero for professionalism. In all Ford's years, he had never witnessed such pointless, joyous cruelty. A similar flaw defined the difference between arson and pyromania. It was weakness. Weakness could be targeted.

Ford stopped beneath the towering chimney, then moved a safe distance away. Hurricanes and the years had twisted it like the spine of a cripple. The damn thing could come toppling down beneath the weight of the stars, or one croaking frog, or a breeze that pushed sulfuric musk across this plain where the diseased had died and were dumped into holes. The air, the earth, and the weeds were contagious with dread. Even Ford, a scientist, could understand why locals avoided this place.

He used the flashlight. Painted the chimney, which was the size of a furnace cupola—a crematorium, possibly. The building's foundation was primitive cement . . . a couple of collapsed rooms . . . a wedge of steps to a root cellar or basement, where rats scampered. Nearby, more rats atop the remains of a well or cistern . . . then, at a distance, a trench lined with bricks, bricks piled everywhere. Several likely locations. "Okay," Ford said. "Show me the bodies."

Vernum didn't move. "Someone was here," he said. He sounded spooked.

"So what?"

"Unlock my cuffs. Man, you saw what they left behind but you just didn't understand. I need the flashlight."

Not a chance. Ford figured it out for himself. Near the steps was a sunflower bound with red ribbon. A little pile of cowrie shells with painted eyes . . . a cigar and an empty rum bottle. At the base of the well, another sunflower, where rats quarreled among the seeds.

"No one comes here," Vernum said. He was scared—but probably more worried about revealing evidence that he was a child killer. Or maybe not, because then he said, "They're in there . . . inside the chimney."

"All five bodies?"

"Isn't that what I just said? There's an opening at the bottom. Hurry up. I want to get out of here."

Ford shined the light. "I don't see it." Gave the man another push, and kept prodding him, until the chimney dwarfed them both, and there it was, hidden by weeds: a brick conduit into the chimney. The outline suggested the shape of an oversized oven. He'd been right. A crematorium.

Ford kicked weeds away. The chimney's base was the diameter of a large room, but the opening was less than the width of his shoulders. "Sit on the ground with your back to me," he told Vernum. He emptied his pockets to streamline himself but kept the flashlight and his phone, which he switched to video mode.

"You're crazy, man. Crawl in there on your knees?" Vernum looked up, the chimney six stories high, rows of bricks missing, whole sections segmented like blocks hanging by a thread. "I don't want to be sitting on my ass if that falls. You bang into it wrong, kick something loose. *Jefe* . . . why you need pictures? Get them later, man, after we do the Russian."

Ford stared at the *Santero* until he dropped to the ground, facing the river. "Don't do anything stupider than you already have," he said, then got down and probed with the flashlight. What he saw caused him to thread his head and one arm into the space. Then attempted to wiggle his shoulders through. The space within stunk of fur and darkness.

High above, a brick broke free, fell for a silent second, and hammered into the ground. Another brick fell.

Vernum's voice: "Shit, man . . . didn't I tell you?"

Ford held his breath even though he knew Vernum was on his feet, running. He lay motionless . . . exhaled, then took a shallow breath and shot video because he didn't want to do this ever again. A slow pan: rib bones . . . swatches from a chiffon dress . . . a femur protruding from leggings that were once a girl's pajamas.

He didn't speak. Even when he remembered the Russian's phone out there with his wallet, but not the keys to the car. Sound was energy. His voice would reverberate up the chimney like smoke or an eroding wind. Vernum, his hands cuffed behind him, would be easy enough to catch.

When he did, Ford's first question would be *What did you do with their heads?*

19

On the road that tunneled beneath Havana Harbor, Figgy couldn't help blasting the horn just to hear the echo. After three years in an insane asylum, he valued life's simple pleasures, and he had never driven a Buick station wagon before.

Tomlinson, who had spent most of the trip looking over his shoulder, said, "Jesus Christ, why not flag down a cop and tell him we're late for our firing squad?" He looked back where the chickens were trying to sleep in their wire cages. "Where the hell did that Mercedes go? It's been twenty minutes . . . no, more like thirty. The commie bastard's toying with us, that's what I think."

Very confusing, the strange things this gringo hippie said, but the shortstop reminded himself that the hippie was also a left-handed pitcher. "It's dangerous to speak with policemen, I think. But if you're sure, you should take off your hat. Rastafarians are illegal in Havana. Well, three years ago, that was true, but"—he laid on the horn again before exiting the tunnel—"the world has changed a lot since I escaped to America."

"It's a beanie, not a hat," Tomlinson said. "More like a hair cozy—a stocking cap with style." A moment later, he added, "Illegal? You're shitting me. What do you mean illegal?"

Figuerito replied, "I asked the chicken woman the same thing." He shrugged. "You think I'm going to argue with a body like hers? Even at her age, a woman who danced at the Copa deserves respect as an expert."

"Olena?" Tomlinson asked. He had no idea what the little Cuban was getting at.

"Of course. How many dancers we know from the Copacabana? I liked her legs. Did you happen to see her *chichis*?"

Impossible, Tomlinson decided, to make sense of a shortstop on a freedom binge. So he let it go, saying, "Can't argue, I guess. Olena wouldn't do me wrong."

They drove up the hill onto the Malecón, four lanes that curved along the sea, crumbling buildings to their left—Old Havana—some adorned with scaffolding that for years had signaled the hope of restoration but was used only for hanging laundry. Traffic sparse, a few cabs and whining motor scooters; a restless farmer in an oxcart, who urged his horse *Faster! Faster!* in the slow lane.

"That's a nice load of mangoes," Figgy remarked.

Tomlinson didn't notice. He was trying to orient himself. It had been several years since his last stay in Havana. Not that much had changed, but cities built by Conquistadors were always a directional challenge. Streets converged like spokes of a wheel, designed to capture the wind in hot, tropical regions, which was ingenious— air-conditioning via architecture—but also confusing as hell if you were in a car, not on a plodding horse.

"Are we near the Hotel Plaza? That's where Doc would stay if he's here."

"Who?"

Tomlinson went through it again, making the connection with Gen. Juan Rivera. A minute later, they were off the Malecón, driving past totems of the Revolution: tanks, debris from a U.S. plane, and Castro's motor vessel, *Granma*, mounted within glass like a trophy. The Hotel Plaza was on the left, across from a park, only one security guard at the door. Tomlinson got out, spoke to the guard, then said to Figueroa through the window, "I've been a Rastaman for, what, two hours? And the screws are already disrespecting me. I need some paper to leave a note."

"Your friend's not there?"

"The guard won't say, which tells me Doc checked in

but he left and hasn't come back yet. It's a sort of sensory connection thing we have."

In the glove box, Figueroa found a receipt book and a stub of a pencil. "What kind of car does he drive?"

"That he rented, you mean?" Tomlinson began scribbling a note. "Knowing him, something beige with seat belts."

Next stop was the Masonic Grand Lodge of Cuba on Avenida Salvador Allende, west in Vedado. The building was an Art Deco Gothic from the '50s, eleven stories tall, crowned by a lighted, revolving planet Earth. Two guards stationed here. Tomlinson got out, carrying the card given to him by Raúl Corrales. "These guys meet at weird hours, you never know, but keep an eye open for the Mercedes," he said to Figgy. "If they let me in and I give you a thumbs-up, that means you can haul ass inside if you need to hide from the Russian."

For fifteen minutes, Figueroa sat there, long enough to roll a joint and light it. He checked and rechecked the mirror, alert for the Mercedes, but didn't notice two motorcycle cops parked down the street, which also happened to be downwind. That's who he was talking with, the cops, when Tomlinson exited the building and did an immediate about-face. But then turned around—he couldn't just go off and abandon the little guy—despite an ingrained aversion to men in uniform, especially with the scent of good weed in the air.

Figgy, though, had the situation under control. "They feel you should drive," he whispered. "Do you have twenty dollars American?"

"You bribed them? Thank god."

"And the chickens, they wanted them all, but I talked them down to two."

Tomlinson smoked the last of the doobie while he followed the cops to their apartment on Zapata, a street that skirted a cemetery so large that mausoleums and lighted statuettes accompanied them ten blocks before the cops pulled over. They switched off their headlamps, checked the street both ways, and waved for Figueroa to help them with the poultry cages. Gad . . . it reminded Tomlinson of a bizarre drug deal from long ago. Tabs of mescaline, an undercover narc, and a conga line of Hare Krishnas had somehow intersected. Details were sketchy, but he remembered thinking the bald men in robes were skinheads and was terrified of whatever crazy shit came next, yet he'd remained fixated on the dazzling lights of Berkeley . . . or was it San Francisco Bay?

Didn't matter. The sick feeling in his *hara* is what mattered. Same with his fixation on the cemetery, a dazzling grotesquerie, well-lit, a forest of cathedrals, crypts, and crosses, a gated community for the dead. His instincts warned him not to look away, but his battle for clarity won—and there, a block behind them, was the black Mercedes.

Figgy reappeared, slapping at bugs . . . no, pinfeathers on

his shirt, and saw the car, too. Instead of getting in the Buick, he jogged toward the cops, who didn't want to be bothered—not while lugging cages up the stairs—but the good cop relented . . . placed his chicken on the ground and listened while Figgy talked and pointed at the Mercedes.

Brilliant, Tomlinson thought, yet futile. It was a finesse that could not work. But, my god . . . it did work. The cop drew his weapon, signaled his partner, and they both trotted toward the black car.

Figgy jumped in and slammed the door. "Drive fast, brother."

Tomlinson was already in second gear. "Christ, what kind of crazy bullshit story did you give them?" He shifted to third and checked the rearview mirror: the Russian was out, hands up, a man so big he dwarfed the Mercedes and the cops.

"Story?"

"Dude, if there was ever a time to make up a story, this is it." Now, in the mirror, the Russian, instead of handing over his wallet, was gesturing impatiently like a VIP without a driver's license or even an ID.

Figueroa, looking out the side window, said, "Damn . . . I wanted to drive through the cemetery. You think Key West is nice? There's a cathedral in there full of dead famous people. It's next to the baseball memorial, and I wanted to show you—"

"The cops," Tomlinson interrupted, "try to focus, man. What did you say?"

"I told them"—he plucked a feather from his tongue and spit—"I told them the Russian wants to kill me. That he's a fat *bolá* who hates Cubans, especially me, 'cause I defected to the *Estados Unidos* to play in the major leagues. But I came back to help my *abuela*."

"To save your 'grandmother,'" Tomlinson translated.

"Yes, I'm fairly certain. To save her from embarrassment."

"They bought it? I'll be go to hell."

"Perhaps," Figgy said, "but what I told them is true." He twisted around in his seat. "Next time we're in Havana, we'll buy beer and visit the grave of Dolf Luque, Cuba's first major leaguer."

Gad, he was still talking about the cemetery.

"There's an area where left-handed pitchers are buried, a nice place to lay in the grass. But even before crazy prison, I couldn't enjoy my trips because the bad *Santero* followed me. Others sometimes, too."

"To a . . . geezus, why?"

Figuerito became uneasy. "Could be that people believed I knew where things of value were hidden, but I don't. I mean, I *do*, but that's not where they are."

"What the hell are you talking about? Does this have something to do with why every narc, cop, and bad guy in Cuba is after us?" He glanced at the briefcase on the floor. "The cemetery—is that where you found the letters?"

"That's where some people looked for them, brother.

I'm fairly sure. Same with the motorcycles and machine guns."

Tomlinson needed a time-out. "Let's not talk for a while," he said.

FIGUEROA'S GRANDMOTHER, Imelda Casanova, whom locals called the Dowager and feared as a recluse, lived in a gabled house that in a village as small as Plobacho was considered a mansion.

Driving west into the foothills of Sierra del Rosario with the sea to their right, Figgy explained that villagers also feared his grandmother because after the Revolution wealthy Cubans were evicted and their mansions were turned into apartments. Except for one woman. And one house.

"Why?"

"You'll have to ask my *mu-maw*. Think she'll be surprised to see me? I'm kind of worried, brother, 'cause I didn't leave under what you'd call real good terms."

They discussed Figueroa's grandmother awhile before Tomlinson got back to it. "Was your father famous? That might be why Fidel let her stay. You said he danced for the Moscow Ballet." Another motive came to mind, but it was better to get all the options on the table.

"I never met him. Why else would my mother live in Russia when I was a boy living in Cuba? Before I was kicked out of school, children teased me, saying it was a lie: Cubans didn't dance ballet, especially in Moscow, where all men are fat except for soldiers and *maricóns*. Oh, brother, did that make me mad."

Uh-oh, Tomlinson thought, and pictured Figgy as a schoolboy tossing bullies off a cliff. "How did you, uhh, deal with the situation?"

"The multiplication table ended the problem," he answered.

"Excellent, a great way to deal with anger." Tomlinson nodded. "Doing math problems in your head. Know what? I'm going to suggest that to my friend Doc. A nice guy but a lot of repressed anger, I think, that manifests itself in tight-ass behavior. You know, always on time, has to follow through with every little promise. The guy won't even smoke a joint."

"Who?"

Tomlinson had to go through it again, an abbreviated version.

"Smoking *pitillo*, sure, it might relax your friend, but I don't know about his ass. What I was talking about was getting kicked out of school because of arithmetic. I couldn't get past three times three—three being my lucky number, as you know—so I didn't have to listen to their shit on the playground no more. Your friend the doctor, is he good at arithmetic?"

Tomlinson slipped a baggy from his pocket. "Be judicious when you roll the next one," he said. "We're low on papers—and that's the good news."

They were on a winding road not much wider than the station wagon, the Rosario Mountains not yet cascading into the sea. Dark out here in the countryside: sugarcane and stars, tiny houses with goats, an occasional ox grazing in the yard. "Do you mind driving for a while?" Tomlinson asked.

For the next half hour, using a flashlight, he skimmed through more love letters, all to the same address in Plobacho, Pinar del Río, although the pet endearments varied: My Adored Gaitica, Beloved Angelica, Dear Little Ducky, My Sweet Galleguita. More often, My Beautiful Elma. Elma seemed a shorter form of Imelda, but was it? Were the letters all to the same woman?

"Did your grandmother have a sister?" Tomlinson asked. "Or a cousin—a niece, maybe—who lived in the same house?"

"She had maids and a housekeeper. Just a housekeeper the year I was sent away." Figgy looked over from the steering wheel. "I was told never to open those. She didn't mention you, but I . . . well, as long as I'm here to watch, I guess it's okay." A passing cottage caught his eye. "Have you ever owned a goat? They have eyes like snakes, but they're very good in stew."

"Your grandmother told you not to read these, huh? Then how did General Rivera get his greedy paws on the briefcase?"

"It was a deal we made before he bribed the warden and got me out of crazy prison. Now I'm worried she might be mad. But I told you the truth. They were never hidden in the Colon Cemetery no matter what I said to others."

"That's what you meant back there? Oh yeah, I asked about the letters."

"You don't remember that either? All the marble statues and tombs, the most beautiful cemetery in the world. After a doctor checks your brain, maybe we'll go."

"Geezus, please, no more with the cemetery. What about your grandmother?"

"That's what I'm telling you. She never cared about baseball, so I doubt if she'll understand." The little man fretted for a moment. "I haven't seen her in more than three years. She can't cook either."

Tomlinson returned to the letters, his eye sharpening as he skimmed through several. Fidel's penmanship had more flourish than his brother's, but his notes were shorter, seldom more than a few lines, and often cryptic. A couple of times Tomlinson asked Figgy for help with translation but soon realized that the multiplication table was not the shortstop's only academic failing.

"I understand most words written in ink," he explained, "as long as I know the person and can guess what they want to say. And certain books because they're typed out. You know the thin ones with nice pictures?" He couldn't talk without taking his hands off the wheel to gesture or indicate size and this time they almost went over a cliff into a river.

After that, Tomlinson stopped asking for help.

The letters were arranged haphazardly, no regard for dates or whether they were from Fidel or Raúl. Envelopes from 1953 to '55 were all from federal prison on the Isle of Pines. Each first page contained illegible initials in red and sometimes a circular stamp CENSURADO. Aside from Fidel's fantasy about his Galleguita bathing naked at a washbasin, Tomlinson was struck by the consistent formality. Each missive was respectful, mindful of decorum, but with love hidden between the lines. The same was true of letters posted after the Castros were free men.

He was impressed by the eloquence of the writing, especially Raúl, who wrote of his "embryonic love" and of his "auto-analysis" regarding Fidel's behavior when, in 1957, they both went into hiding. These letters were not authored by ignorant thugs. They were written by articulate, well-educated men who were mindful of the social niceties due a woman, mistress or not. Two distinctive voices: Raúl rambled and strained for lyricism; Fidel snapped orders or lectured, often as a martyr or victim, and always in a superior tone.

But so far, not one single damning or controversial line, save for the one from Raúl, written from prison, that hinted at Fidel's inept baseball skills—no, it had been softball. Certainly nothing worth killing for.

Tomlinson skipped ahead, seeking anything written during the political turmoil of the early 1960s, but correspondence had dwindled. He found several from Raúl, but only two from Fidel, who by then was revered, or feared, as the *Máximo Gran*, the leader of all Cuba.

An envelope leaped out. Tomlinson held his breath while he opened it to find a telegram:

MY FRIEND. DESTROY WHAT YOU HAVE SAVED AND FIND A SAFE PLACE. SAY NOTHING. THE SWAN LIES. MONTHS MUST PASS. F

It was dated 9:18 p.m. 22 November 1963. A Friday, Tomlinson remembered. The day John F. Kennedy was killed in Dallas.

The Buick's roaring muffler vanished as he reread the lines several times. Fidel was ordering his mistress to destroy all letters. Or destroy all of something. That seemed evident. A respectful period of time had to elapse before they could resume their relationship. Made sense, as did instructing her to find a safe place, which anticipated a nuclear attack by the U.S. But what the hell did THE SWAN LIES mean?

"Brother, why are you so quiet?" Twice, Figueroa had to ask.

SWAN . . . ? The chances of Figgy knowing a Cuban acronym from 1963 were slim. Tomlinson switched off the flashlight. "These were written to your grandmother, weren't they?"

It had been obvious for a while and it was time to put it out there.

"Maybe." Figueroa shrugged. "Others are to women named Little Ducky and My Sweet Gingersnap and strange names like that."

"But it was your grandmother who told you to guard the letters, wasn't it? That's cool, man. I'm just trying to understand. Did the general read these? He knew what was in the briefcase, that's obvious, but did he actually *read* them?"

Figgy, concentrating on the road, said, "If he had, I would have had to kill him."

Tomlinson sat back. "Say what?"

"That worries me, brother, now that we're shipmates. My *mu-maw* doesn't understand baseball and cares less about ships than she does cooking." He glanced over. "But a promise is a promise. You know?"

IMELDA CASANOVA inhabited an upstairs room in a house that smelled of cobwebs and lavender, a wooden time capsule where the table was set with silver and china for two, napkins folded, as if awaiting a guest from 1959 who might yet appear.

That's where Tomlinson waited, in the formal dining room, while Figgy stood at the stairs and called, "Guess who's home, *mi abuela*? I brought a friend, but don't worry, he's not really a Rastafarian and doesn't eat much."

No answer. Figgy started up the stairs but lost his courage. "Maybe *yayah* is asleep," he whispered.

"Your grandmother?"

"*Yayah* or *mu-maw*. It's the same, but she doesn't like those names—even from me."

"It's almost eleven," Tomlinson reassured him, but was thinking, *The poor guy's scared shitless of the old woman.*

Only now did he understand why.

The housekeeper, if there was one, hadn't come to the door, so they'd entered through the root cellar into the basement. Oddly, Figgy's room was down there, next to an old washing machine, the kind with a crank and wringers. He had lived in a cubicle with a steel door and only one window that looked out onto weeds at ground level. Except for some shelves and a homemade bong, it resembled a prison cell.

"How did you and your grandmother get along personally?" Tomlinson had inquired. The room reminded him of a Colorado drunk tank where he'd once spent a night.

"She treated me pretty good as long as I worked and brought home money" was the reply. "And, of course, did what I was told to do. But don't make that woman mad." The man's expression read *Wow.* "Many times she locked me in here for all day. Once, almost a week."

"Geezus, that's terrible."

"Not as bad as cutting off my rooster." He motioned vaguely at his crotch. "She always gave me a choice, though, so you can understand why I'm still thankful. It's better to be locked up, I think, or beaten with a cane stalk."

Tomlinson had been looking forward to meeting Castro's mistress. Not now. "This was after you moved from the village near Cojimar?"

"Hell yes. I'd have run away, but I still had bad memories of drowning. And lots of bad hops, as you know. Plobacho has a much better baseball field. Look—you can see it from here." He moved a stool, stood on it, and opened the window. "This is how I got out at night. If there was a full moon, we'd play until morning." For a moment, he was happy. Then, from a higher vantage point, he surveyed his old room and realized something was amiss. "Those *maricóns*," he said after a moment. "Someone stole my best shit."

Tomlinson nearly winced. Weed that was more than three years old? No . . . Figgy was missing a sports coat he claimed almost fit, and a shrine to his patron saint, Eleguá, and a baseball trophy. On the shelf was a photo of the thing: an ornate silver cup with seams like a baseball and an inscription plate too blurry to read.

"You won this?"

"How old do you think I am? That's a valuable antique, brother. Nobody won that game. I wouldn't have felt okay stealing it if they had." Figgy had placed the photo against the wall in a respectful way before tying on a pair of old sneakers. "If they stole my best shit, I bet they took other shit, too."

Tomlinson had to ask, "What do you mean, no one won the game?"

Too late. Figgy went out the door, saying, "She's going to be mad. There's nothing my *mu-maw* hates worse than a thief, and that was my job. You know, protecting her valuables. But not everything valuable would fit in here."

The briefcase, he meant, which he carried against his chest like a pillow, or a shield.

Upstairs, the house was spacious, though not large enough to cloak the poverty of its owner. A penniless woman lived here, but a sickness inhabited the place, too. Figgy switched on lamps that had no bulbs. Closets had been thrown open and emptied. Walls once adorned with art were scarred by outlines of missing frames. What little furniture remained was littered with fallen plaster. Yet, in the formal dining room, undisturbed, was a table big enough for candelabras and a dozen chairs, plus fine china and silverware—and place settings for only two. In the middle, a wilted sunflower.

"Does she ever come down here?" Tomlinson kept his voice low, spooked by it all, the craziness of ageless and interminable yearning for something long dissolved by time. It scared him because the same crazy yearning burned within him.

Figgy, at the foot of the stairs, tilted his head and called, "It's me, Figueroa. I'll find the men who robbed you. I won't let the Guardia take me away from you this time. But, uhh . . . I'd like to say hello first. Oh—and I brought this to make you feel better."

The briefcase—he held it up.

Tomlinson put his hand on the shortstop's shoulder in a comforting way. "I'll go up and check on her. Stay here, if you want."

Figgy let him pass but said, "I'm coming, too," then took the lead when they got to the landing because there were halls and many rooms. "She lives in there," he said.

Tomlinson entered through double doors into a circular room with so many windows it reminded him of a lighthouse. Antique lamps and furniture . . . the scent of lavender even stronger than the scented letters opened here sixty years ago by a girl who was in love. Not a girl . . . a beautiful young woman. Tomlinson, looking at a framed photograph, said, "That's her—Imelda," because it could be no one else. Stunning. A teenage mistress dressed in virginal white, black eyes that projected a yearning spark across the decades.

He stood fixated while Figgy cracked a door, then another door. "She's gone," he said, and walked to a window that opened into stars and a breeze sweet with trees and a nearby river. "Damn it," he muttered. Then swore again, louder. "Son of a mother . . . you see that?"

It was enough to yank a man back to reality. "What's wrong?"

"She's there"—Figgy pointed—"she goes there at night sometimes. But that can't be her. She carries a candle or a lantern, not a flashlight. Last time men with flashlights were there, well . . . you know what happened. I had to throw my best bat off the cliff."

Tomlinson was completely lost. "What in God's name are you talking about?" But then he saw it: in the distance, a beam of light. Someone a quarter mile away panning a bright LED vertically up and down an industrial-sized chimney that had no roof or building to support it. "Is that an old factory or what?"

"You can't stay here," Figuerito said, "but you can't see where she is either." He rushed across the room, then stopped with an *I've got it!* expression on his face. "Follow me." He grabbed the briefcase and took off.

Tomlinson ran after him. "Where are we going?"

"There's a place in the cellar. No one will find you there. Me, I'm going after those men with flashlights."

"And do what?"

"I already told you."

"Kill them? Gad. Just because they're trespassing? At least you could pretend to be undecided."

Figgy didn't know what that meant. "Do you like home movies?" he asked, and vaulted the last three steps.

"You're not getting rid of me that easy. Let's take the Buick. Hey . . . what's the rush?"

"The old kind that you crank on a projector," the shortstop replied. "If someone hadn't stolen the projector, but they must have. *Mu-maw*, she wouldn't like you seeing her movies, so don't make any noise."

"You can't be serious, man. Watch a movie while you go off and kill people? Dude . . . slow down. Christ, you're going to pull a hamstring. Figueroa . . . ?"

The little Cuban didn't stop until they were in the cellar, where he opened the washing machine, removed several blankets with *Copacabana* embroidered across them, then a metal film canister. The canister was old-style, huge. "Here," he said. "There are some parts about baseball you'll like."

Odd, the look on the shortstop's face. Figgy was not a man who communicated via clever subtext, but there seemed to be a message there.

"Baseball?" Tomlinson asked.

Figgy pointed to a bare bulb hanging from the ceiling, the cellar's only light. "You'll have to hold the film up to that and sort of strip it through your fingers. Do it fast." He pantomimed to illustrate. "It's almost like watching TV." He placed the canister on a chair next to a couple of candles. "Don't let anyone see this, and be careful if you light a match. Film burns fast, brother. You've got to promise. I won't be gone long."

Tomlinson realized, *He thinks he might be killed by whoever is out there.* "Amigo," he said, "let me tell you something about your grandmother. She's crazy as three loons. Let's leave the letters—that's what we came to do—and get the hell out of here."

Figuerito was in a hurry. "Don't tell her that. If you're lucky, she'll only lock you in my room."

20

If not for stomach cramps, Anatol Kostikov might have reacted differently when the Cuban cops forced him against the car and tried to cuff him. The last thing he wanted was a confrontation because he had been looking forward to following the hippie and the traitor into the cemetery. If Vernum Quick, the deviant worm, was right, they would lead him to a mausoleum where, locked inside, was something the Russian had wanted all his life.

Oh yeah—plus the letters. Official business came first. Afterward, he could enjoy his private time.

Anatol had been reminding himself of that when the stupid cops ordered him out of the Mercedes. Their timing could not have been worse. Later, no matter how he explained what happened to Cuba's DGI, the only thought in his mind was *If I'm cuffed, I won't be able to wipe when I find a toilet.*

The cramps had made a fool of him already. Like at the stadium that afternoon when someone—an American CIA agent, he suspected—had stripped off his pants and robbed him. Until now, money and his IDs were secondary. It was the loss of his top secret Vul pistol that worried him most.

Humiliating for a direct descendant of legendary Terek Cossack warriors. He'd stood there by the stadium urinals, hands cupping his genitals, while he tried to convince an army lieutenant to do an immediate lockdown before the Yankee bastard escaped.

This embarrassment could never be revealed to anyone, let alone explained to two Cuban cops. However, after getting out of the Mercedes, Anatol did offer them his satellite phone and say, "Call embassy. You get big promotion, I think, you help me catch traitor. Perhaps American spy, yes?"

Not these two hard-ass motorcycle bulls. Their big mistake was a knee in the kidney after berating him for having no passport, no ID. Then the talkative cop had revealed what this was really about: "What you got against Cuban baseball players, señor? That little man you after, he's half your size. He's a shortstop, not a traitor—already got a contract for the major leagues. Try saying the same shit to us, you dick-sucking *bolá*.

Now, give me your goddamn hands and let me cuff you."

A knee under the ribs ended all attempts at diplomacy. Anatol crouched, spun with his elbow extended, and crushed the cop's nose. The key, as he'd taught hundreds of agents, was to move fluidly and continue the attack until the situation was stabilized. The second cop was reaching for his pistol, unprepared for an unarmed suspect to charge. Anatol shattered his knee with a side kick and caught him before he fell. Did a simple duck-under, then framed the cop's head with forearms and hands that resembled a figure four.

"You lazy turd of shit."

Those were the last words the Cuban heard. Anatol twisted so violently that, before he killed the talkative cop, the one with the busted nose, he looked at his hands: no blood. Good. No severed head there either. Even better.

It had happened to the Russian before.

Then he stepped back and felt something akin to horror when he realized what he'd done. As a senior intelligence agent with diplomatic immunity, he could get away with just about anything—except this. That's why he had recruited that little worm Vernum Quick. Murder the traitor from the insane asylum, and the hippie, too, or anyone else who got in his way, until he had what he'd been sent to find—plus a few other items the Russian considered spoils of war.

A fall guy . . . He had to find Vernum.

Anatol didn't linger over the bodies. Normally, he would have taken their IDs, their weapons, and pocketed whatever cash they had. Under different circumstances, he might have shipped home their shitty rice-burning Kawasakis, too, just for the fun of it.

Anatol was crazy about motorcycles.

Not this time.

He confirmed the talkative cop was dead—a man could survive a broken windpipe—then stripped off the Cuban's duty belt: pistol, magazines, mace, and . . . *handcuffs* . . . Where the hell had the handcuffs gone?

Anatol retrieved them from the side of the road and hurried to his Mercedes. But try to find a public restroom in this third-world banana republic . . . Desperate, he kicked down the door of a house, ripped out the phone, and told an old man who had refused to let him enter, "Fool. Now must kill you."

This time, he did a sloppier job. Vernum Quick, after all, was an amateur.

EARLIER, at a pharmacy, the Russian had bought two bottles of pink medicine that resembled Pepto-Bismol, and a packet of loperamide—*Warning,* the directions read, *do not exceed two tablets daily.* The pills had brought him a few hours of relief, so he tossed back four more, washed them down with half a pint of vodka, and refocused.

He knew where the hippie and the traitor would go next—Plobacho. Not much doubt about that. Russian intelligence had a large file on Imelda Casanova. For decades, the KGB had known about her love affair with the Castros. The agency was also aware that much of their correspondence was unaccounted for. While the brothers were alive, the old woman had remained an untouchable, politically speaking.

Things were different now.

Officially, Anatol's orders had been to confiscate the woman's personal effects in the interest of "preserving the history of the Socialist Party." In fact, he'd been sent for political reasons, as he damn well knew after thirty years in the clandestine services. If he had to guess, his guess was this: Vladimir Putin feared the Castros had let an uncomfortable truth slip in one of their letters. There were many ugly secrets from those early years. Many? Hell, thousands. One dated back to 1963. Cuban intelligence had recorded Lee Harvey Oswald's wild threats at their embassy in Mexico City six weeks before the assassination of JFK.

Even uglier secrets might have been revealed, but none had more cachet. Anatol turned west toward Plobacho and thought about that. If the truth came out, it wouldn't cause an international firestorm, but there would be headlines. Headlines would cause more suspicion, more media surveillance. That might hamper Moscow's plans. America's right-wingers, of course, wouldn't concede the obvious: embassies worldwide rejected crazy aspiring traitors on a daily basis. It was impossible to predict who would do what. If the rantings of every applicant were printed and shared, governments would choke on paper. That was as true now as it was in 1963.

Anatol, however, could admit to himself that Havana and Moscow should have taken a former Marine Sharpshooter a bit more seriously. If they'd dropped a friendly line, perhaps, to their comrades at the CIA, it might have changed history.

Funny. Pills and vodka had settled his stomach. Anatol, hunching over the steering wheel, laughed at his own joke.

He drove through Miramar into the embassy district, past his favorite restaurant, El Aljibe, which served the best *pollo* and black beans he'd ever had. Now, though, the odor of chickens roasting on a spit made him want to vomit. He burped and tasted the jerked sandwich he'd eaten on the plane.

Vernum, he remembered, had bought it for him.

That deviant freak. I will crush his head when I'm done here.

But not yet. First, he had to find the bastard.

On the passenger seat was a handheld GPS locator. The Russian had followed Vernum's travels with mild indifference until a little after ten, when he'd received a suspicious text: *Dropped phone in water. Messages garbled cannot call. Meet you where?*

Seconds later, the Cuban's transponder had gone dead. It was now ten fifty-eight and the screen still showed only Vernum's last location. Or . . . maybe Vernum, the sex pervert, had switched off the transponder because he wanted privacy.

Anatol thought, *I'll teach you to hide from me,* and hit *Destination.* The computer responded with estimated travel time to the pervert's location: twenty-three minutes.

Eighteen minutes later, Anatol Kostikov drove up a dirt lane to a house where a woman—a very pretty Latina—and two screeching whelps ran from the porch to greet him, one of them in baggy pink-and-white pajamas who called, "Marion . . . I knew you'd come back!"

They're expecting a female friend, he thought, then decided, No, a Cuban female couldn't afford a Mercedes, but a CIA agent could. *Marion* . . . in America, it might be a name for a male *pizdă.*

Kostikov got out.

The whelp in pajamas turned and fled, but the woman stood her ground.

KOSTIKOV, IN HIS best Spanish, said to the woman, "I am friends with Marion. How else I know sex deviant was here? Vernum Quick, that is sex deviant's name. Marion, he is gringo. Tell me where is my friend and Vernum Quick."

The woman, arms folded, backed away. "Describe what he looks like."

"Sex deviant, he is puny. A Cuban—"

"No, tell me what the American looks like."

Kostikov thought, *Thank you, stupid woman.* "Oh . . . you mean my good friend, Marion?" He laughed while he recalled what he'd been told after the bathroom incident. "He is strong man with glasses. Often, a green hat he wears on head. I have idea . . ." He watched her face carefully. "Tell me where Marion is found. You and me, I will drive. He will tell you we want the sex deviant arrested. Is good, no?"

The woman didn't buy it, but her reaction confirmed she knew where the American was. Or, at least, knew more than she was willing to reveal. That was useful. Now that the cramps were gone, it was pleasurable to look at her standing in the headlights of the Mercedes, her body visible through a cheap cotton robe. All but her breasts, which were concealed by her arms. The Russian tried to change that by extending his hand. "I am Anatol. What are you called?"

Defiant bitch. She shook her head, arms still folded, and asked, "What is Marion's last name?"

The Russian looked past her into the house. The youngest whelp was on the porch holding what might be a machete. That told him they were alone. Even so, he asked, "Where is husband?"

"He's . . . asleep . . . And it's none of your business anyway. He's a soldier. My husband won't like you being here."

"Husband is fool and you are liar." Kostikov pushed the woman aside when she tried to block his path, then pushed her again too hard and she sprawled sideways onto the ground—nice what the headlights revealed when her bathrobe flew open, but only for a second.

The Russian stared at her face, her legs, mindful he had packed condoms and a Viagra tablet somewhere, along with the name of an expensive prostitute. Damn . . . they were in his stolen wallet. But no reason not to strip off the Latina's robe by pretending to help her up—a memory he could save for when he felt better. He smiled, leaned, and offered his hand . . . then stood abruptly, aware that the child was charging him, a kitchen knife, not a machete, in her hand.

The woman screamed, "Sabina, go in the house!" while the girl screamed something about a fascist gringo who would feed him to the sharks.

The Russian grinned, amused, while his hand located the pistol he'd taken from the Cuban cop. It was in his back pocket, a 9mm Glock with a magazine that held eighteen rounds. He waited until the whelp stopped beside her mother and looked up, threatening him with the knife. Hilarious—she was the size of a bee. "Who is this dangerous gringo?" he asked the girl. "Is my good friend Marion?"

"Leave my mother alone," the girl hollered, then realized what she'd just heard. "Do you . . . you really know him?"

The woman, getting to her feet, told the girl to hush, but the girl kept talking. "I don't believe you. If you don't go away and leave us alone, he'll do anything I tell him to do."

"Go in the house," the woman ordered. "Don't say another word."

Yes, the girl also knew where to find the American. Kostikov used his gentlest voice. "Is important I find our friend Marion. Tell me, then we will all laugh before he feeds me to . . . did you say 'sharks'?"

"If that's what I want," the girl said. She yanked her arm away from her mother. "He has the fastest boat in Cuba and it's invisible. I'll tell him to tie you up and throw you in the sea if you don't leave right now." She lunged with the knife. The Russian, still grinning, held up his hands in surrender and backed a step. Didn't protest when the mother took the knife from the brat and herded her back to the house. Yet, something about the way the woman moved bothered him—so purposeful and suddenly in a hurry.

He let it go, thinking, *An American with an invisible boat?* It was a fairy tale no one would believe. But Kostikov, after thirty years in the clandestine services, was convinced, CIA.

Worse, the son of a whore had his silent pistol.

From inside the Mercedes gonged a persistent chiming. The satellite phone. He reached in and had a look. It was a text from Vernum, but just a string of garbled letters. Maddening . . . But wait . . . that meant the man's phone had been switched on. This was confirmed by the GPS locator, which he held up for better satellite reception. The sex deviant—his phone, at least—was nearby, somewhere to the northeast. He zoomed in so that Google Earth showed the roads and terrain. Cross-country, only two kilometers, near what appeared to be the ruins of a collapsed building. By car, due to Cuba's terrible roads, five times the distance and over two bridges.

Better to walk; quieter, and he wouldn't have to cross the river—but how long would he be free of the stomach cramps?

That goddamn chicken sandwich.

No, he would have to drive. On the way, he'd take more pills and finish the vodka.

Kostikov tossed both handsets into the car and, when he turned to check the house, reached for the pistol in his back pocket. Couldn't help himself. The mouthy little girl, in the glare of headlights, was on the porch, taunting him with her middle fingers, both jabbing at him, while she stuck out her tongue and made grotesque faces. One of Santa's elves dressed in pink-and-white—she reminded him of that. Inside, he could see the mother rushing from window to window as if searching for something—a weapon better than a knife, he guessed.

Kostikov took a breath and sought a reason to stay and punish the whelp for her insolence. Easily done. Finding Vernum was important—he needed a scapegoat—but so was recovering his stolen pistol. The girl knew more about the American than she had admitted. Same with the mother, if it came to that.

Kostikov started toward the porch. He despised children. He had never killed one, but it was exactly the sort of thing a sex deviant like Vernum Quick would do.

When Vernum heard a car backfiring in the distance, he collapsed in the bushes, fearing the gringo had spotted him and started shooting. After several seconds, though, and two *bang-bang*s rapid-fire, he realized the reports came from some faraway road.

Vernum was as shaky as he was suggestible. Except for air force training, he had never heard gunshots in Cuba. Only police and the military had weapons, and, as he knew, very few policemen were issued live ammunition. The *Fidelistas* stayed in power by limiting venues of power, and even their opponents could not criticize the country's remarkably low crime rate. A senior Russian agent, however, could pack any damn weapon he wanted.

Kostikov, Vernum thought. He got my text and figured it out.

That would explain the gunshots, but where was the
giant Russian? And why fire a gun from a distance . . . if
it was a gun.

A signal, he realized.

He's searching for me.

Vernum's wrists were raw, hands shackled behind
him. He rolled to his side and felt around for the satellite
phone. Blindly, he thumbed letters on the keypad, then
rolled away, looked at the glowing screen, and memorized the control buttons. He wiggled until he felt the
phone under his back and pressed *Send*.

Zoom. A second message of gibberish to the Russian,
but it would confirm his location and, hopefully, com-
municate the shitty situation he was in.

Vernum lay still and listened. Risking those few seconds to grab the phone while the American was wedged
in the chimney had been the smartest thing he'd done
after a long day of stupid mistakes. Make another mistake, he knew, the gringo would kill him with the indifference of stepping on a bug or snuffing out a candle.

Something is missing inside that man, he thought—
and not for the first time. Kostikov at least takes pleasure in his work. The American is *Desamorado*.

Desamorado—"coldhearted"—Vernum capitalized
the word when he thought of the man.

For ten minutes, perhaps longer, the American had

been conducting a methodical search. That's what Vernum's ears told him. The man moved quietly through the bushes, stopped often and abruptly as if to trick him into running a few more yards. Then he would arc away as if following a grid. That's when Vernum would put more distance between them, but slowly, choosing every careful step. At first, of course, he had run like hell toward the tree line that marked the river. Now, though, he was circling back toward the chimney and the dirt road three hundred meters beyond it. His old car, the Lada, was there. Vernum didn't have the keys—they hadn't been with the gringo's wallet or the phone—but it wouldn't matter when the Russian finally appeared in his Mercedes.

Kostikov.

A frightening thought popped into his mind. What if that Russian replied to his text? The phone's chimes would give away his position.

Changó, damn you.

He flopped onto his stomach and pecked at the power switch with his nose, then tried with his chin. No good. So he wiggled the phone beneath his belly and forced his weight down to muffle it like a hen incubating eggs. As he waited, he listened for footsteps.

Not a sound. Nor did the Russian reply.

After another minute, he was on his feet and struggling to secure the phone in his pocket, but he dropped it. Rather than get to his knees, he squatted to retrieve the thing but lost his balance and fell back on his butt.

Only then, seeing the handcuffs so near his ankles, did he realize what was obvious to anyone not scared out of their wits. He lifted his knees to his chin, threaded his feet through his arms, and brought his hands up in front of him. *Free*—almost. It was easy now to get to his feet and pocket the phone.

Vernum decided to run while he could. He stayed in the trees by the river for fifty meters, then angled out along an old fence where bushes grew tall. To his left, the chimney spired skyward. Ahead were more trees, then the road. Vernum sprinted across an open space into trees, where he stopped in the shadows. No movement behind him, just frogs screaming from the river. No roar of a Mercedes either, but that was understandable. It would happen soon enough. For the first time, he felt confidence returning. All that stood between him and freedom were two hundred meters of open ground and that goddamn American killer— *Desamorado*.

A text to Kostikov would solve the problem.

As he took out the phone, Vernum's eyes strayed. On the ground not far away he noticed what might have been the rim of a barrel . . . or, possibly, a coil of wire. To his left, near the ruins of the building, a flicker of movement drew his attention. He hunkered low and watched. For an instant—only an instant—he saw, or imagined he saw, a willowy figure draped in white . . . or a pool of mist about the size of a young girl. Then it was gone.

Jesus Christ. Vernum, staring, reached for his necklace and whispered a welcome message to the dead as required of a *Santero*: *"Bienvenido espíritu santo . . ."*

For long seconds, he crouched there, the phone in his hand, yet he saw nothing more. Thank the gods. No matter what his brain told him about Santería, in his heart he believed. This place terrified him. Only the demon that lived in his head was comfortable here and that demon was undependable—unless hungry.

The phone. Vernum braced it against his thigh and typed: *Come with gun. Handcuffed by U.S. agent but have escaped. Will wait for you . . .*

Nearby, a twig snapped. Before he could turn, a deep voice asked, "Why did you do what you did to those girls, Vernum? What was going through your head at the time?" The words seemed to flow down from trees that created an awning above, only a few stars visible when he peered up, then spun around. Nothing there.

"Jefe . . . where are you? Man, I never said *I* did it. Just because I happen to know where some crazy peasant hid their bodies? That don't mean nothing."

Silence. He did a slow pan, expecting to see one glowing eye but didn't. *"Jefe . . .* they were just stupid *chicas.* What do you care?"

A shadow moved, bushes rustled with a sudden breeze. He strained to isolate details, but all he could hear was his heart pounding and the screaming frogs.

The voice said, "You turned on your phone, I see. When does your buddy Kostikov arrive?"

"He's not," Vernum insisted, "but that's exactly what I was doing. *Really.* We're going to kill him, right? I think he suspects something because he didn't answer me." Vernum's chuckle resembled a sob. "But don't worry. I know where he stays in Havana. Plus, that other thing I told you about—the cemetery. I bet he's there right now with that crazy fool Figuerito—"

"Drop the phone," the voice said, "or I'll shoot you where you stand."

Click-click. Distinctive—the hammer of a pistol.

Vernum let the phone fall from his hand—but, first, he hit *Send.* Risky. Blood thumping in his ears made it difficult to speak. "There. See? I'm cooperating. *Jefe,* I thought the goddamn chimney was gonna fall. It scared me, you know? That's why I—"

"Shut up and put your hands behind your head. Do it. Now face the river."

"What?"

"Return to something familiar, or maybe there's a key hidden in your car. Either way, I knew. Behavioral patterns are predictable. It's what people like you do to imitate sanity."

Vernum was thinking: *Run, he can't catch me and he knows it. That's why he won't show himself.*

"The river, Vernum. Turn around. Or tell the truth about Kostikov. Do you want to go for another boat ride?"

Slowly, Vernum contorted his hands behind his neck and pivoted toward the tree line, brick ruins and the chimney on his right. Where was that goddamn Russian? He had to do something to stall for time. "You're right," he said. "There were more than five. Girls. I already explained why."

"Don't give me that bullshit about purification. I saw what you did to them."

"*Huh*? That wasn't me. If what you found, if certain bones were missing, what do you expect out here?" With his head, Vernum motioned to the vastness of the sky but was also deciding which way to run. "There are starving dogs. Rats, man, you saw all those rats. Don't blame me for—"

Distant gunshots stopped him—*ker-WHACK* . . . *ker-WHACK*—two, the reports sharper, heavier, than a car backfiring, but still far enough away to echo through the valley.

"*What the hell?*" The gringo sounded confused at first, but then put it together. "You son of a bitch. That came from the direction of Marta's house."

Vernum was just as confused. Why had Kostikov, still kilometers away, fired a gun to acknowledge his text? Then *he* put it together. "*Whoa!* You've got this wrong, man. I never mentioned Marta Esteban—"

"If he hurt those girls"—a light flashed on, blindingly bright—"no one will ever find your body."

That was enough. Vernum ducked his head and

sprinted . . . made it four quick strides before he hit a trip wire strung at thigh level. He was struggling to get up when a hand snapped his head back, then sought his jugular.

A WILLOW'S MIST floated a candle toward the *Santero*. She materialized from the earth beyond the chimney. Female, translucent as ice.

Vernum smiled in a dreamy way. The child-like ease with which she moved triggered the first carnal stirrings within him. Comparisons sparked through his brain. A ballerina on tiptoes, a flame carried on butterfly wings. A prima dancer not yet soiled by the inevitable—adolescence, confidence, contempt. A girl who possessed fire in her fingertips.

Vernum tried to focus, anticipating the child's beauty. But it was the flame that hammered through his eyelids, a searing, thumping pain. The pain radiated, scalded his arms, his wrists, his head, until he lifted his head, finally conscious.

What happened?

His eyes did a slow inventory. He was strapped to a tree, his hands cuffed behind him. No . . . *wired* to a tree. He tried to speak, attempted to force his tongue through the stench of epoxy—his lips, once again, sealed with glue.

He gagged and coughed through his nose. His nose couldn't pump air fast enough to stem the terror building inside.

Don't leave me alone.

In his mind, Vernum called out to the gringo, or the Russian, anyone who might hear, but the sound that exited his nose resembled a howl. He inhaled to try again but caught himself.

Don't frighten the child. Another howl might send her running. The child was his only hope—if she was real.

Vernum braced his head against the tree to steady his vision. And there she was, a willowy creature clothed in white—Santería white, a virgin initiate—tiny, fluid in her movements. Yes . . . and dancing, but with an invisible partner, a lantern in one hand, her partner's hand in the other. They did a slow waltz: one, two, three . . . step . . . one, two, three . . . glide . . .

His eyes widened. Exquisite, the hope this girl aroused in him. But when she lifted the lantern higher, he saw her face, and the light went out of Vernum's world. It wasn't a girl and she wasn't dancing. It was an old woman, shuffling toward him, using a cane.

One, two, three . . . the woman stabbed at the ground for support. One, two, three . . . stab . . . Then she dragged her back foot.

Over and over she repeated the process until she was close enough to crane her head and look up. In a voice tinted with lavender and decay, she said, "Who are you? You have no right to be here." She looked him up and down. "*Fool.* Do you have any idea who I am?"

Vernum made a mewling sound of apology. The Castilian accent of Cuba's noble class had gone extinct after the Revolution. Just from her voice, he would have known, even though he had never actually seen the woman. Few in the village had. Just a glimpse or two, a silhouette through the mansion windows. At night, sometimes, music from a phonograph. Duke Ellington, tunes too aged to recognize. Old vinyl records scratched from use that popped and snapped like meat sizzling or a broken clock.

The rumors about Imelda Casanova were known to all who could hear or whisper. Only the Dowager lived alone in a mansion while most Cubans lived jammed together in tenements. Only Señorita Casanova was permitted to have maids and a housekeeper, while, even in Havana, neurosurgeons and attorneys competed for bartending jobs to make a little extra money.

Señorita Casanova. On the streets, gossipers stressed that maidenly prefix in a biting way because she had never married, yet the woman had raised a retarded cane cutter and handyman who claimed to be her grandson.

The most dangerous rumors concerned a child—or was it two or three?—who had been aborted during her trips abroad. Others said she had given the newborns away before returning to Cuba. Or worse.

The most dangerous rumor of all was a truth no one doubted. This withered old woman peering up at him had been Fidel's mistress. And she still lived under the protection of Fidel's ghost.

Only a powerful woman could have saved that simpleton Figuerito from a death sentence. Vernum despised the Dowager for that. Despised her even before the incident in the cane field. For years, he had been searching for a way to topple the bitch from a station so lofty that even a *Santero* had reason to fear her.

Now here she was, but it was Vernum who was at her mercy.

The lantern was a tin box with glass, a candle in the middle. She raised it high as if curious about the stitches in his face, then placed it at her feet. Tiny leather shoes . . . legs of onionskin within a robe that suggested the body of a much younger woman.

I'm hallucinating, he thought. She's an Egun, the spirit essence of a young girl that I . . .

Murdered.

Rather than complete the thought, he turned away and closed his eyes.

"You," she said. "You're the filthy *Santero* who had my maid's bastard child arrested. I know you. I've seen you before. Had him arrested for murder, didn't you? Yet, it was you who killed those irritating peasant girls."

Vernum made a groaning sound of helplessness—a play for sympathy—but cut it short. *The maid's bastard?*

Was she talking about Figuerito? Yes, because then she said, "Thanks to you, they took him away to the insane asylum."

Thanks to you? My god . . . it sounded as if she actually meant it. Was that possible? He opened his eyes. The woman's face was a mosaic of shadows and candlelight, her hair a rope of woven silver. A cameo seen out of focus. Real but not real. Like some women shrunken by age, she had regressed to the dimensions of childhood. Slowly, phonetically, Vernum moaned through sealed lips, "I . . . am . . . sorry." He blinked with remorse to hide the frail hope he felt.

She understood. "I bet you are."

Her inflection told him nothing. "Very . . . very . . . sorry," he repeated.

Beside the lantern was a bag. Much too nimbly for a woman her age, she knelt and spread a cloth on the ground, then began removing objects and arranging them as if preparing a picnic.

That frightened him. An Egun, as the essence of a child who had died too young, possessed the power to inhabit a youthful body, but only for short periods of time. Something else: she hadn't mentioned the American killer who had vanished. Surely she had seen him from her hiding place.

The woman kept her head down as she worked. Paused only once to look at something lying at the base of the tree—his satellite phone. The American had left it behind for some reason. He couldn't deal with what that meant, not while he was staked out like a sacrificial goat.

The old woman . . . He still hadn't gotten a clear look at her face. Vernum waited, hoping the truth would be revealed by her eyes.

"Figuerito had the brain of a turtle," she said finally. "At night, he fouled my father's house with the smell of marijuana, and he would rather play baseball than eat. Not that I cared—there's been no cook in my home for thirty years—but, come time to pay his rent, he had no money. The ungrateful son of a slut. A filthy slut who bedded baseball trash and . . . and *others* above her station. And what good is a man if he has no money?" Bitterness required her to look up for understanding . . . but Imelda Casanova did not look up.

Vernum felt a chill.

She reached into the bag and placed a thimble next to three tiny cups. "I loathed Figueroa. All through his whining childhood, then his pimple-faced teens, I loathed him. I would have put him in an asylum years ago, but for one thing"—her head tilted, but then she reconsidered—"Figueroa knew . . . *something* about me. So I tolerated the brainless bastard. But . . . I suppose even stupid boys have useful qualities. He did whatever I told him to do. Very obedient, that child. He protected me, my personal privacy, which is important to someone like myself. Tell me"—she dealt four small white shards onto the cloth as if dealing cards—"do you know what these are?"

For a moment, Vernum strained against the wire, then went limp. Yes, he knew. Four pieces of coconut rind, each sliced as round and white as a coin. Coconut represented Earth's own flesh. Life fed on life. In the little cups would be ground cowrie shells, turpentine, and powdered bluestone. This was a purification ceremony.

"Do you feel guilty about the things you did here—and in the cane fields?" The woman's voice different now, purring like a young girl in love.

Vernum nodded eagerly.

"Do you believe in redemption? Or justice? We can't have it both ways . . . Or can we?"

Vernum had to think about that before he nodded again.

"The guilt in your head, late at night," she asked, "does it pound like it's trying to escape through your eyes? Do your thoughts cut flesh and scream for purity? Do they ask what you might do to make yourself pure again?"

The body voids excess liquids when panic overwhelms. Vernum's head tilted up, then down, and he began to cry.

The woman removed an empty gourd from the bag, a sunflower . . . a fillet knife. Then she suddenly turned to look at the chimney as if surprised by an old friend. She beckoned with her hand. *"Chino Rojo,"* she called.

"*¡La Chino!* Come . . . it is time." Laughter in her voice, as if summoning her lover to the picnic.

Chino—a "Chinaman." That, at least, wasn't part of the ceremony. But then she added, "Hurry up, Raúl."

In Cuba, there was only one Raúl.

Insanity.

The woman approached with the knife in her hand and placed the gourd between his feet at the base of the tree. By then, Vernum knew that the truth didn't matter, but he struggled and wept and finally looked into her face—a face layered with wrinkles and the skulls of seven dead girls.

"When Figueroa was bad"—she smiled—"I always gave him a choice." Her fingernails sparked like flint as they struggled with his zipper, then stretched him like a chicken neck. "Why don't you sing while you make up your mind? You know the words." Her smile showed fangs. "Your favorite song. I've heard you sing it many times here."

Oggún shoro shoro, the verse went.

The knife had been cleaned and specially sharpened. When she offered the knife to Vernum, he screamed through his nose.

22

Tomlinson was startled by the bellow of an animal in the distance. He fumbled the canister and loops of film came peeling off in his hand. Black-and-white Kodak celluloid from the 1950s. He recovered and rewound the spool, careful to handle it by the ratchet tracks so as not to smudge the frames.

He took a last look at a moment in time, held the film to the light: a soldier on his ass, hat askew and embarrassed but still holding the bat after attempting to hit a . . . *softball?*

No. That couldn't be. Tomlinson was so disillusioned, his sense of justice demanded a replay. He stripped through four previous frames.

Damn . . . it *was* true. Just as Raúl had hinted in a

letter a few years before this film was shot—and probably later letters. Brother Fidel, instead of a major league
prospect, had been a spaz on the baseball diamond.

Correction: *softball field*.

But so what? It didn't matter when compared with
the achievements of a visionary leader who had done his
best to help the world change its profit-drunk, thieving
ways.

The animal bellowed again. It was a sound so primal
that Tomlinson grimaced while he tapped the canister
closed. A cow, probably. Certainly not Figgy, who had
been gone only a few minutes. Or was it Figgy's next
victim, some poor bastard who had wandered into Imelda Casanova's web of madness? Gad, what a sickening
turn of events. If the film hadn't riveted his attention, he
would have been on the shortstop's trail already. Now he
had to hurry to catch up.

There were two candles on the chair and a trusty Bic
lighter in his pocket. He went up the root cellar steps
and outside, where there were stars and a Gulf Stream
breeze but no longer a distant flashlight to mark Figgy's
destination. When his eyes adjusted, though, the chimney was visible, a black spire against a tropic sky. Behind
him, the village of Plobacho slept.

Tomlinson went down the hill with the canister
tucked under an arm, alternately fretting about his
friend and the film's contents.

The hell it doesn't matter, he thought. Baseball wasn't

just a part of Cuba's history, it was a keystone. An unrealized triad was implied by the era—Mantle, Maris, and Fidel—icons of a generation, but one of those icons had sacrificed every man's dream for the betterment of everyman.

Damn this film. The footage unmasked a lie, a generational fraud that would wound fellow travelers to the bone. It would loose a pack of right-wing hounds, a visual blood track that would craze them until they had savaged and befouled a legend who had lived the truth, a truth brighter for the flame of one small deception.

Flame.

Film burns fast, Figgy had warned him.

Tomlinson felt for the lighter in his pocket.

Why not burn it? Imelda Casanova wasn't the victim of a tragic love story. She was nuts. A child abuser who had perverted her own grandson into slavery and made him a lackey who killed on command. And for what? To protect letters and film that gave her power over the past and guaranteed her future. This was political extortion, nothing less. What other damning secrets did the crazy lady have hidden in her arsenal?

Why not, indeed?

On a path that wound along the river, he didn't stop but imagined himself stopping as he flicked a flame to life. The film canister was leaden beneath yellow foliage. For the first time, he noticed a date written in pencil: *12 Nov. 1958.*

Gad. Only weeks before Fidel and Che had led a peasant army into Havana, they had been eating hors d'oeuvres and playing slow-pitch. The context took the wind out of Tomlinson. It was the equivalent of Bob Dylan pirating lyrics, or Hendrix commuting from suburbia to fake guitar riffs.

History. He held it in his hand. He wasn't naïve. He knew that minions of the future often revised the past to fit the needs, or fears, of the present day. But destroy history? That, he could not do.

Well . . . he might, but later. There was a possibility he would need this film to buy Figgy's freedom a second time.

In Cuba, apparently, it all depended on who he had killed.

SWEET LORD ABOVE . . . the mad shortstop had struck again.

Tomlinson, for the first time in his life, hoped he was suffering the horrid flashbacks a counselor had warned him about decades ago, but this was no hallucination. He stood among bricks, a long throw to the chimney, and watched Figgy's silhouette pull a lifeless body away from a tree. Then he dropped the body as if it were a sack of potatoes and swiped his hands together like a workman congratulating himself on a job well done.

Reason enough to yell, "If he's not dead, don't kill

him, for god's sake. Figgy . . . ? I *mean it*." Tomlinson set off at a run but soon slowed because it was dark. A lot of holes and bricks to trip him. He stumbled anyway, and the film canister went careening down a grade into more darkness, where there were bushes and god knows what else in a place where the air had the weight of illness. He had to use the lighter and hunt around on his knees. By the time he found the canister and confirmed the film was okay, the shortstop was close enough for Tomlinson to speak in a normal voice. Impossible to sound normal, however, under these conditions. "Is he still alive? I know CPR, if he's alive. But if he's dead . . . Christ, I don't know what to do. What's the plan? Take him to your usual spot and throw him off a cliff?"

Figuerito cast a long shadow in the lighter's flame. "There are nice mango trees on the way to the sea," he said, "unless you have a better idea. I hope you do. At the house, I didn't see the donkey, so it won't be so easy this time." He paused, staring down at Tomlinson. "Brother, I warned you about lighting matches around old film. You trying to get us in trouble?"

The Bic went out. Tomlinson got to his feet. He walked toward the body, which was hidden by distance and weeds. "You're sure he's dead?"

"Oh yeah. Anyone lose that much blood, they gonna die. Two big gourds full, plus what the earth drank as an offering."

Tomlinson stopped. *"Gourds?"*

Figuerito's mind was on something else. "Did you watch the film?"

"What do you mean, 'gourds'? Oh. Well . . . I held it up to the light. Just a few dozen frames, but I know why your grandmother wants the footage protected." On tiptoes, he got a glimpse of one dead hand. "Any idea who that person is?"

"It's the bad *Santero*," Figgy said. "I didn't kill him, she did. But I took his phone and his money. His phone was next to the tree." He patted his back pocket to confirm both were safe.

"The guy, his name's Vernum, you said. Vernum attacked you, right? Self-defense. You had no choice in the matter. An open-and-shut case. I mean, no one in their right mind would . . . Well, you know what I mean." Tomlinson felt faint.

"In Key West, sure, that was true. You don't remember? His face is still a mess from my baseball shoe. Lots of stitches. It made me happy, seeing that. I wanted to kill him, but my *abuela* is still very quick for her age." Figgy started toward an open space between the chimney and a crumbling brick wall. "Come on. You can help me look for her since you understand about the film."

Tomlinson hurried after the little man. "You're telling me your grandmother—she's, what, seventy, eighty years old?—that she murdered the guy?"

"Either her or the spirits came out of the ground. That happens in this place sometimes. The Egun spirit, she can inhabit a human person to, you know, do her bidding. Have sex with a man, if she wants. Or steal his shit or even kill him. My *abuela* was a Santería *novia* in her youth. Ask her, but"—the shortstop turned to stress his point—"do not make her mad."

Tomlinson thought, *No shit, Sherlock*, while his brain debated *Are they both nuts?* No jury in the world would believe the little Cuban's spiel. But he also remembered hearing gunfire. "Oh . . . Oh! She shot him, you're saying. Okay. It's a little easier to picture a woman that age—"

"Brother," Figgy interrupted, "what she did was cut off his rooster. I always wondered if she would do it. Now I know." He turned left past the wall and angled down a hill shaped like a bunker. "The place I'm going to show you I promised I never would, but I'm worried because you're right. Even three years ago, she had lost a few steps. Her bad leg, you know? They built it for her back when she could dance."

"Built her . . . a prosthetic leg?"

"I don't know what this is, *prosthetic*. I'm talking about the place I'm taking you. There were bombs in those days. Like a shelter, you know? This was before I was born and before my mother left for Moscow because I was so much trouble."

"*Whoa!* amigo. You can't blame yourself for that."

"If it's true, why not? Stupid boys get what they deserve. The shelter, though, they built that back when there were bombs."

They, Tomlinson translated, were the Castros. The cruelty of Imelda Casanova was equally apparent. "No child deserves to be called stupid. That was a shitty thing for her to say, Figgy."

"My mother? She didn't say anything. How could she? They don't have telephones in Moscow where she lives." Figuerito stopped. "Strike a match," he said.

Tomlinson used the lighter and watched his friend descend into a trench lined with bricks that was more like a ramp, bushes all around. Beneath camouflage netting was a metal gate with a chain and padlock, the gate open. "Wait here," he said, then looked back after opening a steel door. "If she comes out holding a knife, don't ask questions, just run. You're faster, but she might make me kill you anyway."

FROM WHERE Tomlinson stood on the side of the hill, he couldn't see a road, but he knew a road was there when he noticed headlights ricocheting between the trees and sky. A bad road with lots of bumps, for a car traveling so fast. Beyond, to the southeast, distant flames were a candle in the darkness. A peasant's house on fire, it looked like.

Shit-oh-dear. The Russian came into his mind. The *Santero*'s Key West wingman in the black Mercedes. But what was he, or anyone else, doing out here in Fumbuck, Cuba, at this hour?

Tomlinson didn't need a watch to feel the starry weight of midnight.

His logician brain shifted to the phone in Figgy's pocket while his extrasensory powers probed the horizon. Not easy because, first, his receptors had to pierce a veil of agony; a century of pain lingered here. His lens soon broke free and there was contact: heavy . . . very heavy—a human presence out there. A gelid void: intelligence with a functioning heart.

Was it Ford? The biologist, in certain moods, transmitted a similarly scary vibe. Possible. The message Tomlinson had left with the hotel doorman read *En route biggest house in Plobacho to return what was taken. Meet there or No Más anchored Cojimar. PS: Giant Russki chasing us. Float on and watch your ass.*

Tomlinson concentrated on the road and fine-tuned his reception. No . . . it wasn't Ford. The biologist drove like an old woman, even in a rental. Yet, Ford was out there somewhere—a green aura, blue-tinted—and seemed to be pressing closer.

The cell phone, his logician mind reminded him. That's the problem, dumbass. The phone Figgy's carrying has a GPS in it.

Something else he noticed: the odor of woodsmoke, sudden and fresh. Very close. He changed angles and saw a spark spiral out of the bushes not far from where he stood. The chamber within was vented, and someone had lit a fire. Once again: shit-oh-dear.

Tomlinson tapped at the steel door, then opened it a crack. "Figgy . . . ? Oh, Figuerito, I think we might have company."

No response. He flicked the lighter and went through into a hall made of rebar and concrete, walls three feet thick, with a ceiling so low he had to duck. It actually was a bomb shelter. A second steel door was open. Down a ramp, along another hall, where a light allowed him to pocket the Bic before his thumb blistered.

"Figgy? Uhh . . . Miz Casanova? I'm not armed, just a decent man trying to help a shipmate."

He exited into a room that was a small office. A steel desk, military green, maps on two walls, kerosene lamps on hooks in the ceiling, only one lit. On a table, a portable shortwave radio next to a battery-operated phone, the old kind with a crank. Wire snaked through a hole in the wall—antennas. Another steel door at the back of the room was closed. The rivets reminded him of a watertight hatch on a ship.

Damn. No wonder Figgy couldn't hear him. This was more than a bomb shelter. It was headquarters for a few high-ranking survivalists. Only two names came to mind—or three, counting Imelda Casanova. But why, during a nuclear war, would the Castro brothers seques-ter themselves with only one mistress?

They wouldn't. In a space this small, mayhem could be guaranteed.

He placed the film canister on a chair and sniffed. Faint odor of lavender, and woodsmoke from the fire that had to be in an adjoining room. It was quiet down here below ground. A good spot for a nervous man to breathe deeply while his heart slowed to normal. On the desk by the radio was a logbook, pages yellow with age. He removed a lantern from its hook and flipped through a few entries, then several more. Ham radio gibberish, mostly, but one grabbed his attention:

25-10-62. Radio SWAN Island. Pro-fascista tráfico. U.S./CIA 19:23 hrs. Putas mentiras . . . All entered in a flowing, feminine hand.

Putas mentiras meant "lying whores." The date was in transposed Latino: 25 October 1962. A dangerous period. The Cuban Missile Crisis. It was the Kennedy-Khrushchev era, when the world had teetered on the brink of nuclear holocaust.

Tomlinson considered the concrete fortress. Hell, no wonder they had built this place. There were probably simi-lar bunkers spaced around Cuba in case bombs fell while the Castros were on the road. The logbook entry explained the letter Fidel had written on the day JFK died. Swan Island, as sailors who had transited the Canal knew, was off Honduras. Tomlinson hadn't made the connection. Apparently, the CIA had transmitted radio propaganda from there.

The SWAN lies.

So what else was new?

Fidel had also instructed his mistress—perhaps his former mistress by then—to destroy everything. Imelda Casanova had obviously ignored those orders. Tomlinson closed the book and moved around the room. It was a small space, cluttered but orderly, and a treasure trove of Castro memorabilia. Somehow, Juan Rivera had learned that Figuerito had access to such things. He had bartered freedom in trade for blue-chip collectibles to be sold on the Internet.

Comrade, my ass, Tomlinson thought. *Yet another soul bites the big green weenie.*

On a shelf was a stack of stuff: a cartoon of Uncle Sam with fangs like Dracula, *Look* magazines, 1960 to '63, Marilyn Monroe, John Wayne, LBJ on the covers . . . Oh, and the Buddhist monk who had set himself ablaze to protest U.S. involvement in Vietnam. Very heavy and sad, sad mojo. Time had stopped in this bomb shelter. All inhabitants had turned to dust.

Stored in a box was happier news, the trophy from Figuerito's photo: an ornate silver cup with seams like a baseball. Big; tarnished with a greenish black patina. Tomlinson lifted the trophy and read the inscription:

INTERNATIONAL LEAGUE CHAMPIONS
1959

That was all. The name of the winning team hadn't been added. Inside the cup was a *Miami Herald* clipping from the same year. Dateline: Havana, Cuba.

> During a game between the Havana Sugar Kings and Minneapolis Millers, a late-inning celebration degenerated into firecrackers and gunfire. Minnesota's third-base coach, Frank Verdi, was struck, as was Leo Cardenas, the Sugar Kings' shortstop. Neither was seriously injured, but three U.S.-born pitchers for the Kings fled the stadium and are still missing. The game and the series have been canceled according to . . .

Tomlinson stopped reading when he heard the door to the next room open.

"Figgy," he said, turning. "Look what I found." He hoisted the trophy.

Figuerito grinned and made a fist as if he'd just sunk a long putt. "Now the old woman has done two good things."

"Yeah?" Tomlinson looked past him, seeing a woodstove and a table set with china for two. "Can I meet her?"

"That's the first good thing," the shortstop replied. "You don't have to. She's dead. Now there's no promise to break when I show you what I've been lying about."

Tomlinson was so untracked and confused—then fascinated by what awaited on the other side of the door—that he wasted several minutes gawking before he remembered to say, "Figgy, we've got to ditch the *Santero*'s cell phone. Or . . . how about we move our asses and hide?"

23

Anatol Kostikov, leaving Marta's house, watched flames in his rearview mirror and ruminated over a likely investigative tagline: *Sex deviant sets fire to destroy evidence.*

Workable if he pitched the theory to the right Cuban official. Someone sloppy enough not to bother with DNA, or interviews, or details that had more to do with arson than sex crimes. The key was killing Vernum first; make it look like self-defense, then planting evidence enough to stifle an investigation. To hell with what anyone else thought or said. He was a senior Russian agent, by god, and Cuba, once again, was in his country's debt.

On the passenger seat was a bag. It contained all the

evidence he needed. Under the seat was another pint of vodka. He needed that, too, plus a few more pills.

The vodka went down with a nice burn.

On the dashboard, the GPS tracker marked the location where Vernum's phone had gone dead ten minutes earlier. The would-be spy was two kilometers away, if pursued on foot, five kilometers by road, but driving was still the only choice. Stupid to leave his Mercedes near a crime scene. Plus, along with stomach cramps, Anatol now had something else to worry about. He was bleeding. Not badly, but enough. A bullet had furrowed the fat on his left side when a pistol magically appeared in Marta's hands. She'd shot him. Fired three times, eyes closed, before he'd slapped her to the ground.

The Russian gulped from the bottle and watched the scene repeat itself in his head. The obnoxious brat screaming when he grabbed her, teeth snapping like an animal. Then the mother was there, her face ashen in the headlights, bringing her hands up, up, up, which should have been warning enough, but he had been complacent in a country that didn't allow even Party members to own guns.

It was his only excuse for what happened next. Those scenes, Anatol did not want to replay in his mind. Among the worst was later, when he tried to put a bullet in the woman's skull, but the stolen Glock was loaded with dummies that wouldn't fire because even cops weren't trusted in this tropic shithole nation. The Latina and girls had bolted, while he rushed to pilfer a few bullets before they got to the trees. The scene had stayed with him, Marta's expression of horror, and the burden of his own sloppiness.

Goddamn . . . *disgraceful*. In the same day, he had been robbed in a public restroom, then shot by a peasant female. Him, Anatol, the descendant of legendary Cossack warriors.

To spare his reputation, if nothing else, he had to find Vernum. This time, do every little thing right. Place the evidence just so and cover his tracks. Once that was done, he was free to turn his attention to Fidel's letters, then the CIA agent. If he was methodical—and his luck changed—he might even ship home an antique Harley or three when his job was done.

Another gulp of vodka allowed him to linger on the lone masterstroke in this long, shitty day. After so many screwups, he had stepped back and rallied. The seasoned professional had asked himself a professional's question: How would a sexual deviant kill three victims and cover his tracks?

The resulting finesse was a nice touch he would share with that worm Vernum.

The answer: burn them all alive.

ANATOL SKIRTED a cluster of trees, his eyes on the GPS tracker, while the house burned in the far, far distance. He was so intent on his quarry that had it not been for the scent of blood, he would have kept going up the hill, past a derelict chimney, then another sixty meters.

Metallic iodine and brass. Distinctive, that odor, if the sample was large enough. Some of his most satisfying achievements were linked to the smell of blood, but it could also signal danger.

He crouched and pocketed the tracker but not the pistol. Even though he had dimmed the LED screen, his vision required several seconds to adjust. Head tilted, he inhaled . . . moved a few steps; sniffed again, and followed his nose into the trees. A penlight came out and threw a red beam. On a blanket were cups, seashells, and a sunflower as if spread for a picnic. A couple of pumpkin-like vessels nearby. Then what looked like an empty garbage bag, but it wasn't a bag—it was the goddamn stupid *Santero*.

I can make this work, Anatol told himself. He believed that until he was standing over Vernum and saw how the would-be spy had died.

Idiot. What brand of stupid sex deviant allowed himself to be wired to a tree so an even crazier sex deviant could cut off his cock? Closer inspection added to the puzzle. Vernum's wrists showed abrasions, but his hands were free, and there were no defensive wounds. So . . . he had been unconscious during the assault, or—Anatol had to project himself into the mind of a sick deviant—or Vernum was such a masochist, he had welcomed his own mutilation.

Either way, it would be tough to convince authorities that the murderer of two cops and an old man had, while taking a breather, parted with his own cock willingly.

Shit.

Profanity was better in Russian. He stomped away from the body, hissing, *"Der'mo. Der'mo. Der'mo!"* Then the finale: *"Eto pizdets!"*

Total screwed-up madness. This sort of crap didn't happen to Anatol Kostikov. Never had he experienced such a streak of bad luck.

To hell with it. Vernum *had* to be the fall guy. There was no other way. If a senior Russian intelligence agent couldn't fool these Caribbean hicks, who could?

He stretched on surgical gloves. Then did a slow recon of the area in darkness. Insects and frogs cloaked the sound of his weight. He moved from tree to tree, knelt for long seconds in the weeds. In the distance, the saffron flicker of Marta's house was useful. With only four bullets in his gun, a brighter backdrop made for better target acquisition.

There was no target. Even so, Anatol returned to the corpse, thinking, *Someone is out there.*

It was more than intuition. Vernum's body was still warm.

He popped the last of the wire bindings and went to

work. The scenario was this: he had surprised the Cuban, who was with another sex deviant. They had bragged about assaulting some local girls and their mother. Because of his status with the embassy, Anatol had an obligation to Cuban law. They had argued. Vernum had shot him. As to how the idiot got his cock cut off, why ask a respected Russian agent? No goddamn idea—that must have happened after he'd left to seek medical attention.

Into Vernum's hand went the little Sig Sauer pistol taken from Marta. Fingerprints would register on the barrel even though the dead hand failed to grip it. Three brass casings were scattered nearby. He added subtle touches: a bit of hair from Marta's brush, hair from the two girls. Then a swatch of cloth from the obnoxious brat's pink-and-white pajamas, and a robe he had torn off the mother—this was just before the goddamn Glock had misfired. He spattered each with Vernum's blood—just a little—then smeared footprints.

Enough.

He took out the GPS tracker and went up the hill. Stopped twice to grimace and clutch his side. The bullet wound was insignificant. The cramps had returned.

A BOMB SHELTER . . .

Anatol recognized the construction immediately. A Type 4, Level 1-A Complete, designed by Russian engineers, then reassembled in Cuba. He wasn't old enough to have served during that period, but he was old enough to remember, and to appreciate, similar shelters he had seen on the island and in what was becoming the New Soviet Union.

Who knew? Maybe bomb shelters would be needed again.

He started down the ramp, then dropped to a knee and waited, pistol ready. Someone was following him. He felt sure, even though he hadn't seen or heard anything. On a night as dark as this, there were two possible explanations: he was either paranoid or there was someone out there wearing night vision. Not the cheap third-generation stuff either. CIA-quality.

Yeah. To a thirty-year vet of clandestine services, the explanation felt right.

Under any other circumstances, he would have called his contact at Cuban intelligence. The DGI could have a chopper here with an ops team hanging out the doors before the American escaped. But he couldn't risk that. Not now, with Vernum lying out there, dead and dickless, and Marta's house ablaze.

A better idea was to drop everything and turn the tables. Hunt the hunter. He was, after all, the expert who had taught the world's elite to track and kill. In his soul, in his marrow, that's what he wanted to do. But there was another problem: the stomach cramps were worsening. The last time Vernum's phone had pinged a

signal was twenty-eight minutes ago. The ping had orig-
inated from here, the entrance of the shelter, but there
was no guarantee the phone was somewhere inside.

Vernum certainly was not.

To hell with the phone. A Type 4 shelter contained
everything four or fewer people needed to survive a nuclear attack. That included food, storage, sleeping cells,
a kitchenette with woodstove—which was not a require-
ment in Cuba—and, of course, a chemical toilet with a
septic tank.

That's what Anatol required, a toilet, and he required
it soon.

Three minutes he stood guard, which was less than
protocol demanded, then slipped inside—but, first, removed the padlock and chain to reduce the risk of being
trapped within. Clearing a room couldn't be rushed, especially a room already lit by a kerosene lantern. Someone had been here, or was still here—Vernum's killer or
killers, judging from footprints. Bloody smudges suggested a person with small shoes had been accompanied
by a man with feet almost thirty centimeters long. He
peered around a concrete portal, then followed his pistol
into an office area crammed with old military furniture
and hardware.

Fidel, he thought, or Raúl. This was one of their
hideouts.

It made sense. Their mistress Imelda Casanova lived
nearby.

Check under desk and table. Stop, listen, sniff the air. All clear, and the door to the next room was open wide. He repeated the process and entered the kitchenette, where the woodstove was still burning. But why on a balmy November night?

Burning evidence, he decided.

The stove could wait. The cramps could not.

He carried the lantern to the next door and placed his ear against it. These prefab shelters were little more than sewage culverts designed to be dropped into three trenches that intersected. When the trenches were covered, occupants enjoyed the illusion of spaciousness because the tunnels branched into wings that could be sealed as private rooms. He had yet to reach one of those terminals. A moment later, he did. To his right, behind a vinyl curtain, was a cramped bathing area with a hand pump. In an adjoining stall was a Russian-made commode that resembled a wedding cake.

Thank god.

Training, though, demanded that the entire shelter first be secured. There were two doors here, both made of steel. One sealed an intersecting branch. The other continued along the length of the tunnel. He placed the lantern on the floor and chose the tangent branch. It opened into a dead-end room that was damp and smelled of mold. He thought it was empty until he retrieved the lamp. Inside was a religious shrine: sunflower and cane stalks tied into bundles, beads and cowrie shells, a statuette of the Virgin Mary on a ledge streaked with candy-colored wax from a thousand spent candles.

On a lower ledge were bottles of rum that had evaporated and cigars rotted to dust. Except for one bottle that was full, recently uncorked. A fresh cigar was balanced on the bottle's lip. They sat apart above three loaves of concrete that appeared structural until he moved closer.

No . . . they were tiny crypts, infant-sized. Long ago, names had been scrawled in wet cement. Anatol didn't care. He was more interested in what lay at the foot of the graves: a stainless fillet knife streaked with fresh blood.

Perfect. Fingerprints would validate his story.

Santería. It fit with the murder of a *Santero*.

THE LAST ROOM he cleared was the largest. It was a double concrete cell, where an old woman gowned in white lay sleeping, he thought at first, but then realized she was dead. Candles, burning in sets of three, sat on abutting nightstands.

Fidel's mistress?

On the walls, photos in ornate frames proved that, at the end at least, Raúl was the only Castro she had cared about.

Good riddance, he thought. All of you. Burn in hell.

The room stunk of lavender and old age. Woodsmoke added an acidic edge. His stomach churned. All he wanted to do was use the commode, complete his search for the letters, then get the hell out. Protocol, however, demanded the basics. He'd already checked the bed and behind curtains that served as closet space. All that was left was a grated bulkhead that, he guessed, housed pipes, pumps, and conduit required for survival underground.

He took a last look at the old woman. Attractive, possibly . . . for a Cuban—six decades ago. Dusty sheets, no splattering of blood visible. This dried-up crone hadn't killed the *Santero*, but details of her condition might be useful. He didn't touch the corpse. He used his nose and eyes. Body fluids stain. Decomposition starts when the heart stops.

Convinced, he hurried to the steel grating that was flanged like a door, but wider and lower. It was locked. *Strange* . . . No lock was visible. He rattled the bars and raised the lantern. Yellow light spangled the floor within. Anatol squatted. He pressed an eye to an open square . . . and, for the first time that day, he grinned, and marveled at his sudden good luck.

"So beautiful," he whispered. "So very, very . . . oh my god. You are mine."

Hypnotic, the graceful lines that greeted him: a duo of Harley-Davidson Sportsters from 1957 . . . possibly '58. The year was unimportant. Same with the patinas of dust. Same with his mild, fleeting disappointment when he saw there were only two, not three, motorcycles. Otherwise, it was better than finding gold. Step back half a century and these machines were fresh from the showroom floor. Tires were flat, of course, but, my god, even the rubber looked pretty good.

Dazed, he stood. Had someone been maintaining these fine machines? Apparently so. Vernum had lied to him from the start, the freak. After all, the Harleys were here, not hidden in the cemetery west of Havana. Either that or the old woman's grandson had lied to everyone. That made sense. Figueroa Casanova, as a traitor, would be a shameless liar. Details were unimportant now. The Harleys were his—or would be after he snuck them aboard a troop transport disguised as a cruise liner.

Anatol couldn't take his eyes off those sweet, sweet classic lines. Pristine, the motorcycles leaned on kickstands with a gangster swagger. Spoke wheels, *Sportster* in italics cast in steel. Chrome everywhere: hydraulic forks and drums, swooping handlebars and headlamps. Fenders and fuel pod on the nearest bike were brilliant jet-stream blue. The other Sportster was red—candy-apple red of a hue that pained his heart and knotted his stomach.

No . . . it was another goddamn cramp.

He grunted, clutched his side, and groaned. Kostikov wasn't a garrulous man. It was unlike him to speak to leather motorcycle upholstery, but he did, saying, "You would be ruined. I'll get you out of here before she starts to stink."

Imelda Casanova had been dead for at least two days, probably longer. He had seen enough corpses to know.

Running was risky, so he hurried through the tunnel, taking short, fast steps, until he was close to the commode and out of danger. His belt buckle required both hands. He placed the lantern, then the pistol, on the floor and closed the curtain. Once he was seated, stomach cramps took charge. Finally, when he was comfortable enough to retrieve the pistol, he had to snake an arm under the curtain to find the damn pistol.

It wasn't there.

What? The pistol *had* to be there.

His fingers probed until they finally made contact, but what they found wasn't a Glock 9mm. He snatched the object anyway and held it up to see . . . his stolen wallet.

Shock—rare in KGB veterans, yet his thoughts mired as a voice said in Spanish, "You're a big target, Kostikov. If you have other weapons, slide them under the curtain. Slowly. I can see you just fine from here."

The lantern. Because of the damn lantern, Anatol realized, his silhouette was visible from any angle, yet he was blinded from seeing anything *but* the curtain. Well . . . that and his own shoes where pants were piled around his ankles. Never had he discussed such a predicament with aspiring agents. Bluffing, congenial manipulation, however, were part of daily fieldcraft. Even he could decipher the accent of an American speaking Spanish.

"Ah," he said, "how are my friends at Langley? Forgive, I am expecting you, but have—how you say?—a case of shits bad."

The lantern. He stared at the thing while he hurried to clean himself. Molotov cocktails, homemade incendiaries. He considered the curtain's fabric: waxed cotton, material used for military tents before noninflammables became popular. A natural accelerant.

The American said, "You don't have the shits. It's uranium poisoning."

Kostikov stiffened for an instant, eyes wide as he listened.

"Vernum Quick, he put a few drops on a sandwich he gave you. He told me all about it. Jerked chicken. Remember what you ate in Jamaica?"

Nauseating, the bile that hiccupped into Anatol's throat. Whether from the sandwich or the possibility it was true could not be distinguished. "Is lie," he said. "You think I not know symptoms? What you expect if you torture such a liar as Vernum? Torture"—he used a scolding tone—"is illegal from Geneva Convention. Too bad if international headlines you are in. But only I see body out there, huh? Is possible I might forget. You understand?"

The voice replied, "Guilt has killed better men than Vernum Quick. Cooperate, maybe you'll live long enough to get to a hospital. Last chance, Kostikov—if you have a weapon, slide it under the curtain."

Anatol crouched, hoping for movement, a sound. Several seconds passed. "See?" he said. "Is okay. Only my phone I have here. Is how I know Cuban military is on way." His hand moved to the wall, then down the wall, where he slipped his fingers around the lantern's wire handle. "Me, I have much time. You, my friend, not so much. Unless a deal we strike, perhaps. Would you like see phone as proof?"

"Reception fifteen feet underground?" The American found that amusing. "Here's the only deal you'll get." An old logbook fell from somewhere and slapped the concrete at Anatol's feet. A ballpoint pen rolled free from the pages. "You're going to write a confession. Marta Esteban and her daughters, Sabina and Maribel. You set their house on fire. You killed them. Write it down, then sign it. In Spanish, not Russian. Or English, if it's any better. What happened to the KGB? You used to be big on language skills."

The woman and her brats were dead? Finally, some good news. It was something he could work with, but then another cramp caused Anatol to lose focus. Recovery time, a moment to think, was needed. He snatched up the book, asking, "How are names spelled?" Then scribbled them down before adding *Yo mató estas mujeres*—"I killed these females."

He signed with a false name that was close enough to fool an American and pushed the book under the curtain—but only halfway. As he did, he slipped one foot clear of his pants, then the other. He was free, ready to move.

The lantern. Anatol lifted it, as if to show he was done, while his eyes were fixed, waiting for a hand or the American's shoes to appear.

"Your Spanish sucks, but the signature looks familiar. Yeah . . . I've seen that signature before. For some reason, I hoped you were smarter. Weird, huh? Two grown men and we're still playing the same goddamn stupid game. Fool's Mate."

Where the hell was that voice coming from? Tunnels echo. Anatol's ears tried to zero in . . . until he realized what the American meant. Another stupid error. The name he'd used was on a false ID in the wallet the American had stolen.

"I left your emergency money," the voice said. "Think of it as professional courtesy. Now sign the goddamn paper again. Your real name . . . *Anatol*."

"But I did—" A searing contraction cut off his air. "I did, but you haven't looked at it closely." Sweat beaded, slid down his cheeks, as he nudged the logbook another inch into the hall. "I'm sick. You speak of professionalism. You, whose head I own when DGI comes, but I would not give you to fools of DGI. A deal we will make, huh?" His knuckles whitened on the lantern handle. "You are calling General Anatol Kostikov a liar?"

The voice replied, "Stand up, and I'll make it quick."

Click-click. The metallic latching of a pistol hammer

always, always signaled an end to negotiations. Anatol winced but wasn't afraid. Training took over. When cornered, attack. In Ukraine, the ancient land of Cossacks, soldiers entered battle with the same ancient war cry. A guttural howl. That howl carried Anatol into the hall, lantern slashing, but the goddamn curtain came with him, draped over his head like a shroud.

Snap-Snap. Snap. Three plastic-on-plastic reports. The Russian heard the sounds, but they held no meaning except that each coincided with sudden hammering blows that stabbed him twice in the thigh and once in the kneecap.

Anatol tumbled forward onto the floor, aware in numb consciousness that he was bleeding . . . and that the curtain he could not shed from his body was on fire.

My silent pistol, he realized. *Bastard shot me with my own weapon.*

The humiliation was enough to rally the giant to his feet. "You want fight Kostikov?" He slapped at flames in his hair and roared. "Come, you *pizdă*! Like men!"

24

Figueroa and his strange friend, Tomlinson, were on their haunches, backs flat against the wall, when the Russian peered into the space where they were hiding and saw the motorcycles.

That was several minutes ago.

An understanding of Russian wasn't required to know the giant would return. He wanted those Harleys. In Figuerito's life, only two outsiders had ever seen them and they had lost their lives during their first attempt. Big men, difficult to drag, but it had to be done. He had loved these pretty blue and red machines since childhood. His earliest memory was of someone—his grandmother, possibly—revving the engines as he lay in a crib, or box, too young to talk but old enough to cherish the vibrations and the sleepy odor of exhaust fumes after she had closed the door tight.

His next memory: darkness, alone and thirsty, but too content to make a sound when someone—*definitely* his grandmother—entered the bedroom carrying something small and naked and dead while candles burned. The familiar odor of cigar smoke had accompanied the woman's sobbing, then her rage.

For years afterward, dozing beside those rumbling engines was Figgy's favorite way to drift off—and one of the rare recreations the old woman had allowed him.

There was no doubt the Russian would soon return. Even so, the strange gringo sighed a *Whew* of relief when he was gone and whispered, "That was a close one. We should have run for it, man. No matter how drunk some *bandito* happens to be—a pissed-off husband is a better example—hiding is the surest way to get your ass kicked. Next time, you should listen to me."

Tomlinson got to his feet; peeked through the steel grating, then tested the dead bolt at the top of the frame. "Gad, he almost ripped out the damn screws. What a monster. Just gave it a little shake. See for yourself. Dude, we've got to get out of here. He cut the *pinga* off that poor bastard and we both know it. Even with me, superstition only goes so far."

Figueroa, speaking of his grandmother, replied, "Just because she's dead doesn't mean her temper has improved. No blood on the sheets, I understand, but it's different here. Her spirit can come out of the earth and do all sorts of nasty shit. How long you think she's been dead?"

Tomlinson took another look through the grating. "Maybe he's not coming back. Christ, I hope he's not coming back."

Figuerito only shrugged. "Did you hear what he said about the motorcycles?"

"He spoke in Russian, for god's sake. But look—he closed the door, at least, when he left. That's a good sign. I think I heard another door close, too. It's what people do when they're not coming back. A guy that size, what's he want with a Harley? These old classics"—Tomlinson was already coveting the bike of jet-stream blue—"are half the size of a modern-day hogster."

Figuerito was becoming irritated. The hippie was always offering advice or lecturing him on the difference between right and wrong. Surprisingly uncooperative, too, when they had pried open a crate stamped SER-VILLETAS SANITARIAS but which, in fact, contained a pair of old gangster-style Thompson submachine guns.

"We have many bullets," Figgy whispered. "Here . . . see?" He produced a weathered box of .45 caliber Remingtons. "Show me how the guns work."

Tomlinson recoiled as if the box contained *mierda*. He didn't want to hold a machine gun either, although he was impressed with the gold lettering that read LOYAL BEYOND DEATH—FULGENCIO BATISTA.

"Geezus Christ. General Rivera would sell us both into slavery to get his hands on these babies. A tampon crate is exactly where they belong. Put them away."

This was all very confusing. "Would you rather use the guns as clubs? They're heavy enough, I suppose, but he's a big one, that Russian. It's safer, I think, to shoot him."

"Don't you get it? I'm not shooting anyone. There's got to be another way out of here." The hippie, whispering, went to the back wall, where there was an air vent, the wall streaked with mold beneath a low cement ceiling. "You've got to get off this killing kick. Seriously, it goes against every moral code and law—even in the minor leagues. Violence just begets more violence."

Figgy had one of the Thompson machine guns on his lap. "Of course. Why do you think I want to shoot him? The problem is, the old woman didn't mind me playing with the motorcycles, but I wasn't allowed to touch these"—he turned the gun upside down—"and shooting is more complicated than I thought." He pressed a button, gave a yank, and the magazine drum popped free. It resembled the film canister, only thicker. "Hey . . . do the bullets go in here?"

"How the hell would I know?"

Figueroa felt his ears warming, but he concentrated on a lever at the front of the drum. He pushed, pulled, then pried. One side of the drum broke free and clattered like a hubcap when it hit the floor. *"¡Ay, caramba!"*

he said, looking inside. "Lots of little spaces in here." He began inserting cartridges. "Hey . . . they fit. Okay . . . once it's loaded, then what?"

Tomlinson was at a rack of metal shelves, moving boxes to see what was behind them. He didn't bother to respond.

Figuerito didn't like that. They were running out of time. "Brother. You're from Florida. Everyone in Florida knows about guns. Have you forgotten the *bandito* in the parking lot? And the baseball team, the ones who chased me from Texas? Even in the dugout, their catcher had a—"

Tomlinson threw his hands up but kept his voice down. "I swear to god, I don't know how to load a Thompson submachine gun. If we could just wiggle through a crawl space or, hell, fire up those bikes, maybe, and . . . Geezus, the damn tires are flat. What next?"

"There's a bicycle pump," Figuerito said. "In front of you, next to the red can. But don't use it all. Later, that's when I'll need it. The gasoline, after I shoot him."

"Does it work?"

"The gasoline? Three years ago, of course. Harley-Davidsons don't run on diesel. Do they use diesel in the *Estados Unidos*?"

Tomlinson tested the tire pump's plunger a few times, but his attention drifted to something lying atop a box. A baseball card with sewing needles stuck in it like some type of Santería curse. On the back: Iván Bárbaro Figueroa, Birmingham, Alabama, Tigers, 1980. He'd hit .344 in '78, but then suffered a hitless two-year slump that, presumably, had ended his career. Tomlinson's blue eyes moved from the card to Figgy, then back to the card. Too many similarities not to ask, "Are you related to this guy?"

Figuerito was busy reattaching the magazine to the machine gun but glanced over. "*Him?* He was an outfielder. Brother, even in English I know that."

"I don't know . . . something about the ears, his chin, the whole look. Are you sure?"

"To an outfielder? My *abuela* would not have ordered me to chain a relative from the outfield in the cellar if Iván Bárbaro ever came back. He didn't come back, but she kept that ugly picture, so I know what he looks like."

On the back of the card, Tomlinson read *Born Pinar del Río, Cuba. Five feet four, two hundred and five pounds.* "A righty. Geezus, you'd need a backhoe to knock the guy off his pins. Uhh . . . speaking of pins . . ."

"I spit on his name, the thief, and my *mu-maw* cursed him. Before I was born, there were three motorcycles and three nice machine guns. One was painted gold, which, of course, matched these pretty words." His finger traced the inscription LOYAL BEYOND DEATH. "I blame Iván Bárbaro for her dislike of baseball. For firing the maid, too, who, even as a youth, I knew had beautiful pink *chichis.*"

Tomlinson shrugged his understanding. "He stole them both. I get it."

"No, just the motorcycle and the gun. Isn't that enough? Gold's my favorite color."

After a last look at the baseball card, Tomlinson returned to the moment, while, under his feet, the floor vibrated with the sudden impact of a big man falling on cement.

Figuerito didn't notice. He pulled the gun's bolt back and let it snap into position. *Success.* Then bounced to his feet saying, "Hope I didn't put the bullets in backwards. What would happen, you think? I don't want to shoot myself. If I shoot myself, then it will be up to you to . . ." He froze, crouched, and thrust up a warning hand. "*Listen.* Did you hear that?"

From the echoing distance, through two steel doors, a man's bellow reached them, then one familiar word in Russian.

Pizdă.

Figgy turned to his friend. "The Russian's calling you names again." He pulled the dead bolt clear and pushed the steel grating open. "Brother, that makes one of us mad."

SOMEWHERE IN THE TUNNEL, beyond the bedroom, furniture crashed. There came the thump of heavy flesh on concrete, of hollow bone hitting bone, and the clang of a steel door banging open . . . or slamming closed. No way to know.

Figueroa, with the machine gun at waist level, paused at the foot of his grandmother's bed. Another steel door slammed . . . then silence. Woodsmoke carried an unfamiliar chemical odor. He sniffed the air, turned, and spoke silently to the dead woman: *Stop nagging. I'll burn everything, just as promised. Letters and movies and photos. Even the motorcycles. But*—he stepped back fearing a sign of protest—*I didn't say when I'd burn them . . . did I?*

Candle flames twitched, the woman lay motionless. He pressed ahead.

So . . . I'm going to use the motorcycles for a while. Probably drive to baseball games. Keep this nice gun, too—if it works.

The corpse did not budge.

Good. Finally, she approved.

Behind him, Tomlinson stopped, made the sign of the cross and whispered, "Safe passage, Imelda Casanova."

Strange words, even for a left-handed pitcher, but at least he had stopped lecturing about the evils of shooting the Russian. Fear of losing his *pinga*, Figuerito suspected, had opened the man's mind to new ideas.

Now all he had to do was kill the Russian, then figure out how to transport the dead giant and the bad *Santero* to the special place high above the sea. The mule was missing, but they had that nice Buick station wagon. Re-move the chickens and there would be room enough.

Tomlinson, after waiting through more silence, said, "The Russian, he's gone . . . or maybe he passed out. Did you smell his breath? Smirnoff, a hundred proof."

"Drunk?"

"Yeah, and I'm envious. Figgy, this is batshit nuts. Hell, if he wants the letters, let him have them. They're not worth dying for, and your grandmother is beyond caring." His eyes drifted away from the bed. "We don't even know if that gun works or not. Amigo"—Tomlinson took a big breath—"sometimes talking is best. Wait here. I'll see what I can do."

Strange as the man was, he was thoughtful and some-times made sense. "You're worried the bullets are in backwards." Figuerito smiled. "That I'll shoot myself. Brother, I've never had a friend as devoted as you. We'll go together."

He cracked the door a few inches, intending to sneak a look, then said, "Uh-oh!" and tried to squeeze through in a rush because he saw flames. The machine gun, with its wide magazine, snagged and the gun went off, a deaf-ening chain of explosions that rang in the shortstop's ears even after he'd stumbled into the hall. It took an-other second to realize he had to take his finger off the trigger to stop the weapon's wild convulsions.

"Wow," he said, looking back at Tomlinson. "This is some gun."

The gringo, fingers in his ears, was yelling, "Holy Geezus shit! Have you lost your beaner freakin' mind?" and other words in English, to which Figuerito nodded agreeably.

"That's what I think. If the Russian's out there, I've killed him by now. Come on." He jogged toward the fire, which turned out to be only a blanket or bedsheet burning. No . . . it was a shower curtain. He stomped out the flames, then, turning toward the next room, saw that the door to his *abuela*'s shrine was open. In the doorway lay the giant.

Figuerito aimed the gun at him. "Bring the lamp," he said but didn't wait. When he was close enough, he nudged the Russian's foot with his sneaker. Then nudged him hard enough that a conscious man would move. But the giant didn't move.

Tomlinson arrived, carrying the lamp above his head. "Oh shit. Now what are we going to do?" Then said, "I know, I know—the cliff. Or . . . maybe he's still alive." He knelt by the Russian. "Christ . . . you shot him at least three times. See his legs? Help me roll him over. There have to be other wounds."

"Shot him, yes, but I didn't steal his pants. Check under his shirt. I wonder where they went." Figuerito leaned to see into the shrine, which was busy with Santería offerings, and the crypts of unknown children his *abuela* had forbidden him to discuss or ever mention to outsiders.

"Those are the only bullet wounds," Tomlinson said. "His burns . . . I don't see anything that bad. But his head—such a weird angle. And at least one arm broken. Gad"—he moved the lantern a little—"a compound fracture. And that hand . . . his fingers aren't much better." He turned to Figuerito. "You didn't kill him."

"Are you sure?" He motioned with the machine gun. "I'll do better now that I know how this works. Don't you think you should move?"

The strange gringo tried to yank the gun from his hands, but Figgy was too strong. "Go get your own— but I'm only loaning you the other gun. When you come back, maybe our problems with the Russian will be done. After that, we have work to do, so bring the briefcase. Oh, and the movie film. The film will help the gasoline."

"Listen to me!" Tomlinson put his hands on Figuerito's shoulders. "He's already dead. *You* didn't kill him. That crashing sound we heard? Someone else was here. Someone beat the hell out of this guy, then broke his neck."

Figuerito raised the machine gun and turned a slow circle. *"Who?"*

"That's not the point. You didn't kill the guy, and you didn't kill that poor bastard out there by the tree. Dude, it's like freedom. See? We're not guilty of anything. You're still a Cuban citizen, and I've got a visa, so—"

Figgy didn't want to hear any more. "We've got to find this violent person. He couldn't have gotten far."

That was true. They both waited, ears alert, but heard nothing. Finally, Tomlinson said, "Let me think for a second. I want to be sure before we do anything crazier." He squatted by the body. Got on his knees and crawled around, using the lantern to see. He found a pistol but didn't touch it. "A Glock," he said. "I didn't hear any shots."

Figgy thought, *You were smart to put your fingers in your ears.* Bells in his head were still ringing. He left the strange gringo and checked the bathing area, grimaced at what he saw in the commode. Then crossed the hall, stepped over the Russian, and entered his grandmother's Santería shrine.

The stainless fillet knife was gone.

Tomlinson continued his search. In the breast pocket of the Russian's shirt was a folded piece of paper; the paper was old and resembled the pages in the radio logbook. Tempting, but he didn't touch that either. Bundled against the wall was a woman's robe. Nearby, he found a ribbed collar torn from a child's shirt, or pajamas, the material pink with white checks, the checks spattered with blood.

"Don't touch a damn thing," he said. "This is a crime scene. A setup. Very, very orderly." *Orderly*—he mouthed the word again. "Gotta be. That devious bastard. Maybe he didn't realize we were in here."

Peculiar, the gringo's tone. It was as if he were puzzled but already knew the answer to the puzzle.

Figuerito stepped into the hall, where Tomlinson was cleaning his hands on his shorts. "I need to check on something outside. Won't be a minute."

"Not without me," Figgy told him. "Whoever it is took my *abuela*'s knife from her shrine. The man who could do this"—he indicated the Russian's contorted arm, his broken neck—"that man is dangerous."

"Sure, if you want. The knife—probably seeding more evidence or destroying it. Who knows? There's always a reason with him." Tomlinson looked back. "Leave the gun. Mostly, Doc's a nice guy."

FIGUERITO WASN'T GOING to part with the beautiful Thompson submachine gun even for his close friend and shipmate, the strange hippie who, once again, was mostly wrong but a little bit right.

There was no dangerous man waiting outside. There was no dangerous man waiting in the trees near the body of Vernum Quick, the dead *Santero*. Someone had visited recently, though. The fillet knife lay atop a pile of clothing at Vernum's feet.

Tomlinson, holding the lantern, said, "Here they are, the Russian's pants. You could make a circus tent out of—what?—probably size fifties. And look—"

In the sand was a pistol, its handle brassy-colored like a cigarette case. Strange in appearance when compared with pistols seen on TV.

"Planting evidence," Tomlinson said, "didn't I tell you? With him, there's always a reason." He did a slow circle, his head swiveling as if expecting to see a familiar face.

It didn't happen.

"I have things I must do," Figuerito said.

"Go ahead. I want to do another lap." The hippie stopped. "In the bomb shelter, you mean? We haven't broken any laws. Remember that. There's no need to get rid of anything, especially off a cliff. *¿Comprendo?*"

Tell that to the old woman, Figuerito thought.

Twenty minutes later, he was in the shelter, filling the tires of the red Harley-Davidson, when Tomlinson returned, saying, "We need to talk."

Figgy watched him enter. "I'll loan you the blue motorcycle, but this red one is mine. We can't both ride tonight anyway. Olena, the chicken woman, will want her chickens back, so one of us has to drive the Buick. I like that Buick, but I was never allowed to drive the motorcycles. Just start them, you know? I'd sit on the seat and twist the handles. Do you know how the gearshift works?"

Tomlinson squatted so they were face-to-face. "Listen to me. We've got a decision to make. If you want to go back to the United States, you've got to leave tonight."

"Huh?"

"I found my friend, Doc. Well . . . he found me. I

358

don't know what hellbroth he's stirred up, but that's the deal. You leave now or risk another week while my sailboat's repaired. I guess I could go, too, and fly back to Havana in a few days." Before Figuerito could respond, he continued, "I know, I know . . . they've got no reason to arrest us. On the other hand, there's no predicting what Cuban cops will do if they check, and you don't even have a birth certificate. And the American immigration cops—gad, don't get me started. It's up to you . . . brother. He's waiting for us at the river."

Figuerito put the tire pump aside. "Doc? Who is this friend of yours, 'Doc'? And why is he in the river?"

Tomlinson sighed, picked up the tire pump, and moved to the blue Harley. "Okay. Let's go over this one more time."

25

Marion Ford—lights out, engines burbling—
waited at the mouth of the river until his
electronics showed that both Cuban patrol
boats had returned to base in Mariel Harbor.

It was three forty-five a.m.

He went over the checklist a last time: radar-absorbent
bow shield in place; chaff buoys behind the seat; fuel,
water temp, oil pressure okay; items on the bow trimmed,
blanketed, and secured; night vision monocular within
easy reach. If the worst happened, his P226 semi-auto
was beneath the wheel. In an ankle holster, the mini Sig
Sauer he'd loaned Marta—and had recovered from the
Santero's body—was loaded, wiped clean of blood, and
ready if needed.

He popped the boat onto plane, exited the river, and hugged the westerly shoreline for two miles, then turned north and punched the throttles.

Running speed: forty-one knots.

No trouble until he neared the twelve-mile limit. An aircraft appeared on radar. Cuban, out of Mariel Harbor. He watched the flashing red icon until he was sure it was a helicopter. He killed all electronics, pulled the inflation cord on a chaff buoy and dumped it.

Rubber ducks, they were called in naval jargon. His were surplus, not the expensive version, with a battery-powered chip that would seduce incoming radar with a signature resembling a much larger vessel.

The buoy would buy him an hour before the battery died. Two hours before the buoy sank.

Top speed, as read through a night vision monocular: fifty-three knots.

Slower than normal because of a heavy load, most of it under the bow shield.

IN PEARLY LIGHT before sunrise, he passed west of the Dry Tortugas. Loggerhead Key was a single drifting blossom of cumulus cloud. The brick fortress on Garden Key resembled Montana sandstone, a low escarpment on a waterscape of jade.

A seaplane appeared from the direction of Key West. By satellite phone, Ford had contacted his pilot friend

Dan Futch, but it wasn't Dan's plane. He turned to Figueroa Casanova, who was munching peanuts beside him. "Get under the cover," he said.

The Cuban's expression showed pain. "Again? It's quieter out here with you."

"You won't have to stay long," Ford replied. "Take the peanuts—and don't forget to share."

He put the boat on autopilot, a compass heading of 54.12 degrees, and watched for sea turtles. He spotted three loggerheads, and a hawksbill, its shell an iridescent prism of caramel and green.

He slowed but did not stop.

SOUTH OF MARCO ISLAND, Florida's coastline is sixty-five miles of wilderness creeks, mangroves, and shell antiquities interrupted by three dots of habitation: Everglades, Chokoloskee, and, to the north, the mudflat village of Mango.

Ford had lived there as a child with a crotchety cowboy uncle, Tucker Gatrell, whose sloppy approach to life had cemented Ford's allegiance to meticulous routine and coherent patterns of thought. It was this bequest that he valued far more than the shack and cattle pasture he'd inherited, property he seldom visited but on which, of course, he paid taxes annually, and always on time.

At Demijohn Key, he cut east, crossed the flats inside Sandfly Pass, and threaded a backcountry matrix past

Panther, Tiger, and White Horse Keys, then burrowed deeper until he exited into a bay northeast of Dismal Key. Ahead in the mangroves, a clearing of low shell mounds, a few trailers, docks, and a house with a tin roof, a pole barn, and pasture. It had been years since cattle had grazed there. Weeds dominated the fence line, but, beside the house, clothing had been hung out to dry on this sunny November morning.

Ford maintained speed, and found a rivulet of wheel tracks that served as a channel. The water was thin here, constricted by oyster bars and rocks.

From behind the house, an old woman appeared, carrying a laundry basket. Mariaelana, her name. She had been his uncle's Cuban mistress and was now Ford's tenant who paid no rent but took good care of the place. Near shore was a deep-water basin. He backed the throttles until the boat bucked on its own wake, then idled toward the dock while he scanned for a seaplane.

Figueroa poked his head out from under the bow shield. "My ears, they're hurting, and I have to pee. Are we there yet?"

No, they wouldn't get to Sanibel Island until after sunset. Possibly tomorrow morning, depending on how things went.

Ford took out his cell phone, dialed, and asked his pilot friend Dan Futch, "What's your ETA?"

· · ·

Sunday, the Office of Citizenship and Immigration on Colonial Boulevard, Fort Myers, was closed. Ford told Figueroa, "If you're going to live in the United States, it has to be legally, so do us all a favor and try not to get arrested—for the next twenty-four hours anyway."

Figuerito asked, "It's illegal to play baseball?" He was thinking, *The strange hippie is a lot more fun than this man. I hope he arrives soon.*

They were inside Marion Ford's unusual house. Two small houses, actually, built on posts over the water, which made a nice platform to stand and spit over the railing or pee designs in the water. In glass boxes, the man—who everyone called Doc—owned a lot of fish too small to eat, yet he was protective of them and had many rules regarding their treatment. Already, Figgy had learned to stay out of Doc's lab.

"I'm trying to arrange a meeting for tomorrow afternoon," Ford said. "I've called in every favor I have to expedite the process. By Friday, maybe earlier—I'm not sure how much paperwork is involved—you should be free to do whatever you want."

"Is true? I like that. Anything, huh? Yes, brother, of course. I'll do what you say."

Ford's assessment of Figueroa Casanova: a good guy, but a pure spirit unencumbered by the strictures of duality, abstract thought, and other cortex functions, possibly due to injury or deprivation during childhood.

Otherwise, very bright, but in the way feral children have a genius for survival. He replied, "I should have put that differently. Wait"—he went to a desk where there was a computer—"I'll type out a list of what you can and can't do."

"Another one?" Figueroa asked. He had yet to read the list given him last night. "I like Key West. I should be there when the hippie comes in his sailboat. There's a nice baseball field there, that's all I meant. So, you know, while I'm waiting, play some ball, but don't worry about the witches. I already know about them."

"Witches?" Ford looked up through his wire-rimmed glasses.

Figueroa nodded. "How many days before he returns, do you think?"

Tomlinson, who was unencumbered by sexual morals, combined with the Cuban's zest for direct action, were a combination so volatile, potentially, that Ford didn't want to deal with it right now. "I'll let you know," he said, and went out the screen door.

Figueroa waited respectfully for a large, curly brown dog to go, too. He followed them across a boardwalk to the shore, where Doc's nice blue truck was parked. Three men were there, working in the shade, tools scattered on a blanket. *"Caramba,"* Figgy said, "can you teach me how you did that so fast? I already know how those machines come apart."

Jeth and Alex, two fishing guides, and Mack, who

owned the marina, were all smiles even though they didn't understand questions asked in Spanish. Jeth, stuttering a little, said, "Doc, any cha-cha-chance there are more of these? I've always wanted to go to Cuba." He stepped back, and big Alex Payne did, too. Leaning on its kickstand was a 1957 Harley-Davidson Sportster, candy-apple red, 300 pounds of chrome, steel, and gangster swagger, fully assembled except for the leather seat Mack was sweating over now. On a tarp in the shade, the jet-stream-blue Harley was in pieces, each piece wrapped in a blanket embroidered with *Copacabana* in gold thread.

Gold. Ford had forgotten something—something important, in light of the little Cuban's new infatuation with firearms. He and the dog jogged back to the lab, where he had hidden the Thompson submachine guns in one place and their empty magazines in another.

When he returned, he spoke to Jeth, Alex, and Mack in English—not giving orders, exactly, but close—then said to Figueroa, "You see that gate?" He pointed to the parking lot. "Don't go outside that gate. And wear a helmet."

FORD DROVE toward Captiva while the dog, with his head out the window, let the wind turn his ears into wings. *I've never liked Sundays,* he thought. *Mini-holidays without purpose. Government offices not open on* *the one day people can afford to take off—what a pain in the ass. Fewer boats on the water, at least*—the Gulf of Mexico, to his right, proved that. "Thanks to pro football," he said.

Ford's sentence fragments no longer earned the retriever's attention.

Another Sunday benefit was that the Mad Hatter Restaurant was closed, but its back parking lot, Gulf side, was open. He pulled in and switched off the engine under the guise of needing a moment alone to think.

It was a lie. Beyond sea oats and palms were The Castaways beach cottages, red, yellow, and green. Maggie, the lonely tourist, was putting a suitcase into the trunk of her rental compact, unaware of Ford in his blue truck. Possibly also unaware that, according to the radio, the Midwest was covered in snow.

"Of course, I'm rationalizing," he told the dog. "At least I'm aware of my adolescent bullshit devices. I have totally screwed things up. I admit it. That counts for something."

He wasn't referring to his relationship with Maggie—if that was her real name.

Earlier, after a few hours of sleep, he had made good on his promise to call Hannah Smith. Until then, it had been difficult to think of Hannah, who was rangy, beautiful in her way, and plainspoken, as an ex-anything, particularly his ex-lover.

The first thing out of her mouth was "I could stand

here and pretend I didn't know your boat was gone for four days. I could also pretend I didn't pick up clients at Castaways on Tuesday morning and see you sneak out of one of the cottages. That was before sunrise. You have to get up pretty early in the morning to fool a fishing guide, Doc. She's an attractive lady. I'm surprised you didn't take her with you."

He could have contested the word *sneak* and tried to parlay that into a counter-accusation—"Now you're spying on me?"—but his respect for Hannah, and himself, wouldn't allow it. There were only four options in Marion Ford's world: deny, deny, deny, or change the subject.

"I need your advice," he had said. "It's probably better to speak hypothetically. You'll understand when I explain."

"Are you in trouble?" The way she had asked the question—worried, eager to help no matter what—still squeezed his heart.

"Let's say I brought back a guy from Cuba. No birth certificate, no papers, nothing. I didn't notify customs before I left, and I certainly didn't check in on the way back. Now, because it's Sunday—"

"You went to Cuba? In *your boat*?"

"I wish to hell I'd taken you," he'd said. "Last night off Naples, I almost fell asleep at the wheel. I can't think of anyone I trust more."

The remark, although sincere, had received a frosty response. "It's nice you hold my boating skills in such high regard, but I'm prone to pickiness when it comes to breaking federal maritime laws. Hypothetically, of course. How can I help you . . . Marion?"

He had hoped to discuss dinner, or a boat ride beneath the stars, but heard himself shift to objective mode: two professionals discussing options and legalities. "Cubans who enter the country illegally are treated differently than those from other countries. It's not favoritism, it's law—the Cuban Adjustment Act from back in the days of the Cold War. Immediate political asylum is guaranteed the moment their feet hit dry ground. Even so, I wouldn't bring in someone I didn't trust. Now I'd like to expedite the legal process. Or smooth it out, at least. Some of your clients are wealthy power players. And your family has been in Florida forever. So I . . ." By then, Ford was thinking, *Just shut the hell up before you make it worse. Or, at least, tell her the whole truth.* But he had stumbled along into an elaborate network of bullshit that included a list of possible names.

Hannah had taken the high ground, of course. "Harney Chatham, yes. Former lieutenant governor. He's a client—and a good friend, I'd like to think. Nobody knows the system better than Mr. Chatham, and he's on a cell phone basis with every important official in the state. I have his number. Or would you rather I call him?"

Amazing. The woman had single-handedly elevated his deception into an unexpected opportunity. But, first, he'd had to admit, "Hannah, there's a bunch I left out," to which she replied, "Why am I not surprised?"

After that, a full explanation was required.

OVER THE NEXT HALF HOUR, the woman's empathy and interest had warmed to the problem, but her coolness toward Ford hadn't changed. "Traumatized, of course, by the boat ride and everything else. Then to be put on a bus and driven to some holding facility in Miami and asked a bunch of questions by people in uniform. Personally, I'd need more than a few days in a quiet place to decompress. I understand why you did what you did."

Ford's response: "Thanks. I'd like to believe I'm not always an insensitive jerk."

Not the faintest wisp of a smile did that earn him.

Beyond a crop of sea oats, framed by palms, Maggie—if that was her real name—had closed the trunk and was returning to give her vacation hideaway one last look.

Ford drummed his fingers on the steering wheel. Left hand only because he'd bruised, or broken, his right hand on Anatol Kostikov's head.

Should he get out and say good-bye to the lady as required of a gentleman?

No . . . it was too late for that.

I wish you all good things, he thought as he watched her. *Your husband, too.*

Ford, when Maggie was safely inside, started the truck and drove to Jensen's Twin Palm Marina and Cottages, which was bayside, Captiva Island. The next morning, that's where he was, on the porch of Cabin 8, when Hannah and the former lieutenant governor arrived in a limo. Sitting beside Ford were Marta and Maribel Esteban. In his arms, still crabby from lack of sleep, Sabina lifted her head from his shoulder and said, "My god, Marion. Now what have you done?"

Doc Ford and Tomlinson find themselves in the part of Central Florida known as Bone Valley. Neither Doc nor Tomlinson realizes what they've gotten themselves into—and in a region built on a million-year accumulation of bones, there is no shortage of spots in which to hide a corpse. Or two.

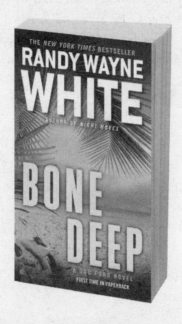

"A descent into the world of overzealous and unethical fossil collectors leads to a boat-napping, stolen artifacts, and increasingly dire threats." —*Publishers Weekly*

AVAILABLE IN PAPERBACK

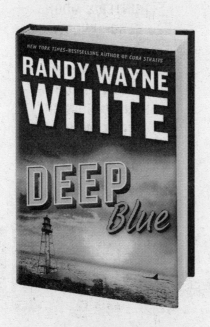